THE ACCIDENTAL BRIDE

What Reviewers Say About Jane Walsh's Work

The Inconvenient Heiress

"This book is so tender. It's soft and aching and delicate while at the same time being all the things I ever want in a historical romance novel—dramatic and lush and dynamic. Each word is so steeped in culture and convention and then with some magic flick of her wrist she's flipped it all upside down onto its head. Jane Walsh writes with such a reverence for women and womanhood while embracing a vast and wondrous queerness.

Reading a Jane Walsh novel is a dream with every page. It's a reminder that we have always been here, that we have always been finding community and finding love, that we have always risked it all and been rewarded for our bravery, that queer love is about the quiet moments as well as the loud ones, that we deserve to wear flowy gowns and make our art and find our future, that we deserve to have our love and care returned to us in spades, that we deserve and deserve and deserve."
—*The Lesbrary*

Her Duchess to Desire

"One of Walsh's strongest points is her ability to build a strong, positive queer community in a time period that is known to have sometimes been hostile to them. …I love an Ice Queen heroine who melts in the hands of the right person, and Anne is a great personification of that."
—*Courtney Reads Romance*

Her Countess to Cherish

"This book was a nice surprise to me in its portrayal of gender fluidity, along with a delightful romance between two sympathetic characters. If you love queer historical romance, you should absolutely check this out."—*Courtney Reads Romance*

Her Lady to Love

"If you are looking for a sweet, cozy romance with grounded leads, this is for you. The author's dedication to the little cultural details do help flesh out the setting so much more. I also loved how buttery smooth everything tied together. Nothing seemed to be out of place, and the romance had some stakes. …Highly recommended."—Colleen Corgel, Librarian, Queens Public Library

"Walsh debuts with a charming if flawed Regency romance. …Though Honora's shift from shy curiosity to boldly stated interest feels a bit abrupt, her relationship with Jacquie is sweet, sensual, and believable. Subplots about a group of bluestockings and a society of LGBTQ Londoners add depth…"—*Publishers Weekly*

"What a delightful queer Regency era romance. …*Her Lady to Love* was a beautiful addition to the romance genre, and a much appreciated queer involvement. I'll definitely be looking into more of Walsh's works!"—Dylan Miller, Librarian (Baltimore County Public Library)

"…it's the perfect novel to read over the holidays if you love gorgeous writing, beautiful settings, and literal bodice ripping! I had such a brilliant time with this book. Walsh's novel has such an excellent sense of the time period she's writing in and her specificity and interest in the historical aspects of her plot really allow the characters to shine. The inclusion of details, specifically related to women's behaviour or dress, made for a vivid and exciting setting. This novel reminded me a lot of something like Vanity Fair (1847) (but with lesbians!) because of its gorgeous setting and intriguing plot."—*The Lesbrary*

By the Author

Her Lady to Love

Her Countess to Cherish

Her Duchess to Desire

THE SPINSTERS OF INVERLEY SERIES:

The Inconvenient Heiress

The Accidental Bride

THE ACCIDENTAL BRIDE

by
Jane Walsh

2023

THE ACCIDENTAL BRIDE

ISBN 13: 978-1-63679-345-0

THIS TRADE PAPERBACK ORIGINAL IS PUBLISHED BY
BOLD STROKES BOOKS, INC.
P.O. BOX 249
VALLEY FALLS, NY 12185

FIRST EDITION: MAY 2023

CREDITS

EDITOR: CINDY CRESAP
PRODUCTION DESIGN: SUSAN RAMUNDO
COVER DESIGN BY TAMMY SEIDICK

Acknowledgments

Many thanks to everyone at Bold Strokes Books for all their hard work. I was delighted to finally have the chance to meet the publishing team and some of my fellow authors in person, and it was a major highlight of my year. I couldn't be happier that my queer Regencies continue to have a home at BSB.

Special thanks to my editor, Cindy, for all her support and for making me a better writer with each book.

And as always, thank you to my wife, Mag. You give me so much love each and every day, with so much grace. It would be impossible not to be inspired to write romance with you in my life to show me the way.

Dedication

For Mag, with happy memories of all
the trips we've taken together

CHAPTER ONE

London, 1813

Thea Martin wiped the sweat from her brow with her forearm, careful to avoid touching her face with her dirt-stained gloves. Spending hours in her new conservatory would be all well and good in winter when the wall-to-wall glass magnified the heat of the sun, but it was a noble sacrifice in the name of science to bear it during the heat of August.

She snipped a bud on a bright pink dahlia, hoping to encourage a larger bloom to form, and let it fall to the table crowded with plants, buckets of soil, and discarded clippings. Life at its finest, new growth emerging from the muck of its surroundings.

There was nothing more satisfying.

Thea made a notation in her journal, then glared at the dirt that smeared across her words. She had forgotten to remove her blasted gloves. She tugged them off and tossed them onto the table amid the mess before losing herself in details of petal length and stamen placement.

A shadow darkened her journal, and a stack of letters landed with a thwack on the table.

Startled, she looked up to see Anthony. "You're back!" She threw herself at him, clutching him tight enough to wrinkle the wool of his expensive coat, but she couldn't restrain her joy. Anthony was dearer to her than her own brothers.

"And I've brought presents." He nudged the envelopes.

"Of course you did, you darling man." Thea drew the pile closer and cracked the seal on the first letter, then nodded as she scanned the contents. There were notes scrawled around landscape illustrations of fields and flowers, instructions on how to pick and preserve the plants. A sachet that had been tucked inside the pages fell out, and she peeked inside it. "Ah, *Lobelia cardinalis* seeds. Wonderful." The vibrant red cardinal flower was known to reduce swelling. Another letter included *penstemon hirsutus* seeds, a purple flower with a hairy stem, but she was most delighted to find a packet of *dichorisandra thyrsiflora*. Thea clutched the seeds to her chest. She didn't know of anyone who had cultivated blue ginger in England yet. "These are marvelous. Thank you."

"You paid the crew well enough for them. They send their thanks, by the way. It was a good bonus on a long journey."

Seeds and cuttings from other countries were of vital value to botanical study. To Thea, it meant she could cultivate the foreign plants that fascinated her. She could barter seeds with other collectors, further diversifying both of their stocks. Botanical interest had a far reach these days—comprising of scholars, physicians, florists and their nurseries, estate gardeners, and more—and she could be the center of their discussion if she could grow something that had never before thrived in England.

Anthony prowled around the room, peering at every corner. He was a short compact man with a round chin, and he often lamented that it was most unfashionable these days to sport a beard. He compensated for it by growing his sideburns long enough to meet the high points of his starched collars. Anthony had a presence that brightened the room more than the sun that dazzled through Thea's windows. "The conservatory was in the planning stage when I left. It's impressive, but already you are out of space."

Satisfaction coursed through her as she looked around. The high domed ceiling made it seem airier than it really was. It might be snug, but the addition took up over half of the back garden of her Chelsea townhouse. Pots and vases lined the tables along the glass walls, overflowing with plants and flowers—bright fuchsias, cherry pink begonias, sunny yellow chrysanthemums, and an orange tree heavy with fruit. The padded bench with its cushions waited for her to curl up with a cup of tea and her notebook at the end of the day.

Thea gazed at the *camellia japonica variegata* that took up the other half of her garden. It was a magnificent shrub, five feet wide and about as tall, but so far only glossy leaves rustled in the summer breeze. Camellias bloomed inside in carefully cultivated environments, and were a popular sight in conservatories and greenhouses. She was determined to be the first to grow one *outside*, however, all the way from seed to flower. Yet it was proving difficult to pin her hopes on a bush that took six years to blossom, and which hadn't yet done so in the seven since it had been planted.

These blue ginger seeds would be an excellent project if the camellia never bloomed.

"The conservatory is wonderful, isn't it? It has exceeded my expectations."

Anthony tapped on a square of windowpane. "And the budget, too, I imagine. Wise choice to use mullions instead of sheets of glass. It would have cost you twice as much otherwise."

Thea waved a hand. "Yes, it drained all the money I had saved over the years. But it was necessary."

Every farthing that furnished the conservatory and paid for the seeds and plants that Anthony's crew gathered for her was worth it. She hadn't thought twice about making the decision, extravagant as it was. Someday, she would succeed in growing something that England had never seen before.

Thank goodness her allowance was due in a fortnight.

Plants thrived in the wild with naught more expense than nature's bounty of water, air, and soil, but they were dashed expensive to keep as a source of study.

Thea tapped the packet of blue ginger seeds into her palm and frowned at their texture, hoping they weren't too dry. Three-quarters of the seeds that Anthony brought back tended to lose their germination during the voyage. It was a common agony among botanists as they sought to understand the ideal conditions in which to transport and grow plants from afar in England's climate. Some of the seeds that Anthony had collected this time were sealed in their own drop of wax, which he explained was to prevent moisture from entering it. It was a novel technique, and one she hoped would improve the yield.

"I was worried about you," she said without looking up. "You were gone a month longer than I expected."

He shrugged. "You know me. Born with a silver spoon in my mouth, and itchy feet that my father despairs of."

Anthony's spoon was more gold than silver, providing endless streams of luck and wealth. Properly speaking, he was Mr. Robinson, the youngest son of the Earl of Eastmoor. To her, he had been Anthony since the first time they had slept together a lifetime ago and deemed it a disaster.

"We did interesting work around the St. Lawrence River." He was a mapmaker and led a team of geographers though expeditions of the Americas. "Most of the seeds are from the area."

"They will brighten England's gardens by the time I am finished studying them."

"You and our friends here brighten my thoughts when the seas are rough." He raised her hand to his lips, but instead of kissing it, he crinkled his nose. "Potting again, Thea?"

She snatched her hand away. "I wear gloves and you know it!" She picked one up and swatted him with it.

"My valet will be cross if he discovers even a hint of manure on my coattails."

"Well, Polly doesn't raise a brow if she sees dirt on my skirts."

"Your maid is doubtlessly accustomed to it. But mucking about in the soil does not give any excuse for your gown to be so wrinkled. You look like you arose from your bed a quarter-hour ago."

"You exaggerate. But tell me, what use does a scientist have for the latest styles? Should I have the maids waste an hour to set my hair in curls before I work?" She patted the chignon that she had twisted up that morning.

"You take such excellent care of your plants but of nothing else around you." He frowned. "It might behoove you to take an interest again in things beyond botany, you know."

"There is nothing more interesting or more important than the study of nature." Thea swatted him again for good measure, then picked up the next envelope. It might as well have contained deadly nightshade with how fast she flung it back onto the table.

Anthony glanced at it. "Your housekeeper gave me your correspondence to bring in with me. Who is it from?"

"My parents."

It was a shame that she hadn't received it before finishing the conservatory. She could have added it to the newsprint that insulated the wall abutting the townhouse. That would be a far better use for the letter than reading it would be.

Thea's allowance was mailed to her by her father's secretary each quarter, banknotes stuffed into an envelope that contained naught else but a curt greeting. But this letter was thin as well as early, and her name had not been written in the secretary's hand.

"Ah, Mr. and Mrs. Martin." Anthony clasped his hand to his heart and bowed in the general vicinity of the letter. "Do convey my worst wishes if you choose to reply."

It was a blessing to have friends who loved her. Unlike her family, who considered Thea a scapegrace of the first order.

He draped an arm over her shoulders and pressed a kiss to her temple. "Best to open it swiftly."

She slumped against his chest. "Take me away from all of this on one of your adventures instead, please."

"You get seasick at the sight of a boat on the gentlest of lakes, Thea."

She sighed and picked up the letter but took her time about it, easing her thumb beneath the seal and watching the wax break apart before unfolding the page and smoothing out the creases. Her mother's hand was sloping and elegant, but the words on the page were spiky and cramped. Dread pooled in her belly. If it had been Mother instead of Father, the letter might have contained nothing more than an engagement notice for one of her brothers.

She propped her elbows on the table and read it.

Then she leapt to her feet, swearing, sending the stool sprawling behind her and crashing into a copper pot with a bang.

"Thea! What in the world—"

"They've done it." She banged her fist on the table, scattering the cuttings. "Hell and blazes, they've finally done it."

"What?"

"Summoned me home."

Jubilation was her first feeling. But it was choked and swallowed up by hurt, like ivy smothering an abandoned house. Father wouldn't call her back to Inverley for the pleasure of seeing her again. She would bet her best chrysanthemum on it.

"You're not going, are you? They've been wretched."

"I haven't heard from them in years." Usually she gleaned her news of them from her brothers, who enjoyed London more than either of their parents. An uneasy feeling settled over her. "What if one of them is ill?"

"I can come with you, if you wish."

"It's nothing like the adventures you're used to."

He grinned. "All of life is an adventure. You don't have to go anywhere for that to be true. Besides, I'm between voyages, and these feet of mine are still itchy."

To not want to go meant that somewhere, somehow, she still cared what they thought of her. But that was impossible.

"I can't leave my work." The camellia wouldn't bloom for months yet, if this was indeed to be its year. But it was a fickle shrub, and much could go wrong if they had sudden rains or prolonged heat.

"The servants can care for your plants if you leave them instruction. And any ladies you may be entertaining these days could survive without your attentions for a week, can they not?"

She hadn't had a lover in ages, despite her reputation. "I suppose."

He offered his arm. "Then to Inverley we shall go."

Grace Linfield watched the foamy waves wash up onto the beach, scattering pebbles and seashells across the sand. The sun was hot on her neck where neither her bonnet nor her hair covered it, and the air was clean, fresh, and invigorating. She had been in Inverley all summer and thought it might be the very best place she had ever lived.

Lady Edith stood at the shore, staring down at a rock in her hand. She tossed it into the water with poor enough form that proved her governess hadn't paid much mind to calisthenics in her formative years, and watched as it sank.

"Mr. Martin told me that he could make the stones skip," Edie said, biting her lip. "But he was an awful tease about it and wouldn't let me in on the secret. I think maybe he was funning me."

James Martin was the reason they were in Inverley. As far as Grace was concerned, he was a fly in the ointment of an otherwise perfect summer. He was snide, foppish, proud—and the heir to the wealthiest family in the area.

Which meant that an unmarried lady like Edie was meant to be fawning over him in pursuit of a wedding ring.

Especially unmarried ladies like Edie who were hiding a secret from their recent London Season.

Grace smiled at her. "Maybe stones aren't meant to dance across the water. We had best save such miracles for the churchmen, should we not? Now, we must return to Martin House."

Edie nodded and they crossed the beach to the road that wound its way past the edge of town and up the bluffs to the grand manor house where the Martins lived.

"Oh, a penny," Grace said, and stooped to pick it up from the cobblestones. "That's good luck, Edie."

Edie smiled. "If one believes in such superstition."

Grace tucked the penny into her reticule and gave it a pat for good measure. There were never enough opportunities to improve one's luck in life, so what was the harm in trying to find more where one may?

Grace was a lady's companion in the employ of Edie's mother, Lady Harriet, and had been charged with chaperoning Edie through her first Season. It hadn't ended in matrimony, but at least it also hadn't ended in scandal.

Yet.

Lady Harriet had not been impressed by that interpretation of events.

Grace had endured scathing lectures on her failures as a chaperone and had been given one final directive to fix things—find a wealthy husband for Edie. Immediately.

They had been lucky enough to receive an invitation to Inverley when the Martin family had decided to extend the social whirl beyond the Season and host a summer house party at their estate. Edie was a likeable young lady and would make anyone a delightful wife. The task should have been easy.

But time was running out.

After dressing for dinner, Edie floated down the main staircase in her airy muslin like a cloud.

"Edie, I received a missive from your mother this morning. She is coming to Inverley at the end of the week."

Edie's answer was a sigh and an eyeroll, which she would never have dared do in London. Grace felt a pulse of alarm. Edie's friendship with some of the local girls was having an ill effect on her, filling her head with airs and fancies and—worst of all—talk of *love*.

Grace stopped Edie on the steps and rearranged the bow in her hair, which had become lopsided as she rolled her eyes again and added a shake of her head for good measure. "You must hide your feelings better," she said. Thank goodness they were alone on the staircase. "You must look and behave irreproachably. Do not under any circumstances allow *any* of the Martins see such poor behavior!"

"I know," Edie said, her eyes downcast. "Mama expects me to marry Mr. Martin. I had a letter too."

"You can always trust me to help you. No matter what."

But what would Lady Harriet think of them both if she saw that Edie's manners had deteriorated over the summer?

Lady *Harridan*, as Grace sometimes thought of her. Sometimes, in her most private moments, she allowed herself to use the name that had been denied her during her whole life, and which was still a secret to everyone. Including Edie.

Aunt Harriet.

But the familial connection, once so yearned for, was now a perpetual thorn in her side. She never liked to think of her aunt as anything other than Lady Harriet.

They were a dozen to dinner tonight. Grace counted, relieved it wasn't thirteen with the addition of new guests who had arrived that afternoon. Mr. James Martin walked past his usual place near his father at the head of the table and headed toward where they sat. Despite her promise to help Edie, Grace half hoped he would continue walking, but he shot a smug grin at Edie and seated himself beside her with a flourish of his coattails.

Grace stabbed at her shellfish. Enduring the tedium of gentlemen full of their own importance and very little else was the worst part of being a lady's companion. Gentlemen never paid any mind to *her*, of course. Her station was too low, her style of dress too simple, and her face was only a notch above plain. She was happy enough to be overlooked, having no interest in being courted, but it meant that she was forced to listen to them yawn on about their every opinion to Edie.

"Ah, the lovely Lady Edith. Your beautiful countenance is a delightful counterpart to my wit and charm, if I may say so myself," he drawled, hitting all the right notes of insouciance and puffed-up consequence that made him popular in London, though not a whit of it made any sense.

Edie's smile didn't reach her eyes.

Grace didn't like the idea of Edie marrying him, but it was Lady Harriet's command. Edie had gritted her teeth and agreed to abide by it, and Grace had gritted hers and promised to facilitate it.

Mr. Martin was far from the biggest catch of the London Season, being from the younger branch of an earl's family with a modest country estate. But he was the biggest catch that Edie would be able to get now that the Season was finished, and eligible gentlemen had dispersed from the capital.

To fail meant ruination.

Not just for Edie, but for Grace.

Grace smiled at Mr. Martin. Years of employment as a companion had served her well in being able to paste a serene expression on her face at a moment's notice. "Lady Edith *so* appreciates your attentions, sir. She is too delicate of manner to express such a thing directly, of course, but I must tell you that the pair of you together pleases the eye indeed. Such natural beauty paired with"—she struggled to fish a compliment from her brain—"such *elegance* of manner is wonderful indeed."

A dish of soap to rinse the lies from her mouth would be more fitting than the beef soup that the footman set down in front of her.

Mr. Martin gave her a bland smile and turned his attention back to Edie. "My brother, Charles, and my sister, Dorothea, are coming to Inverley this week," he told her. "You will be pleased to meet the rest of my family, I am sure. I dare to hope that my close relations will be delighted at the most excellent news that I hope to share with them. One always likes to hear of a family increasing in size, and it is a particular pleasure when one is to add beauty to its ranks. May I hope that you feel the same?"

Mr. Martin was insufferable, and Grace wanted to roll her eyes herself at the tedium that his siblings were sure to bring with them. But then she realized what he had implied, and she could have leapt across the table to hug him. This must mean an engagement was nigh. If she had less self-control, she would have sagged in her chair with relief. The penny had proved lucky indeed.

"I look forward to meeting them," Edie said. To her credit, she seemed genuine enough.

All Grace had to do was make it through a few more days without Edie's scandal being revealed, and then she and Mr. Martin would be engaged and Lady Harriet would be happy.

Grace had to guarantee success, for Lady Harriet's wrath could not be borne.

CHAPTER TWO

Inverley was much the same as Thea remembered it. In the spirit of scientific accuracy, she acknowledged that more shops lined the main street now, and newer houses hugged the shoreline compared to in her youth, but the scent of the ocean and the bustle of the visitors felt eternal. Steeped as she was in memories while Anthony's coach rumbled through town, she could almost forget that she had been away for fifteen years.

But not quite.

The countryside hadn't changed in essence, but she had. Otherwise, she would be pressing her face against the carriage window, anxious for a glimpse of home. She would be poking her maid Polly awake and regaling her with stories of her childhood. Instead, Thea sulked against the padded bench, fretting that the housemaids wouldn't follow her instructions for the camellia and the conservatory.

A week was a long time to be away. It was enough time for a shoot to grow a leaf, or to witness the first unfurling of a petal. Or for rot to attack a root. Thea frowned and pulled a loose thread from the cushioned seat.

"Interesting topography," Anthony remarked. "Those cliffs must be sandstone. I'd be keen to map them."

"You may keep your cartographic comments to yourself." She turned away from the seascape that sped by through the window. "Inverley is as dull as I recall it being. Far too many seagulls, and I can smell the fish drying on the nets from here."

"It's *marvelous*," Polly announced. "The sea isn't anything like I expected. It's almost like a living beast."

Polly had a face that looked peaky no matter how many nourishing bowls of soup that Thea pushed at her, and her eyes were more enormous than usual as she gazed at the glittering waves.

Thea swallowed hard as Martin House came into view, a square manor cradled by the bluffs outside of town. Her great-grandfather had built it to be the biggest and best in the area. Its three storeys were doubtlessly still filled with neat and tidy rooms, and its windows looked onto fastidious lawns that had been designed in the old style of Capability Brown. One could hardly stroll ten meters without tripping into a ha-ha or a folly.

The butler greeted her with warmth, but the footman who hauled her carpet bag onto his shoulder led her to the wrong room.

"My suite is at the front of the house," she told him as he sailed past it.

He stopped and blinked at her.

"Perhaps you did not catch my name, but I am Miss Martin." No answering noise came out of his mouth. "The daughter of the house?" she added.

"You've been set up in the Green Room, miss."

The Green Room? Nonsense. "There is some mistake. I have had a long day of travel, so please do air out my own chambers at once."

He glanced around as if looking for help, but they were alone in the hallway. "I can't, Miss Martin. There's another young lady in your rooms. We've had guests all summer."

Guests? Her parents didn't enjoy houseguests. Oh, they were hospitable enough, and dutiful, but they had never entertained more than they could help it. Not even during hunting season when the land was flush with grouse and their London friends wrote pointed letters longing for an invitation to experience the charms of the country and the health benefits of a fine sea air.

"It will have to be the Green Room, miss."

Shaking her head, Thea followed the footman into a small room at the back of the house, its walls papered in a color that she had always felt was best described as bilious.

Polly found her not long after, round-eyed at the grandeur of the room. A London maid ought to be used to better, but Thea didn't keep a fashionable address. Besides, she had found Polly through unorthodox means, and this was her first position as a lady's maid. She was a florist's daughter and knew plenty about plants, so she doubled as an errand runner and correspondent with the nurseries.

"If I had grown up here, I would have never ever left," Polly said. She rustled around Thea's trunk and shook out a crumpled silk dress. "Dinner attire?"

Thea pursed her lips. Her clothing was in dire need of airing and pressing after the journey. She didn't much care, but Mother would be aghast if she was less than presentable at the dinner table. "I shall order up a tray."

Polly nodded and began to unpack. "Sensible enough choice."

Sensible. Thea had abhorred the word when she had lived here and discovered she didn't much like it now either. It reeked of self-satisfaction and prudence, and nothing in the least bit fun.

She unclenched her jaw. "I find I am in need an evening gown—oh, anything would do, Polly, it can be my plainest muslin if need be. I won't dine downstairs, but if I am to survive this visit, I shall be in dire need of spirits to revive me. Best if I find a bottle of cognac after dinner and tuck it up in here for the week." A bottle might not be enough. She wondered if there was space to hide two.

"Davis said there's to be dancing tonight." Polly's eyes turned dreamy, and she sighed down at the frock that looked the least crushed from travel. She draped it over the back of a chair.

"Davis?"

"Oh, he's the footman who brought your things up. He was telling me that there's been more dancing this summer than all the previous ones combined. Almost every night, unless folks wish to attend the local assembly rooms of an evening." She clattered a silver-backed hairbrush onto the dresser.

Another mystery. Thea had made her share of turns around the Martin House ballroom when she was younger, but it had been a matter of once a month in the summers—not almost *every night*!

The dinner tray came as they continued to unpack, Thea giving as much of the guinea fowl to Polly as she would eat, knowing that the servants' fare would be plentiful and healthful but not terribly exciting.

And what was life without excitement?

Well, she supposed that summed up life rather well at Martin House.

Thea yawned and checked the clock on the mantel. It was late enough that the formal dinner should be over. No one would notice if she stole downstairs to the parlor where she recalled the liquor was kept.

But before she reached the parlor, she found Mother and Father talking to the housekeeper in the hallway near the ballroom. She brightened. If they spoke now, then maybe Thea wouldn't have to stay the whole week as they had requested in their letter.

Even though Polly had told her there would be dancing, Thea was still surprised to hear music swelling, and laughter from what sounded like a considerable crowd.

"Ah, Dorothea. Good evening." Mother nodded at her as if they had seen each other this morning instead of four years ago when they were last in London.

Mother was small and spare and elegant as always, her hair pinned up without a stray strand out of place. Her satin brocade gown was as crisp as if the dressmaker had dropped it off this afternoon, but that was how Mother always looked. Perfect in her never-ending efforts to impress.

Father's eyebrows met in a scowl above his eyes, and Thea wondered if it was only perpetual in her presence. His cravat was impeccable, but she knew that before the evening was over he would be yanking it from his neck as Mother tsked at him.

Thea stuck out her hand for a handshake because she knew Mother wouldn't appreciate such a modern gesture but her manners would force her to accept it. It wasn't well done of her, but in this house, she felt the rebellion of being seventeen again. She willed herself not to feel anything as her mother's hand touched hers for a quick limp shake. Certainly not because she still wanted Mother's approval. The idea was preposterous.

"To what do I owe the pleasure of an invitation to Inverley?" Thea asked, with neither preamble nor sincerity.

Father shook his head. "Impatient as always."

"I thought to spare you the pain of excessive conversing with me by approaching the matter at hand directly."

He cupped her elbow and steered her down the hall toward the library. "If you insist on speaking now, then at least let it be in private."

"The dancing is to start soon," Mother fretted as she followed them. "It's dreadfully inconsiderate of us to hold up the evening's entertainment for our guests. Dear James shall have to do our duty for us." She sighed. "It is good that we have one child with proper filial respect."

The library could have belonged to any other gentleman in any other country manor. All the right things were in all the right places. A bust of King George sat on a squat pillar in front of the window. The works of Shakespeare rested on a prominent shelf, bound in navy blue calf-leather. Latin and Greek tomes lined the wall nearest her father's desk, though Thea had never seen him crack one open.

Near the window was a globe, the same world upon which she and her parents stood as tiny dots when one considered the sheer magnitude of things. The same world that Anthony liked to hop around as easy as walking from here to the neighboring county. She used to spin the globe around as a child, dizzy with the possibility of what lay beyond Inverley's narrow confines.

Nothing had changed from her memory of countless scoldings in this room except for the color of the curtains and the addition of a rug in front of the fireplace.

Thea dropped into the black leather armchair by the desk, deliberate in her gracelessness. Mother perched on the edge of the chair next to hers, hands folded in her lap. Father remained standing behind the desk. The better to glower at her, no doubt.

"Dorothea, we are getting older."

Thea nodded. She had noticed new lines around Mother's eyes and lips, and Father's hair was half gray now. Her heart twinged. What if one of them *was* ill? For all their disagreements, she didn't want them to suffer. "Are you well?" she asked.

He barked out a laugh. "Why, our physician says he doesn't know anyone as healthy as we are. No, we are simply getting *organized*. We wish to ensure that our children are well taken care of, and we want to see you all settled within our lifetime."

This was a good deal more interesting. She straightened out of her slouch. Wild hope took root in her heart, but she tamped it down. Something as earnest as *hope* wasn't becoming of her feckless reputation.

"James will inherit the bulk of the money along with Martin House, of course. He is already well taken care of. In fact, we expect him to announce an engagement any day now."

The estate wasn't entailed, but she had always known that James would inherit almost everything. Making more progressive choices wasn't how things were *done* in the Martin family, and Father had no interest in going against the grain of tradition.

"In the event of my passing, your mother will be settled with a third of the estate."

Thea nodded again. So far, all was as she had expected it to be. Nothing worth hauling her to Inverley to explain.

"We have decided to settle Charles with Westhill Grange, effective immediately. He never settled into church life as we expected of him, so we have been forced to make other provisions. He arrived yesterday, Dorothea. We had sent the same missive to you both."

Charles was her younger brother, not yet twenty-three, and so beef-witted that despite an education at Eton and Cambridge, she didn't think he knew flora from fauna. Westhill Grange was to be *his*? Her great-aunt had lived there until her passing years ago. It was a stone house not far from Inverley, much smaller than Martin House. Thea remembered from visiting as a child that it was beautifully kept with extensive acreage. She hadn't even known it was part of their own holdings, having assumed it had gone to a cousin. To think of Charles as its steward...well. It was nonsense.

And yet—if Charles had received the Grange as the youngest child, what was to be her prize as the eldest? It must be a financial bequest. Perhaps it would be enough to rent a larger townhouse in London with a conservatory triple the size of her own, or even something with grounds large enough to build a proper greenhouse.

A warm glow spread across her chest. She should have known that for all their differences, they were still her parents. She had not been forgotten.

"Dorothea."

"Yes, Father?" She was surprised she was able to speak when her mouth was dryer than soil in a drought.

"You also need to settle down. You need better influences in your life."

It was nothing she hadn't heard before from them.

"You squandered your opportunities in your first London Season and ruined your good name."

She gritted her teeth and waited.

"You have ignored polite society to get up to who knows what kind of hedonism."

It had been the truth for years, though not so much anymore.

"So, Dorothea. What we will do for *you* is cut off your allowance."

What she felt was cut off at the knees.

CHAPTER THREE

Thea gaped. Her mouth was dry and her mind whirred so fast that she was surprised not to see sparks before her eyes to herald a faint. "I beg your pardon?" she croaked.

"You heard your father. You cannot continue to gallivant all over London—you are three and thirty, Dorothea. We have indulged you for long enough."

Ignoring her was considered *indulgent* of them? Anger broke through her shock. "How am I to live?"

"You will have to come home, of course."

"To Inverley?" Thea reeled. "I cannot."

It was out of the question to return to Martin House and live under her parents' roof once more.

"Then you must marry."

Hell and blazes. Panic clawed at her throat. "I cannot do that either."

"What you cannot do is continue to waste away your life without consequence," Father boomed. "It is right for us to provide for James and Charles, but a daughter is meant to marry a man to keep her. We have a dowry set aside for you, if that is your concern. It should be tempting enough for a gentleman to overlook your eccentricities."

No gentleman alive could tempt her to marry. Neither prince nor poet, nor even a botanist of the same persuasion as herself. For a moment she considered Anthony. A marriage between them wouldn't change a thing, chaste as it would be. But it wasn't fair to expect that of him, dear friend as he was.

And Thea Martin solved her own blasted problems.

She squared her shoulders. "If I refuse?"

"Then you are left with nothing."

Dreams of continuing her botanical studies, publishing papers, and joining the Horticultural Society someday all evaporated, burning off like dew in a harsh mid-morning sun.

"And if I agree to settle down?" Her lips felt stiff as she forced the words past them.

"Then you will receive your allowance until the happy announcement of your engagement. But you must wed within the year, Dorothea. We need assurance that you will be settled."

"I shall give the matter a good deal of thought," Thea said with more confidence than she felt. "For now, I shall bid you good night."

She left the room on shaky legs and started for the stairs before remembering the cognac. She swung back down the hall to the parlor, where she could hear the violins and pianoforte and the happy din of guests from the nearby ballroom.

She had never expected to be left with nothing while her brothers, possessing naught more interesting than a stamen instead of a pistil, got everything.

Panic and disbelief had dissipated, leaving her in a towering rage.

She ought to bring the cognac to the ballroom and find the least eligible woman to seduce on the dance floor, shocking the crowd. She recognized it for the youthful impulse that it was, but she was too furious to care overmuch. If she was to suffer the pains of disinheritance, then for one last night she wanted to be every bit as bad or worse than her parents thought her to be. One last chance to indulge, before putting on a sugar-sweet act for the rest of the week to convince her parents to drop their ultimatum.

Perhaps not in such a public venue as the ballroom. But someone in this blasted perfect house with its blasted perfect inhabitants must want to kick up their heels and have a bit of fun tonight?

Grace tapped her foot in time with the music as she watched Edie glide and dip her way across the ballroom. She stood among the wallflowers and chaperones, the married aunts and less-than-merry widows. Being a lady's companion allowed her to be on the fringe of genteel social life, though she had little enough of her own.

She told herself not to be ungrateful. She had worked hard for this her whole life. She was now within reach of positions that would provide her with the best living that she could envision for a companion. Baronesses and viscountesses and even dowager duchesses could well be in her future.

Lady Harriet had all but promised it.

Of course, it was a little less like a promise and a little more like blackmail.

But for a spinster who never planned to marry, the guarantee of good employment was a good bargain indeed.

Grace was watching so closely that she noticed the instant Edie's flounce fell away from her skirt. She continued to dance, as the ruffle hadn't dropped so low as to be a danger to her dancing slippers, but Grace felt her stomach sink along with the drooping lace. This would *not* do. Mr. Martin was a man who demanded perfection of his partners. How many times this summer had she seen him sneer at girls whose sartorial infractions included hems worn a touch too high or hair styled an inch too low?

Mr. Martin had all but said yesterday that a proposal was imminent. There was not one opportunity to waste with Edie looking less than perfect.

Grace slipped away from the ballroom toward the parlor down the hallway. She was sure that she had seen a packet of pins there earlier, and it was faster than going upstairs to her bedchamber. She didn't want to leave Edie for too long, though she knew there must be a half hour before the set ended.

On the other hand, that was plenty of time for a girl to find trouble. And Edie, for all her soft manners and doe-eyed gazes, could slip into mischief as fast as anyone.

The parlor was dark, but she remembered that the packet had been on the mantel. If the chambermaid hadn't moved it yet, then it should still be there. She knew the layout of the room well enough after eight weeks at Martin House that she didn't stumble over the stuffed footstool or bump into the papier-mâché screen on her way to the fireplace.

"Looking for something?"

The cool amused voice took her by surprise, along with the scrape of flint against tinderbox before a candle flamed.

Grace blinked in the dim light. A woman stood a few feet away, candleholder in hand. If she had been at dinner earlier, Grace would have noticed her. Her thick blond hair was swept back in a chignon, and her full pink lips were twitched up into a grin. She was tall, and her bosom and hips were full beneath a gown that was in sad need of ironing. Somehow it made her look gorgeously rumpled. Insouciant instead of slovenly.

"Are you here to pilfer the snuffboxes, perchance?"

That husky voice sent shivers down Grace's spine. She swallowed. "Indeed I am not. I am looking for a pin."

"A solitary pin, alone in the dark? My, what an impossible task you have set yourself. Almost Herculean in scope."

Grace felt flustered. "There was a packet on the mantel this afternoon during tea. There is a ruffle in need of repair in the ballroom."

"I suppose to pilfer a pin is not so great a crime. The pettiest of all larceny, I would think."

"It isn't larceny at all! Those pins belong to Miss Alice and I am going to tell her that I had to borrow one. She won't mind." Then she saw the woman was stifling laughter. Grace sighed. "You're funning me, aren't you? Oh, do bring that candle over here and help me search?"

"I suppose a thief would be attired less charmingly—unless she was here under subterfuge." But she obliged and held the candlestick high.

Grace scanned the mantel and grabbed the packet. She flipped it open and almost dropped it. Thirteen pins were stuck in the thick paper. An unlucky number indeed. Her heart pounded. She ought to have gone upstairs after all to fetch some from her bedchamber.

She forced a smile. "Thank you. I am much obliged, Miss...?"

But before the woman could reply, the door creaked open. She blew out the candle, grabbed Grace's hand, and ducked them both behind the thick curtain covering the large windows. "It might be my parents," she hissed. "Stay quiet!"

Confused, Grace pressed against the windowsill and peeked through the narrow opening between the curtains.

A man and a woman ducked into the parlor, giggling to a degree that made Grace suspect that they were not, in fact, her companion's parents. They bumped into both the footstool and the papier-mâché screen, which made them laugh harder.

"Oh, John! How strong your arms are tonight!"

Oh dear. Young, inebriated, and amorous. As a chaperone, Grace had seen it many times before. If she were in the ballroom, she would have notified the woman's mother, or would have tugged the girl away herself to evade scandal.

But Grace was not in the ballroom.

She was hidden behind a curtain, of all things, with a complete stranger.

Grace studied her companion in the moonlight as she slouched with a hip leaning against the windowsill. Grace was close enough to feel the warmth from her body, to hear the breath from her lips, and to inhale the scent of her orange blossom perfume.

Then Grace noticed the decanter in her hand—had *she* interrupted a thief? Her pulse picked up. She couldn't afford to fraternize with thieves. What if Lady Harriet ever found out?

It made no sense to have hidden behind the curtain like this, but now that they *were* hidden, it felt a thousand times more awkward to pop out and startle the cooing couple. It was best to stay where she was.

But how much time had passed since she left the ballroom?

Grace fidgeted against the windowsill, trying not to disturb the curtains and alert the couple to their presence, and her breath started to come quicker. The woman must have heard her, for she took her hand and smoothed her thumb in a circular pattern across Grace's gloved palm.

The contact sent a shock of awareness through her body. How long had it been since she had been touched like this?

A few heart-pounding minutes stretched into eternity while the couple took advantage of the privacy to share a passionate kiss. Finally, they left, laughing and whispering to each other as the parlor door closed behind them.

"Thank goodness," Grace said, pushing her way through the curtains. She wiped away the sweat that had gathered on her brow.

"You seem bothered," the woman said, her eyes intent on her. She lit her candle again and propped it on a table.

"I've heard such noises before," Grace said stiffly.

"Wanting something of the same?"

"Not the same," she snapped, truthfully—and yet not quite. Men held no interest for her. But women, especially *this* woman…that was something else entirely.

Grace didn't expect her eyes to sharpen and for her to lean in. "What a coincidence. Neither do I," she murmured, her mouth so close that Grace could almost taste the cognac on her breath, the scent of spirits mixing with the orange blossom.

Was it possible that she meant what Grace thought she did? She didn't dare assume. It was too risky to be so bold. She'd been slapped for less.

"I won't be in Inverley for long," the woman said. "I find myself indifferent to most of its supposed pleasures." She must have been invited to Martin House for tonight's dancing. A common enough occurrence this summer. "And yet here I am, surprised to find that Inverley does have its share of charms."

She took Grace's hand again, and now her touch felt sensual instead of soothing.

Grace couldn't help it. She squeezed her hand, delighted when she saw the woman smile. "Oh?"

"A holiday is an ideal time to meet like-minded people."

"Of course. Many who come here have similar goals for their health, looking for a superior air and a curative sea tonic." Grace had fallen in love with the high cliffs and splashing waves, the bathing machines and the firm sand that was excellent for walking.

"I am talking about something rather different." Her eyes moved over Grace's body, and her gaze felt like a caress.

Grace swallowed. This could not be happening to her. The most beautiful creature to ever set foot in Inverley was staring at her— Inverley's plainest lady's companion—most boldly. Almost…*hungrily.* An answering hunger pulsed between her thighs, and the packet of pins trembled in her hand.

Thirteen pins.

It was superstition, she reminded herself. There was nothing in it.

"Different?" She managed not to squeak, but it took a great deal of control.

"Something intimate. I wonder if you have ever had the same thoughts as I have?"

It was safe to have such a conversation here, alone in the parlor with the door closed, but Grace was lightheaded and short of breath. This summer had been the first time she had ever confessed her sapphic desires to anyone except a potential lover, having found a wonderful friendship in Caroline, Arabella, and Maeve.

But no one else knew of her thoughts.

No one else could *possibly* guess.

Until now.

The woman moved her hand to touch Grace's wrist, brushing against her frantic pulse, and then trailed her fingers up her forearm. "I have a room here," she said. "It is quite private."

There could be no mistaking this. "Why me?" Grace whispered.

"Have you no concept of your own loveliness?"

Grace had stared at her reflection enough times to know what stared back was agreeable enough, but perfectly average. "I begin to think you are a flatterer."

"Should we not seize the opportunity where we find it, and discover loveliness in it? Or should people of our persuasions grow old and alone, without ever feeling a lover's touch? That is no life for me, I think."

The pins trembled again in Grace's hand, but this time it wasn't from nerves. It was excitement. Why shouldn't she take the opportunity that she was presented with? Grace's whole life was spent in making other people comfortable. Catering to their whims and fancies. Making things easier for them.

This woman was a visitor, and she would never see her again.

Why not take one night of passion for herself?

If only Grace wasn't a hired companion, but a woman of her own consequence making her own choices. A visitor to town, looking for nothing more than indulgence. Temptation and risk heightened her pleasure to almost a painful degree of arousal, such as she had never felt before.

Maybe she could choose.

For one night.

What was the harm in pretending she was a carefree lady on holiday?

Plain prim-and-proper Grace, the lady's companion, had no such luxury of choice.

But Grace, a lady on holiday...the world lay open before her. She smiled. "It seems we do indeed have the same inclinations."

❖

The woman standing beside Thea had a certain poise about her, but it was tinged with worry that for some unexpected and unexplained reason, Thea wanted to soothe. She was the type of person Thea often disliked on sight. As innocent as they came, she would have thought if she passed such a creature on Bond Street. She wasn't quite pretty, and her face was altogether too serious. Almost pensive. Her eyes were large, but a smudge of purple rested under them as if she were exhausted. Her nose was a touch long, and her lips were a touch short. The curve at her bosom and hip was slight.

Not the usual sort she liked to tup, but she was very fine regardless. And remarkably close at hand. And she smelled exceptionally good. Wholesome. Like lavender, and sunshine.

The combination had no right to be so intoxicating.

This woman looked like she had never committed a bad deed or had an errant thought in her life. Thea had done more than her share of both, and here she was proving it by seducing such an angel.

With her blood still boiling after speaking with her parents, filled with the fury of being financially reliant on a family that was forever disappointed in her—she wanted nothing more than to enjoy an evening of illicit pleasures with this woman.

It was time for one last wild rebellion.

"After such a turn of events, I rather think we should know each other's names," she said. "I'm Thea."

The woman blinked, then dipped into a shallow curtsy. "My name is Grace. It's a pleasure to meet you."

Effortless manners, despite the circumstances. The name suited her. "The pleasure is mine. I think there is none greater than meeting a woman one can admire so much." Easy words of seduction fell from her lips. She'd been down this path many times before.

Grace's eyes narrowed a fraction. "Your admiration might be misplaced. We do not know one another."

Interesting. Her head didn't seem to be turned by the usual flummery.

Thea gave her a smile that she knew had weakened many a knee in her past. "If there is so much to admire about you already, then it should be magnified as we get closer."

"We shall hardly have a chance to become acquainted before we are separated, I am sure."

Ah, she was but a guest for the dancing tonight? Even better. "If we are to be *friends* for so short a time as an evening, then it is a pity to part on such poor terms." She raised the decanter that she still clutched in her hand. She had pilfered it before Grace had entered the parlor looking for her pins. "Please let me pour you a glass of cognac. It's the least I can do after you harbored me from such a hardship as the potential arrival of my parents. Thank you for that, by the way. I had no wish to see them. I would much prefer your company."

Grace hesitated. Thea could tell that she struggled with the answer by the tension in her long limbs and graceful neck, her head turned toward the door, ready to flee. Did she understand that it wasn't merely a drink that Thea wanted to share with her? Maybe her skills were rusty. More often than not, the past few years had been spent knee-deep in plants instead of on bent knee in the bedchamber.

"I should return to the ballroom."

"Eager to dance? You must look beautiful during a waltz." Thea meant it sincerely. There couldn't be a thing this woman did that wasn't perfect.

"I hardly dance, but I am expected to return. My absence will soon be noticed. The set that started when I left must be long finished by now."

Thea poured herself a glass and swallowed her disappointment along with her first sip. She would have to try her luck on the terrace in the hopes of encouraging another woman to try a different sort of romance under the full moon. It was a pity it wouldn't be Grace, though.

"But perhaps you could come to my rooms in an hour," Grace said, twisting her fingers in the lace of her sleeve. "I am in the Rose Suite."

Thea's delight was marred with anger. The Rose Suite? "I know where it is," she said. "I shall see you there."

After an hour had passed, along with a quarter of the bottle, Thea tapped on what she considered to be her own bedchamber door and slipped inside when Grace opened it. She wished for another drink when she looked around. The walls were still papered with the pink flowers that she remembered from when she had been a girl. The mahogany bed frame was still painted white, and even the gauzy white canopy that hung from its four posts was the same as when she had whiled away her afternoons under it, dreaming of the future.

Of course this elegant, calm woman had been put in Thea's old room. Her parents had probably wanted someone like Grace as their child, instead of unruly and rebellious Thea. Too loud, too exuberant, too impatient.

There was a bitter sort of satisfaction in knowing she would take her pleasure here even though the room had been denied her, but she found that she wished to forget being in this house at all. She wanted to forget about being a daughter or a sister.

Tonight, she wanted to be a lover.

CHAPTER FOUR

Thea grinned at Grace. "Well, here we are."

"Here we are." She twisted her hands together and there was a furrow in her brow that warned Thea that she might not have much experience.

Thea took Grace's hands in her own and squeezed lightly. "Don't worry if you have changed your mind. We don't have to do anything."

Grace still wore her evening dress, but she had removed her gloves and taken the pins from her hair. Her hair was brown and rather fine and fell beneath her shoulders in a silky curtain. She smiled for the first time since they had met, and it changed her face completely. Her brown eyes sparkled, and she looked more relaxed as her lips curved upward. "Oh yes, I think we do."

Thea laughed, relieved that she was still willing. "Whatever the lady desires."

Grace stepped forward, bolder than Thea expected, and tilted her face up to meet Thea's, pressing her lips against her own. The shock of it held Thea motionless for an instant, then she parted her lips and welcomed Grace's tentative exploration of her mouth. Her lips were soft and gentle, and her hand touched Thea's shoulder as if to steady herself before a swoon.

Grace was so achingly sweet that Thea hardly knew where to put her hands, for to touch her almost seemed like it should be forbidden. But her kiss turned from sweet to ardent so fast that Thea lost her resolve and gripped her tight, taking up fistfuls of silk skirt to draw her closer.

Grace gasped as Thea moved her hands to caress her bottom, then pressed herself against her once more, her mouth sliding against hers with renewed fervor. Thea had lain with plenty of women over the years, but couldn't remember the last time a kiss had roused her to such heights. The heady mix of lavender and spirits enveloped her like a cloud, and she lost herself in the moment as she touched and tasted and lusted to the point that she feared she might ignite.

Ah, this was bliss. A woman in her arms, a rush of pleasure in her veins. This was what Thea needed tonight. And yet it wasn't simply the need for a woman that made her ache. It was the need for *this* woman, her body slender and smooth against her own, the touch of her tongue against the corner of her lips flooding her with equal measures of desire and happiness.

She couldn't remember the last time she had been happy at Martin House.

Thea broke away when she heard a scratch at the door from the chamber that adjoined this one. "Are you expecting another lover?" She would be astonished if Grace had set up a second assignation. In regular circumstances, she wasn't opposed to a third party in bed, but tonight she wanted this woman all to herself.

"Of course not," Grace whispered, her cheeks pinkening. "That is my—er, traveling companion, looking for a late-night gossip."

"Is there any way to be rid of her?"

"She will think me asleep if I do not answer." Her blush deepened. "We shall have to be quiet."

This wasn't the first clandestine affair that Thea had enjoyed. She blew out the candles on the table, though she would have liked to see Grace in all her glory, candlelight dancing across her pale skin. "Then quiet we shall be."

They fumbled to undress between kisses, their hands roaming over one another as shifts and gowns and bracelets and hair pins ended up in a graceless tangle on the floor. They fell into bed, the covers in disarray under them.

Thea eased herself on top of Grace, pressing wild kisses along her jawline and down her neck as she moved her thigh between Grace's legs, nudging them open. Shifting so that her pelvis was on top of Grace's, she started to move against her, slowly at first and then—

BAM.

The bed slammed against the wall with a thud.

Hell and blazes.

There was another scratch at the door. "Grace?" The whisper was faint.

Thea leapt off the bed with alacrity and shoved a thick feather pillow between the wall and the headboard to muffle the noise. She knelt on the bed, her heart hammering and her body aching for its release as she waited an interminable moment to hear if the door would creak open and signal her to flee.

The moonlight streamed in through the open curtains, allowing Thea to look her fill at Grace. Her hand rested low on her hipbone, her fingers just brushing against her curls, and Thea felt a rush of desire. It must be safe now. They must have remained undetected. She slid against Grace once more, fitting her legs against her until their hips aligned and the sweet friction built up again between them.

God, this woman was *perfect*.

But just as she found a rhythm, the bed started to squeak. Thea fell back, biting back an oath, and saw Grace's shoulders shake with silent laughter.

"Give me a moment," she whispered. If nothing had changed since she had once slept here, then the mattress was still supported with a canvas cloth stretched taut across the bedframe by ropes that wove their way around wooden pegs. One of the ropes must have slipped from its peg, a common occurrence that she remembered from her youth, causing the rope to strain and squeak as it stripped the finish from the remaining pegs.

Thea stuck her hand between the mattress and the frame, feeling her way to locate the slipped rope, and managed to restring it in a trice only to feel it fall away again. Devil take it, the pegs themselves must be loose. It wasn't something she could fix.

But such a sound couldn't be enough to give them away. She returned to the bed, determined to carry on lest she explode, and Grace's arms welcoming her back was reward in and of itself. "Where were we?" she murmured, then moved until her thigh connected with Grace's center, thrilling her.

The bed squeaked again, louder than before, and Thea gave serious thought to setting it ablaze to match the fires that danced in her loins. Well, there were plenty of other ways to find pleasure.

She slipped a hand between them and found Grace's center, hot and slick, and moved her fingers against her to test if there would be any answering sound from the bed. When it squeaked in protest, she moved slower, watching Grace's head fall back and the moonlight glint on the whites of her eyes as she ground her hips urgently against the steady press of Thea's hand. She slid her finger inside, then added a second and thrust as slowly as she could without causing any noise from the bed.

"*Thea.*" Grace bucked beneath her as she moaned her name, then gasped as she jerked her head toward the adjoining door, eyes wide with alarm. Thea wondered if it might be too difficult for her to be silent, and moved her hand gently over Grace's mouth. "Bite if you need to," she breathed in her ear, and heard Grace suck in a sharp breath, the muscles of her lower belly tightening where they pressed against Thea's body.

Her teeth sank into Thea's palm as she moved her other hand against her center again. Thea stroked her firmly enough to cause her to bite down once more before she gasped against her hand and jerked her hips hard. There was something poignant on Grace's face as she shattered, something fierce and unrestrained and yet sad at the same time, and it had Thea moving over her again to try to make it better the second time. She slid her fingers against Grace's quim until she succeeded in wrenching another gasp from her lips, her hips moving beneath her hand, a fine sheen of sweat covering her as she fell back against the sheets again.

Grace's breathing was uneven. Thea tucked her hair behind her ear and pulled the blanket up around them, then lay beside her and took her hand, stroking her thumb against her palm.

After a few minutes, Grace turned her head and looked at her, eyes shining. "That was wondrous," she murmured.

Thea felt a burst of gratitude that it was Grace beside her in bed, and not some other woman tonight. She was just as lovely as Thea had thought her.

Grace either had more experience than Thea had assumed, or she possessed innate skills, because she trailed her hands over her pelvis light enough to tease and then moved her way back up to her breasts. She kissed Thea's nipple while she squeezed her other breast, then moved her hand down to touch her. She moved on top, thrusting deep with her fingers and pressing down slow and hard with her hips, as mindful of the squeaking ropes as Thea had been, and the buildup had been so long tonight that it felt like no time at all passed before Thea fell apart, biting her lip and twisting her hand in the sheets as pleasure coursed through her.

In the throes of brilliant passion, Thea managed to forget that this was her room until she opened her eyes some time later, realizing that she must have slept. Grace slept as well, curled up against her, but Thea managed to extricate herself and find her shift and gown in the dark before finding her way back to the Green Room.

This had been the perfect interlude in which to forget her troubles. It was childish to want to defy her parents at the slightest provocation, but she knew that hadn't been the only reason she'd had the liaison tonight. Grace had been intoxicating enough of her own accord.

Now, it was time to be good for the next week. At least she had good cognac to see her through.

She was going to need it.

Before Grace opened her eyes the next morning, she knew that the mysterious Thea was gone. Common sense dictated that a woman who spent a passionate night in another woman's embrace ought to retire to her own room before anyone was the wiser.

Grace doubted that anyone at this house party would suspect a torrid affair between two women. But it would still be odd enough to raise a brow if a guest left a friend's room at the break of dawn with mussed hair, clad in last night's evening gown.

She buried her head in the pillows and caught the faint scent of orange blossom. Delight shivered its way from her scalp to her toes. Proof it hadn't been a dream, at least. She wasn't sure if she had ever had such an erotic night. She had been lucky enough to have had two romantic relationships in her life, however brief, but had never known the delight of a random chance encounter.

Grace thought of the deep thrill that had raced through her when Thea had pressed her into the mattress and told her to bite her hand. If Thea had still been with her in the room, she might have begged her to do it again.

Thea had stirred up…*something*. She wanted more.

Yet *more* wasn't hers to receive. It was no use wishing for a whole slice of happiness when she only had room for crumbs. She pushed herself out of bed and into her plain blue morning dress without any further indulgence of memory. Thea had said she wouldn't stay long in Inverley. She might already be gone. The thought of never seeing her again panged, but it was better this way.

Grace splashed water on her face and brushed and plaited her hair, then knocked on the adjoining door to Edie's room.

The maid opened the door, and Grace found Edie looking like an angel perched on the stool in front of her vanity mirror. She was still in her shift, and her hair was unbound and curling to her shoulders. Everything about Edie was dainty. Despite being cousins, they looked nothing alike. Grace caught sight of herself in the mirror and was shocked anew that Thea—gorgeously sensuous Thea—had chosen her last night.

How mystifying. How *wonderful*.

Perhaps the penny's luck had been meant for her yesterday.

"I had the best of evenings last night," Edie announced. She looked happier than she had in weeks. "I came to your room to tell you all about it, but you were asleep. Did you sleep well? I thought I heard noise from your bedchamber."

"Bad dreams," she said, pasting a smile on her face.

Though Grace pressed her, Edie refused to say anything further, instead rushing her maid into dressing her and insisting that they be early to the breakfast table.

Breakfast was informal at Martin House and could consist of anything from a cup of tea to a quick sit-down to an entire morning of gossip about the previous night's entertainment. A cold collation was laid out on the sideboard for the benefit of guests who ate at various times, as many took advantage of the novelty of walking to the shore at dawn for an invigorating dip in the sea.

Edie fell into conversation with one of her friends and a gentleman that Grace didn't recognize. Grace moved away and poured herself a cup of tea before selecting a slice of ham and a piece of toast. The salvers were a little skewed, and she frowned. Taking a quick glance around, she nudged them back into place again.

A gentleman with long sideburns was contemplating a dish of eggs at the table, and Grace sat across from him. "I don't believe we have had the pleasure of an introduction, sir," she said, taking a sip of tea. She considered it to be unexceptional to relax one's breakfast manners at the seaside and decided to introduce herself. "I am Miss Linfield. I presume you are a newly arrived guest?"

"I am indeed," he said. "I am Mr. Robinson. I arrived yesterday afternoon from London, as an escort to Miss Martin on her way to her ancestral home."

She remembered Mr. Martin saying yesterday that his brother and sister were to join the party. "Mr. and Mrs. Martin must be delighted to have all their children at home for a visit."

"I'm sure they are," he murmured with a small smile that Grace found curious.

She wondered at the relationship of Mr. Robinson to Miss Martin. Perhaps they had come to Inverley together to announce an engagement. Grace had seen the pressure that Mrs. Martin was exerting on her son to marry this summer, and supposed the same pressure was being applied to the rest of her children.

"How are you finding Inverley?" Grace asked.

"It is pleasant indeed. I thought to climb the bluffs later today and have a look around at the shoreline."

"Oh?"

"I'm a mapmaker by trade, and I find landscape in an area new to me to be fascinating. You must forgive me if I begin to drone on about mineral deposits." His smile was warm.

"I shall endeavor to be a good student should you chance to start lecturing. I find science fascinating." She had always liked teaching it during her years as a governess.

"I shall be much obliged, Miss Linfield."

Grace finished her breakfast and excused herself. She went to Edie's side and smiled brightly at the group. "Lady Edith, did you not mention that you wished to speak to your maid about the bolt of cloth that you purchased yesterday?"

Edie looked cross, but it was fleeting. "Indeed, you are right, Miss Linfield." She beamed at her friends. "I shall see you on the bowling green!"

"I fear Mr. Martin may take it amiss if the woman he is courting is speaking so warmly with another man," Grace said once they were in the hallway. She didn't like Mr. Martin, and part of the reason was his sense of superiority. He rarely exhibited jealousy, being too proud to think anyone good enough to be in competition with him, but he was self-centered enough to be annoyed if he saw Edie fawning over someone. Grace could not allow any flaw, however tiny, to spoil Mr. Martin's good opinion now.

It wouldn't do for Edie to have been so focused on Mr. Martin all summer, and then to throw him over for someone else. Rumors had been building about them, after all. Rumors that Grace had encouraged and helped to spread.

Especially after what had happened in London. With any luck, no one in Inverley would ever find out about *that*.

Edie scowled. "I can talk with whomever I please," she grumbled, but it was half-hearted.

"Your mother is expecting you to be engaged by the time she comes to Inverley next week to bring you back to London. You cannot mean to disappoint her?"

No one wished to disappoint Lady Harriet. Edie blanched at the very idea of it.

Her stomach twisted as she glanced at Edie's downcast face.

It had better be worth it. For both of their sakes.

Thea tossed the oblong wooden ball between her hands, her bonnet tipped back on her head far enough to allow the sunlight to shine on her face. A small enough rebellion that her parents might not notice. With any luck, she could convince them that she had reformed her ways and they would relent on this ridiculous idea of severing her allowance and therefore her independence.

She had never been impatient for a game of lawn bowling to begin, but it was the best way to highlight proper behavior in front of her parents. All she had to remember was that a *good* daughter would be all smiles as she engaged with the guests and cheered on her team.

It made her consider dropping the ball on her toes and pleading injury to get away from the hypocrisy of it all.

At least Grace wasn't part of the house party. She must have been at Martin House for dinner and dancing last night and no more, and had likely left this morning, as Thea hadn't caught sight of her again. It was for the best. She couldn't afford any distractions if she wanted to return to London by the end of the week.

James lifted his brow at her. "Never thought to see you back again to swing a ball down the green, Thea."

Charles laughed. "Nor did I! It's jolly good to have us three reunited, isn't it?"

"Let's see if Charlie can focus on rolling a ball without leaping into a thousand different things instead," James said, and feinted when Charles swatted at him.

Thea tossed the ball again, the heft of it stinging her palm as it connected harder than she intended. "I'm surprised you aren't already lording over Westhill Grange."

"It opens new doors for me, and that's the truth. I'm pleased as punch." Charles shook his hair from his face, a brilliant shock of gold in the sunlight. "Did you get anything from Papa?"

"A warning, and little else." She couldn't keep the coldness from her voice. The unfairness of it all! "He wishes for me to settle down."

"That's as it should be," James said with satisfaction, rocking back on his heels like the pompous self-satisfied ass that he was. "You can't gad about London with the riffraff forever, can you? Father told me it was past time for me to find a wife, so I suppose they want to see all of us leg-shackled. That's the purpose of this endless house party, you know. Eligible brides trotted out before me all summer long. It's been rather diverting. My heart's desire was a local girl in Inverley," he added with a trace of bitterness, "but she wouldn't have me. She's exquisite. These London girls can't compare."

Thea rolled her eyes. "I am happy to hear that the women of Inverley are showing good common sense. I expect any lady to be better off without you."

James's face turned sorrowful. "A temper like that is why you have never even been courted, isn't it?"

Thea liked to think that even if she had fit in with her family that she would still find James downright loathsome. He had worsened with the passage of time.

Charles's expression changed and he loped across the lawn after an abrupt good-bye.

A pretty young lady dressed in frilly white muslin beamed at him as she stepped onto the green.

But Thea barely registered her presence. For next to her was her forbidden Grace, tall and lithe in a high-waisted dress the color of spring violets which boasted no ornamentation but flattered her excessively. It drew attention to the length of her legs, hidden from view but vivid in Thea's memory.

Thea's own dress felt uncomfortably tight. Her straw bonnet, weighing no more than a farthing, was too heavy.

She needed air. She needed water.

"That's going to be my wife," James remarked.

She needed to strike her brother down with her lawn ball.

"Oh," Thea said through clenched teeth. "What is her name, pray tell?"

"Lady Edith. If I can't have Caroline Reeve of Inverley, then I have set my sights on the next most elegant girl I've ever seen."

Grace hadn't even used her real *name*? Thea knew they had agreed to keep things confidential, but she had thought her name was real. More fool she. And she was engaged to *James*?

"I wish you happy," she snapped as the ladies approached with Charles.

"Mr. Martin, I had the pleasure of meeting your brother at last night's ball," the younger lady in the white dress said. "He is a most charming conversationalist."

Thea's eyes bore into Lady Edith's, who looked astonished to see her.

"Charles has the remarkable misfortune to be less charming the longer you know him," James told her, glaring at their brother. "Have you also met my sister, Miss Dorothea Martin?"

Thea wrenched her gaze from Lady Edith, and she nodded to the young lady. "I have not had the pleasure, but it is lovely to meet you."

"I am Lady Edith," she said cheerfully. "And this is my companion, Miss Grace Linfield."

As surprised as she was to have thought at first that Grace was a lady, now Thea was indignant on her behalf that she wasn't. That elegance of form and figure, that light precise voice, that poise—Grace deserved to be a lady in truth.

Shock receded into relief that her brother had no claim on her woman.

Not that Grace was *hers*. They had spent a night together. It had meant nothing.

But then why did her heart feel as light as her bonnet to see her again?

"Miss Linfield, I am delighted to meet you," she said, smiling. "I hope you have enjoyed your stay at Martin House thus far."

This can't have been Grace's first subterfuge. Her cheeks bore no hint of a flush, her face gave no indication of either familiarity or discomfort. "I have enjoyed myself immensely. You and your family have been generous to supply us with countless pleasures this summer."

"We Martins aim to please," she said. "Shall we have a game of lawn bowling?"

Now she truly couldn't wait for the games to begin. All thoughts of Grace being a distraction fled in the pleasure of seeing her again. After all, the daughter of the house should be accommodating to her guests. And if a guest also happened to be last night's lover...well. It was the perfect opportunity to have one's cake and eat it too.

CHAPTER FIVE

With Thea's eyes on her as intense as if Grace was a puzzle to be put together, Grace felt nervous. Not that Edie or either of the Martin brothers would take notice if she breathed a little faster or if she plied her fan a little too briskly. In fact, she wasn't worried that anyone would suspect that her thoughts fell all a-tumble when she saw Thea in the glorious light of day.

Sunlight sparkled on her blond hair and blue eyes and had already turned her nose and cheeks rosy as her bonnet sat too far back on her head to protect her. The straw bonnet's scarlet ribbon was untied and trailed against her bosom, and Grace's mouth went dry as she thought about what lay beneath the thin white muslin of her dress. Thea's hair looked hastily done, long tendrils brushing against her cheeks in the breeze, and her fichu was crooked where it was tucked into her bodice. But the inattention to detail made her look devil-may-care instead of dowdy. Rakish instead of rumpled.

She had seemed so much a voluptuous creature of the night, a woman made for fantasy and shadowy pleasures and rich candlelight. To see her in the sun was like seeing a queen. Confident, commanding, and amused at everything around her.

Grace was only concerned that *Thea* would notice her staring. Was she taking note of the pulse that throbbed at the base of her neck, or the way that she seemed to lack breath in her presence? What if Thea found her less interesting as a companion than as her guise last night as a carefree visitor on holiday?

But she also worried that Thea might find her intriguing nevertheless.

For Grace absolutely could *not* have an affair with the Martin daughter while she was working to promote an engagement between her charge and the eldest Martin son. A relationship between women always carried the risk of scandal, even if it was a brief and secret tryst. How could she know if she could trust Thea to conceal their liaison?

"Yes, I would love to bowl with you," Edie announced.

Grace had been so lost in thought that she had missed the conversation about arranging teams. "Best of luck to you all," she said, and started to move toward the sidelines.

Thea frowned. "But, Miss Linfield, you must join us. It's three to a team, and there are six of us here with Mr. Robinson."

The man who Grace remembered from breakfast grinned at her. "We're going to give you a good trouncing, so I cannot blame you for not wishing to play, Miss Linfield."

His good humor was catching, and Grace smiled back. "It would be best for me to take my place with the other chaperones. I have never bowled before and would be the greatest hindrance to you."

"Never in your life?" Mr. James Martin looked astonished as he looked down his nose at her.

"Then you are in dire need of physical activity," Thea announced. "Your complexion looks like it has never seen a hint of good British sun! I am afraid I must insist on it. For your own health."

Grace hesitated, but it would be impolite to continue to refuse. "I am happy to oblige."

"Capital!" Mr. Charles Martin said. "My team or my sister's?"

"Whichever team Lady Edith prefers," she said, and noticed that he looked at Edie like a puppy. A common reaction from gentlemen.

"Then you are on Charles's team," Thea said, "along with Lady Edith. James, Mr. Robinson, and myself shall be your opponents."

"We shall play against each other," Mr. Charles Martin said to his brother, "and the losers shall endure a forfeit."

Mr. Robinson cast the white jack, rolling it a fair distance down the green, and Grace looked at the ball in her hands which was meant to somehow catch up as close as it could to the jack to win a point.

"You really have never done this before, have you?" Thea asked.

Grace almost dropped the ball. "Never."

"I thought you had exaggerated. I've never met anyone who hasn't bowled."

Thea's shawl was slipping down her arm, and a scandalous amount of ankle was bared as she balled her skirts up in her fist while she walked around the green to better view the jack. As carelessly as she treated her clothing, her dress was a beautiful gauzy muslin edged with fine lace and velvet ribbons. Grace didn't imagine Thea mingled much with those below her station.

"I mean, what on earth were you *doing* during your youth? Lawn bowling is practically a national pastime." Thea laughed as she dropped her skirts and watched her brother's ball as it made a neat curve three-quarters of the way down the green. "Oh blast, that was well done of him."

Grace couldn't answer truthfully. "I grew up with no common green nearby."

Thea went next, and Grace watched the muscles in her arm bunch and contract as she swung the ball, giving a quick unladylike holler as it rolled up just before the jack, the closest anyone had thrown thus far.

She loped toward Grace. "Your turn," she said, and tugged her by the elbow to the field.

There were plenty of eyes on them. The Martin brothers, Edie, Mr. Robinson, and the matrons and chaperones who thronged the edge of the field, gossiping with orange punch in hand and but one eye on the green. *That's* where Grace should be. That's where she belonged. On the sidelines, out of focus. She felt a moment's disorientation. Who was she to be traipsing on the field with the Martin family?

"Your form isn't the best," Thea announced. "Not a surprise if this is your first time."

Then Thea's hands were on her, and Grace squeaked in indigitation, which faded the moment she realized no one would think twice about the entwined arms of two women. Thea moved her gloved hand to rest against Grace's wrist as she adjusted her grip.

Could Thea hear the unsteadiness of Grace's breath?

Was she remembering last night's pleasures?

"This is cheating!" Mr. James Martin cried, throwing up his hands. "We're on opposite teams, Thea!"

"It's not going to improve things much if she is inexperienced," Mr. Robinson said cheerfully. "Let her learn."

Grace couldn't think anymore as Thea moved her hand to her upper arm and guided her into a practice swing. "That's how you do it—nice and slow," she said, her voice low and intimate.

They locked eyes and Grace steadied herself just as she felt her knees buckle. "I think I can manage the rhythm," she said, and was delighted when Thea's lips quirked up into a smile.

Just for her.

Oh, this woman was *magnificent*.

Thea stepped back, and Grace swung.

The ball thundered down the green, made a magnificent curve... and fell short of the jack by what seemed like a mile, but which Thea murmured encouragingly was but half an inch at most.

"You shall be better the next time you try," Edie consoled her, which Grace recognized with chagrin as her own words parroted back to her from countless occasions during the Season.

The rest of the game fared no better, and Grace was happy enough to slip away after a spectacular loss, relieved to get away from the confusion and desire that bubbled inside of her when she looked at Thea. She needed to clear her mind.

Thankfully, she soon spotted her dearest friends in Inverley sipping lemonade near the garden—Caroline Reeve, Arabella Seton, and Maeve Balfour. They weren't houseguests but must have been invited to enjoy the lawn games along with a variety of other townsfolk and visitors staying elsewhere in Inverley.

She looked at the women she had met two months ago and felt her body tense up. The four of them—sworn spinsters and sapphically inclined—had become close friends. How had they become so dear so fast? How was she to leave them when Edie's marriage was announced? She had thought herself resigned to the transitory nature of life as a lady's companion. Even as high as she might reach in terms of her future employer's social status, she was still bound to follow where they would lead.

It was a most inconvenient time to wish to put down roots.

"You look flushed," Caroline said, frowning at her. "Whatever is the matter?"

"Nothing whatsoever," Grace said, but couldn't resist the urge to look behind her where Thea was still talking with her brothers and Edie.

"That is nonsense," Caroline announced, shaking her chestnut brown curls. "My sisters have evaded the truth enough times over the years for me to recognize it straightaway." She had five younger siblings and had her hands full raising them.

THE ACCIDENTAL BRIDE

"You don't have to share with us if you don't want to," said kind-hearted Arabella, her eyes blinking at her behind her spectacles. "But we are here if you want to talk."

"There's nothing to talk about."

She didn't dare express the depth of her longing to stay in Inverley. It was a fool's dream. She must go where she would be paid, and that would be London. Or Manchester. Or Bath. Places filled with rich debutantes, or spinsters not unlike herself, or widows, or the elderly. Inverley was flooded in the summer months with visitors, but for most it was a place to pass through and then go about one's normal life, with fond remembrances of one's seaside holiday.

Maeve studied her, a skeptical look on her face. Arabella and Caroline had been born in Inverley and had lived here their whole lives, but Maeve was from Ireland and was traveling through the various resort towns of Britain with her ill mother. Grace liked to think that maybe she would understand her longing to settle.

"Let's walk," Maeve said. "Fewer ears would be listening if we leave the lawn and stroll the gardens overlooking the sea."

"As long as I remain within view of the green. I cannot let Edie out of my sight." With Mr. Martin so close to declaring himself, it would be best to allow Edie to encourage him. There could be no harm in it as long as they remained within the crowd.

Martin House was nestled among the bluffs, not so high that it was a challenging walk from town, but high enough to have a magnificent view of the sea as it rolled and crashed on the shores. Grace knew her time was running out to look at it. Mr. Martin was sure to come up to scratch any day now, and Lady Harriet was due to arrive in Inverley soon.

Grace could be gone as early as next week.

She wasn't ready.

Arabella and Caroline fell into step, and it twisted Grace's heart further. They had fallen in love this summer and were planning a life together. Grace was happy for them, but envy pulled at her. It was rare what they had found.

Maeve walked beside her. "I don't mean to pry," she said. "But you look like you haven't slept a wink in days. I'm concerned for you."

Grace swallowed. She had missed a considerable amount of sleep last night when Thea had been in her bedchamber. That fact would divert them well enough, she realized, and then she wouldn't have to discuss her feelings about leaving Inverley. "I met someone," she confessed.

Maeve's face was bright with interest. "It is little wonder you didn't wish to say anything on the lawn!"

Arabella and Caroline caught up with them. "What is the news?" Caroline asked.

"I met an intriguing woman." Grace debated how much to tell, then decided there was no need for discretion among friends. "We shared an even more intriguing night together."

Maeve pressed her hand to her forehead. "Am I to be the only one this summer with no romantic prospects? I am delighted for you, but how is it that you have all been so lucky?"

Arabella and Caroline linked hands. "We are indeed lucky," Arabella said, her cheeks turning bright pink as she stole a look at Caroline.

"I am talking about one night, not forever," Grace said. "I shall never have that, I fear." She had little enough leisure time as a companion to live her own life, let alone share it with someone else.

Maeve shook her head. "Maybe someday that will happen for me."

"Who is the lady?"

Grace hesitated. "Dorothea Martin."

She looked across the lawn, telling herself that she was checking on Edie but knowing perfectly well that her eyes lingered far longer on Thea, with her scarlet ribbons and bright white muslin. She was talking animatedly with her brothers, her hands on her hips.

She was bold and outrageous, and the last twenty-four hours had been the most fun Grace had ever had with another woman.

Arabella gasped. "I *thought* you looked rather close when she was helping you throw your ball!"

"Who is she?" Maeve asked. "I know of Mr. Martin—is this his sister?"

"Yes. She has a terrible reputation," Caroline said slowly. "It must have been fifteen years ago now that she left for London for her debut Season, when I was still a girl. I remember folks saying she embroiled herself in all manner of wild and scandalous behavior, and that she wasn't welcome back home until she changed her ways. She never did return, so I suppose she never changed." She frowned. "I never heard any rumors of her enjoying the company of women. But there may be more that we do not know about her."

"Well, I am not going to see her again," Grace said in a rush. "Not in any intimate sort of way. It would be foolish. But I admit I am curious about her."

She couldn't resist darting another look at Thea. Infatuated was closer to the truth than curious. The memory of her hands on her body would stay with her for a long, long time.

"She's a few years older than we are, and she often wouldn't deign to play with us town girls of lowly Belvoir Lane, but she wasn't a bad sort. Impulsive, and rash, but not *wicked*," Arabella rushed to explain.

"Not then," Caroline acknowledged. "But the people of Inverley have kept up the gossip. She lives by herself in London. From the little that Mr. and Mrs. Martin have said of her over the years, it sounds like she busies herself with drinking and reckless behavior at endless soirees."

"Sounds wonderful to me," Maeve said, one brow raised. "I shouldn't mind more parties in my life."

Neither would Grace. How grand it sounded. She thought wistfully of a life lived just for oneself, to do as one pleased. She would grasp at the opportunity in a heartbeat if it was offered to her.

Grace continued to watch from afar as Edie chatted with the Martins, and her heart ached. She needed to encourage Edie toward Mr. Martin—and her being distracted by his sister was in poor taste indeed.

CHAPTER SIX

Dinner that night was a bore compared to the antics on the bowling green. Mother's glare, felt all the way down the length of the table, reminded Thea that she was meant to be on her best behavior. But all she really wanted was to relive the feel of Grace's bare upper arm under her hand. It didn't matter that she had been wearing gloves this afternoon when she had touched her. She knew from last night how that arm felt, and she wanted more.

She wanted sun-dazzled kisses on the bluffs, and the scent of the ocean in her nose as she inhaled the spot just beneath Grace's ear.

It was absurd.

Mother had already lectured her after bowls, telling her to pay less attention to ladies' companions and more attention to the *meaningful* guests. Those with titles, or money, or both.

If only she could be free of this awful dependence, with Westhill Grange in her name instead of belonging to Charles! Her brothers had not been saints in London. It was blasted unfair to be punished for indiscretions that wouldn't have raised more than a brow if she had been a man.

Thea clutched her wineglass and started querying her neighbors at the table about their stay in Inverley. She could at least pretend to be interested. It was a simple matter of nodding one's head every few minutes with a little light laugh. Easily enough done. Her attention to what was being said was limited, with the unhappy result of her neighbor growing dour.

"I say, Miss Martin, have you heard a word I was saying?" he demanded, sitting back with a frown.

"Of course I did, sir. Most diverting."

He glowered. "I was speaking of the war in America. Why, ladies these days have nothing in their heads but cotton wool."

She felt Mother's eyes on her again. "I apologize. You are correct, war is indeed serious. I could not agree more."

That mollified him enough to continue with his pudding, while Thea struck up a conversation with the gentleman to her left.

It was a relief to collapse on her bed later and have a drink with Polly.

"I have no more than a few days left," Thea said. "Not enough time to change their opinion of me. Why, the length of one dinner conversation was enough to prove that."

If only she were good at this sort of thing. Smiling, and dancing, and pretending that one's whole life was a diversion. If only her parents could value someone who found it a bore.

They would never believe it of her, of course. She had hosted her share of soirees and dinners over the years, fueled with liquor and sparkling with wit, and those were the years that her parents knew about. They thought her dissolute, even though she had long since moved away from the parties and the late nights in favor of educational lectures and botanical study.

They had no idea that now she cultivated plants instead of scandal.

"You have plenty of time," Polly told her. "You'll get through this. You always do."

"Your confidence is touching, but I'm worried. I need to find a way to prove to my parents that they can trust me, without requiring me to marry or move to Inverley."

The next morning, Thea kicked at a stone as she walked beside Anthony. The bluffs around Martin House were beautiful. The sea was calm, the meadows were flush with wildflowers, and the town looked as charming as could be along the mile or two of sandy shore.

"I don't reckon you would care to stay for another week?" Anthony asked. "I would be happy to continue studying these cliffs."

"I am leaving the day after tomorrow. With or without you."

"Rather presumptuous of you to think of leaving with my coach."

"You would rather strand a lady where she is so unwelcome? There is no doubt that you may stay, of course. Mother would be happy to keep an earl's son in her house."

He stooped to pick up a flat rock. "There is the imprint of a leaf on the shale," he said, pointing it out to her. "That must soften your botanist's heart."

"I lived here for years, Anthony. I used to chip away the shale from the cliffs and uncovered all sorts of such imprints." It had indeed helped foster her fascination with plants. Her temper was too sour to admit that once upon a time, Inverley had held its charms for her too.

"Can't imagine why you don't like it here. Your family, I can understand. But Inverley? It's utterly delightful."

Inverley was wholesome, perfect, and serene. Everything that Thea wasn't. The seaside encouraged health and ruddy cheeks and stout lungs and all manner of nourishing activity. She kicked at another stone with rather more force.

"I shall get my parents' assurance that my allowance is restored, and then we are returning to London where we belong," she said, knowing her tone was sharp but unable to strip it of the bitterness that she felt.

"Of course." He paused. "I saw you making eyes at that lady's companion at dinner last night."

"Miss Linfield? I was doing nothing of the sort."

But then how else could she remember each curl that framed her face and the exact width of the velvet ribbon around her waist? She could have documented every whorl of the lace on Grace's dress as exhaustively as if she were counting each petal of a dahlia.

Hell and blazes. She *had* been staring.

"You may deny all you like, but those of us who know you best know better." He grinned. "Come now, do you plan to make a conquest?"

"Absolutely not." She never hid anything about herself from Anthony. But as long as they were in Inverley, Thea would do her best to prevent gossip about Grace's inclinations.

"Not your usual type, I suppose."

She paused. "What type is she, pray tell? What do you know of her? What have you heard?"

"Curious, are you?"

"Maybe a little." In fact, she was burning to know more.

"I spoke with her at breakfast yesterday morning. She seemed pleasant and kind, and rather sweet, and, well—"

"Too good for me." Thea felt deflated. Grace had seemed perfect to her, too. Flawless. Like a stone polished by the waves.

"No one is too good for you," he said firmly.

But she refused to speak more about it. "I need to get back to the house now to take tea with the guests. How else can my parents determine my worth?"

"You are worth diamonds to take me on this walk and show me more of the cliffside."

"But if it's not in the eyes of my parents, did my kind gesture even exist? I think not. You may linger among the sandstone and shale if you wish, but I must be back to Martin House."

Two more days, Thea thought. She could handle it for two more days.

After all, it was not like she had much choice.

Thea rested her head against the lip of the bathtub and closed her eyes, grateful for the warm water that soothed her aching thighs after hours of riding side-saddle. She didn't keep a riding horse in London, relying instead on hackneys to get around town.

But she had made a rash decision to prove to her parents that she was responsible enough to take a passel of houseguests through the bluffs along the unsettled parts of the coastline, trusting that she still remembered the way. She had even consulted with the housekeeper and brought a pair of servants on donkeys to carry a picnic luncheon to enjoy with a marvellous view.

It had been tedious in the extreme.

With every careful step that her horse took along the cliffside path, Thea had been haunted by memory. She had yearned once to stay here. Before her parents grew their disappointment with her the way that weeds thrived in a garden. It had been hard to look out at the dazzling sea, the sun glinting off its surface, the whitecaps dancing atop the waves. Too many dreams had died here for her to feel pleasure at the prospect.

Polly entered the room and dumped an armful of towels on the bed. "Have you soaked long enough to turn you to a prune?"

Thea sighed. "I suppose so. My legs still ache like the devil."

"That they would after a three-hour jaunt! You're no horsewoman."

Thea rose, the water sluicing off her skin as she stepped onto the mat beside the copper tub. Polly tossed her a towel and she dried herself. "I used to be when I was younger. Anyway, it was worth it," she said. "I think I saw Mother smile at me when I came home."

Polly shook her head. "They're tough as leather, your folks. Are you so sure you want to impress them?"

Thea stilled, the towel dangling from her hand. "That is the sole reason we are here. I need their support."

"Plenty of ways to make money in London. You don't need them."

"Obtaining seeds, cultivating rare flowers, and studying how to grow them take up a good deal of income. More than I could ever earn with what little marketable skills I have. My plants burn more money than most vices," Thea said. "I should know. I remember how much it cost to run a gambling hell out of my front parlor when I took a fancy to it that one year, and to stock brandy for the soirees I used to host." The gambling hell had been a terrible idea, and she was lucky to have disbanded it before membership grew beyond twenty-odd people.

"You and your plants," Polly grumbled, but her face looked soft when she came over with Thea's evening gown.

"Yes, me and my plants," Thea repeated. "They are the only things in my life to tend to, to nurture, and to grow. I will never abandon them."

They had saved her when her life was in ruins. More than the parties, more even than her friends. They had given her purpose.

She dressed and went downstairs to the drawing room before dinner.

She had accepted a glass of wine from a footman and had half a sip when Grace accosted her, her eyes wild and worried.

"You are back already?" she asked, her face pinched.

"It's nice to see you again so soon as well. Yes, I returned with the party several hours ago."

Grace blanched. "*Hours?*"

"Let me assure you, the outing was quite long enough for my liking. Whatever is the matter?" This was the first time Thea had seen Grace without her usual poise.

"Lady Edith did not return with you?"

"She told me soon after we left that she wasn't feeling well, and Charles escorted her home. She must be in her chambers."

"I knocked on her door before coming down to dine, and she is *not there*!" Grace's voice rose on the last words and a few people turned to look at her.

This was odd indeed. "Let me ask my parents if they have news."

She was reluctant at the thought of raising a potential problem with Mother, but she stole another look at Grace's face. She had no choice. What if Charles and Lady Edith had come to harm?

Mother was horrified when Thea pulled her outside the drawing room, Grace in tow, and told her what she knew. "Charles has an excellent sense of direction. He certainly is not lost!"

"I'm sure he is not, Mother. But something must have happened. One of their horses may have twisted a leg. Or what if one of them took a fall? We should send word round to the neighbors in case they are cozied up somewhere."

Thea wasn't truly worried. Charles may be muttonheaded but he was a *capable* enough muttonhead. He would never allow harm to a lady, let alone to Lady Edith—soon to become one of the family if James was to be believed. He was likely indulging in a whiskey and a hand of cards somewhere without much thought to the practicalities of sending word to Martin House about any mishap.

"A fall? The ground is very safe around these parts. But perhaps you are right, Dorothea. We should enquire with the neighbors."

Thea watched Grace spend the next hour mingling with guests, strung taut as a wire, her eyes darting to the door at the merest sound. Thea didn't want to examine what it meant that her own attention was so drawn to Grace. It was concern for a guest, nothing more.

When the footmen returned from the neighbors', Thea, Grace, and Mother met them in the parlor. But they brought no news. No one had seen either Charles or Lady Edith all afternoon.

"Could he be in town?" Mother asked.

"Not even Charles would wear his riding coat to an assembly."

Grace looked as if she might faint.

"There must be some explanation," Thea said, then hurried to add, "There is no real crime to speak of in Inverley. There's smuggling along the coast, of course, but smugglers would never dare do something so bold in broad daylight with no apparent motive."

"Smugglers!" Grace gasped.

"No, no. I said it *can't* be smugglers," Thea repeated, patting her hand. "You oughtn't worry so much."

Grace snatched her hand away, her eyes blazing.

Mother may like it or not, but Thea caught the footman's eye and jerked her head toward the cabinet where the spirits were kept. He brought a snifter to Grace, who stared at the splash of brandy.

"It's medicinal," Thea said, "and good for the nerves. Do steady yourself, Miss Linfield."

She didn't dare add, even in jest, that her father stocked his cabinet from the same smugglers that were decidedly *not* in question in today's goings on.

Grace sipped and coughed. Thea found herself wishing she could reach out and touch her, to hold her hand or rub her back to comfort her.

"Is there anyone else we could ask?" Grace asked, her voice faint. "Miss Martin, you mentioned that Lady Edith had been unwell. Could we send word to the doctor in Inverley in case Mr. Martin took her there?"

Mother wrote another note and dispatched another servant.

But again, no news returned with him.

Grace pled a headache and retired to her bedchamber after dinner.

Thea followed suit a quarter-hour after. She paused when she walked by the Rose Suite but decided against knocking. Grace needed rest.

Thea went through her evening routine with Polly, but her mind was focused on the mystery. Wherever could Charles be? After Polly left, she sat for a long while on the windowsill staring into the starry night, trying to remember anything from the afternoon's ride that could give any hint to what had happened.

Just as Thea climbed into bed, her door opened.

CHAPTER SEVEN

Grace rushed into Thea's room wreathed in a halo of light, a candle clutched in one hand as she brandished a charred piece of paper in the other.

"It isn't good news," she announced, and perched on the edge of Thea's bed without so much as a by-your-leave, her neat plait swinging over her shoulder. She wore a cotton wrapper that covered her from neck to toes, printed with tiny flowers.

Thea sat up, holding the blanket to her bosom. She slept in the nude. Grace had already seen all of her and shouldn't be scandalized, but it didn't seem quite right in the moment.

"What is it? A letter?"

Grace nodded. "I found it half-burnt in Edie's fireplace. After I retired, I went to her room and tried to find any clue of what might have happened. I couldn't find anything at first, but then I noticed the fireplace had ash in it, which I wouldn't expect in August."

Thea took her candle and put it on the nightstand. "What does it say?"

She wet her lips with her tongue, her chest rising and falling with shallow breaths. "It was addressed to her mother, but I suppose Edie realized her news would be unwelcome and thought better of sending it. Edie and Mr. Martin—Mr. *Charles* Martin, I should say—they have... well. It seems they have fled to Gretna Green. They are eloping."

"Eloping?" Thea stared. "They don't even know each other!"

"It's incomprehensible."

Thea had known Grace for about as long as Charles had known Lady Edith. It had proved long enough to like her, and long enough to be intrigued by her. But to run away to Scotland together on such short acquaintance? She leaned against the headboard. "Eloping," she repeated, unable to believe it. "I didn't think Charles had it in him to do such a thing."

Grace looked miserable. "Her hairbrush is gone, and so are a few of her gowns. I also found this beneath her pillow." She produced a handkerchief from the pocket of her wrapper, and Thea saw the monogram *CM* embroidered in the corner.

Her heart sank. "This is damning evidence indeed."

Grace shook her head. "It's foolish in the extreme," she said. "Her mother is to arrive at the house party by the end of the week. She is expecting Edie to be engaged to Mr. James Martin. Edie is eloping with the *wrong brother*!"

The look of anguish on her face spoke volumes.

Thea was starting to wonder if Lady Edith was an impertinent baggage who oughtn't wed either of her brothers, but that was beside the point. Charles had behaved like a cad. If he had run off with Lady Edith, it would cause an uproar. James would be livid, Father would be mortified by the scandal, and Mother was going to have a fit of the vapors that may very well last the rest of her life.

Thea sat upright.

And that meant *opportunity*.

"I'm going after him," she announced, and flung the covers from the bed.

Grace blinked at her and Thea remembered she wasn't wearing a stitch of clothing. She grabbed a shift and pulled it over her head. She debated ringing for Polly, but it was long past midnight. She couldn't leave Inverley straightaway, but she could at least pack her valise to be ready at the crack of dawn. She hauled her carpet bag onto the bed and yanked her dresser drawers open, rummaging for stockings and her traveling dress and whatever she could think of to last a journey to Scotland.

"What are you doing?"

"I'm going after him," she repeated, trying to find patience. "My parents will be furious if Charles follows through on this fool's errand."

"You don't know what route they've taken!"

"Of course I do. Charles isn't clever enough to take anything beside the main roads. He will have gone on the mail coach to London, then a stagecoach along the Great North Road. If I leave at dawn, then they only have a half day's head start. It will be the work of a few days to catch up. Nothing more than a lark."

"Do you think it's possible?"

"I do."

In fact, she had no idea. But what better way to show her parents how dedicated she was to family than for the prodigal to go haring after the lost sheep? In one fell swoop, she could escape this awful stay in Inverley and do something that would guarantee her place in this family. Triumph raced through her veins. At last, she had found a way to succeed that wouldn't depend on good behavior, but instead on her actions.

She yanked the smaller of her two trunks over to her and worried her lip as she tried to remember just how far away Scotland was. Anthony would have to come with her, of course. He was an experienced traveler and would be her best bet to gain enough ground to stop Charles and Lady Edith. Traveling together would raise brows along the road, but there was no choice.

"I'm coming with you." Grace stood, a fierce look on her face.

There was something almost familial in Grace's devotion to her charge.

Unlike herself. On a personal level, it didn't matter much to Thea who Lady Edith or Charles wed. They were adults and capable of making such decisions for themselves, though she thought Lady Edith was getting the poor end of the bargain, having to put up with Charles for a lifetime.

Far from altruism, it was money that compelled Thea. She felt almost ashamed for a moment. But what mattered the motive as long as everyone would be happier if she could bring them home?

"You won't be comfortable. It's best for you to stay here. In case Lady Edith writes to you," she added, improvising.

Grace was *not* coming with her to Scotland.

Not in a carriage, cooped up together for days on end.

Not staying at inns together along the road, darkness beckoning them to continue their secret affair.

She couldn't gaze at those lips all day and remember where they had been on her body and then be expected to avoid the temptation to lay with her at night.

But Grace stood, resolute, her dark eyes burning from her pale face. "Lady Edith is my charge. I am coming with you."

"Shouldn't you be here when Lady Edith's mother arrives?"

Her lips thinned. "I want nothing *less* than to be the one to tell her the news."

It could be helpful to have her on the journey. They could be each other's chaperones on the road with Anthony. If they were successful, it would be better for Lady Edith if she could travel home with Grace by her side so she could avoid any questions about where her companion had been during her jaunt away from Inverley. Lady Edith would be ruined otherwise.

She doubted Grace knew the first thing about the pell-mell pace that the trip would demand. Maybe Polly could rustle up some smelling salts to bring with them for the inevitable fits of the vapors, though she would go off in peals of laughter if Thea ever suggested such a thing.

"I'm leaving at dawn," Thea said, still hedging. "The days on the road will be long."

"I can handle it," Grace snapped. "I will be ready." She stalked out of the room.

Thea blew out a breath. Would it hurt to have such a lovely passenger by her side? And yet, that way lay dangerous thoughts indeed.

It was dark enough that the owls were still hooting. Grace fidgeted with her reticule as she stood on the cobblestones in front of Martin House, her leather portmanteau at her feet. She hadn't trusted Thea to leave Inverley without her, so she wanted to make sure that she couldn't be overlooked if anyone was coming or going.

She had barely slept for fear of missing her opportunity.

The thought of disappointing Lady Harriet had been enough to keep her awake all on its own. She had been serious when she told Thea that she didn't want to be in Inverley when Lady Harriet arrived and discovered Edie missing.

She pulled her shawl tighter around herself. The sun would burn off the sea fog before long, but in the dark of night it was chilly. She had been waiting for a half hour at least, and her thin shoes were growing damp.

There were bats flying around the eaves of Martin House, and she grew uneasy. They were an ill omen indeed. What if harm had befallen Edie?

She remembered the geography lessons that she had taught when she had been a governess. To make good time, they would need to spend over a dozen hours each day on the road. It would be a difficult journey, and tedious. If they didn't catch up with Edie and Mr. Charles before the border, then they would be on the road for at least a week on the way to Scotland, and then another on the way back.

How much easier it would be if it were anyone other than Thea on the journey with her! She would rather have Mr. James Martin as her companion instead of his sister. As awful as he was, she could trust that he would conduct a thorough search. He wasn't a man to take being embarrassed lightly.

Thea, on the other hand—how could she know what her priorities were? From what Caroline and Arabella had said of her, she wasn't known to be reliable. How could she trust that she would follow through and go all the way to Scotland if need be? Last night she had called it a lark. Grace needed to go with her to be assured that there would be no scandal.

How could Edie have done such a thing? How was it possible that she had planned an escape with so little time? Mr. James Martin wasn't the husband that Grace would have liked for Edie, but to elope with his *brother*!

Grace was lucky to have found the letter in the grate. She hadn't expected to find anything like that when she had looked through Edie's room. Instead, she had been worried that she might find an unsent letter to Lady Harriet referencing her interesting condition, which she would not want any of the maids to find if they came in to tidy the room.

Thea came bustling out the door, followed by Mr. Robinson and a pair of footmen carrying lanterns. She stopped short when she saw Grace.

"Miss Linfield! I thought you would still be abed at this hour. I was planning on packing up Mr. Robinson's coach and then waking you. I must see what kind of horseflesh my father keeps in the stables and then we can begin our journey. I don't wish to lose a moment of daylight, so we shall be off before the rest of the house wakes." Thea turned to Mr. Robinson. "Let's take a look at the stables," she said, marching past Grace.

The footmen followed Thea, leaving Grace alone again in the dark. She shivered in the cool air. What had she gotten herself into? She pressed a hand to her stomach to calm her nerves, then marched after them.

Thea looked up when Grace entered the stables. "We will be on our way soon, I promise, Miss Linfield."

The coach was covered in black lacquer and looked as slick as if it had been raining. It was the most impressive conveyance Grace had ever seen. Thea stood beside the coach, equal to its magnificence in the lantern light, her blond hair bright as burnished gold. Her body was taut and her eyes were shining, as if she were primed and eager for adventure.

A thought struck Grace. "We are not taking two coaches?"

However would they fit the servants? The coach could seat four, but surely Mr. Robinson would need his valet, and they each would take a maid? Though she was no servant, she had assumed she would ride in the second carriage.

"We're already a day behind. We won't be able to catch up if we're waiting on four more horses and another coach to catch up to us at every stage. We need to travel light." Thea studied her. "You needn't come, Miss Linfield, if you are afraid of being uncomfortable. I will have my maid with me. It will all be quite proper." Her tone changed into a sneer on the word *proper*, as if it was distasteful to her.

A prickle of unease started in Grace's belly. She would be in a carriage with Thea all day.

Every day.

For up to two weeks.

That, too, had contributed to her sleepless night.

"It is my duty to bring Lady Edith back to Inverley. I am not afraid of a little discomfort along the road."

The truth was that she wasn't uncomfortable. She was terrified.

What if something happened on the road and they met up with an accident, or—God forbid—a highwayman?

What if the rooms at the inns weren't safe and someone stole into their chambers while they slept?

What if Thea took her in her arms and kissed her again?

She closed her eyes and took a deep breath, willing herself to calm down.

"I will accompany you, Miss Martin. Wherever you may go."

CHAPTER EIGHT

Thea eyed Grace as she stood beside the coach. Her face was pale and her lips were pressed together tighter than a tulip at night. She hoped Grace wasn't the type to fall ill during carriage rides, but she supposed it was time to find out. The sky was lightening and the birds had started chirping. They had no time left to shilly-shally.

The grooms finished hitching up the horses and slung the baggage into the leather imperial strapped to the top of the coach. Thea headed back to the house. She had asked the butler to wake her parents before sunrise.

Father was already standing at the front entrance, dressed for the day as if he always woke at such an hour. As little as she knew of their current lifestyle and habits, she supposed he might.

"I'm off to fetch Charles," she told him without preamble, looking up at him at the top of the stairs. "I'll have him back within the fortnight."

Mother came out and stood beside him. There were heavy shadows under her eyes. "This will be a scandal."

Thea had already come up with a plan. "Not if we keep things quiet. If you and Father tell the guests that Lady Edith had a sudden need to visit a relative in poor health, and that Charles and I escorted her along with her companion, Miss Linfield—then everything is as proper as can be. No one could get up to mischief with two spinsters in tow. I daresay even the notion would put a damper on any sort of young person's fun." It couldn't fail. She felt light and cheerful, eager to go.

Father sighed. "If you succeed—"

"*When* I succeed," Thea corrected him.

"*If* you succeed, you would be saving the reputation of our family."
She stood a little taller and repressed a bounce of her heels. Finally,
some approval. About blasted time.

"I can't tell you what it would mean to us to have Charles escape
this unscathed." Mother shook her head.

"You can trust me to get this situation under control." She
hesitated. "When I do, I wish to review your plans for the inheritance."

Father glowered. "That is not up for negotiation."

"Charles has proved himself unworthy of Westhill Grange," she
said, refusing to back down. "He has betrayed all trust in himself. When
I bring him back without scandal—could my reward be the deed?"

Her breath caught in her throat. Westhill Grange was a far better
prize than retaining her allowance. It may have few rents to sustain it,
but it had a sprawl of lawns. Space enough for two dozen conservatories
if she wanted them.

It felt gauche to think of helping her family as transactional, but
then again, they were not bound together by anything as tawdry and
middle class as *emotion*.

"There is merit to what you say," Father said gruffly. "If all goes
well, you may consider the Grange to be yours."

Thea hurried to the coach as the first streaks of gold started to
brush the sky with the sun's warmth. For the first time in days, she felt
like everything was going to be all right.

This was going to be a most welcome adventure.

Two hours later, Thea's enthusiasm had waned.

Anthony's coach was comfortable enough. It was his best one, and
though he was but an earl's youngest son, the best meant more luxury
than Thea was accustomed to. Thick padded cushions, large windows
with drapes that blocked even the brightest sunlight if desired, oiled
springs that made the seats bounce and glide with nary a creak.

But four people in such close quarters wasn't Thea's idea of a
pleasure trip, no matter how well sprung the coach was.

Anthony yawned on about geology, to the point that Thea wondered
if Polly had thought to pack any laudanum in her reticule, though she
supposed it was about as unlikely as smelling salts would be.

Polly was restless and requested the curtains to be drawn open and closed a half dozen times, trying to get comfortable and catch up on last night's truncated sleep.

Grace remained the picture of perfection. Thea didn't know why she was surprised. Even on the bowling green, when it had been clear that she had the athletic prowess of a shrinking violet, she had managed to look like she *belonged*.

A smile rested on her face as if glued there, unmoved by the bumps and dips in the road. She appeared absorbed in Anthony's conversation, as if there were no better use of her time than to listen to a lecture on cartography.

She was infuriatingly patient.

At the same time, so very kissable.

Thea wanted to unlace the ribbon of Grace's bonnet and thread her fingers through her light brown hair, shaking it loose from her plait. She wanted to tug her linen fichu off with her teeth and press a kiss against her collarbone, inhaling her lavender scent. She wanted to run her hand over Grace's wrist and press her thumb into the sweet curve of her elbow as she moved her arms above her head. She wanted to wedge a knee between those thighs and—

"We are already at our first stop of the journey," Anthony announced, knocking a knuckle against the windowpane.

Thea's heart thudded into place and she wrested her thoughts back to their current predicament. This wasn't leisure travel. It was a hunt.

"We made good time," Grace said, her voice calm. Thea envied her self-control even as it stung her ego. Clearly, their proximity didn't have the same effect on her.

"I reckon it will take a half hour to hitch up a new set of horses, if you ladies wish to refresh yourselves inside the inn."

A stagecoach could change horses in ten, and the mail coach that Charles and Lady Edith had undoubtedly taken could make do in five. Thea hoped Grace didn't realize how much time they would lose in stopping, but there was no choice. The horses couldn't go more than ten miles at a stretch.

"I'm long past due for a cup of tea," Polly announced, and hopped out of the coach as soon as they stopped long enough to open the doors.

"It will be nice to stroll," Grace said, stepping down to the cobblestones with Anthony's assistance. "My legs are stiff."

She arched her back and moved her head from side to side. It was a discreet ladylike stretch, but Thea was aware of every shift of every muscle as if Grace wasn't clad neck to ankles in a sturdy twill dress. Her traveling clothes were as unadorned as her day dresses were. She was primly buttoned up, but the dark brown fabric was rich against her skin and made Thea want to reach out and touch.

Thea wanted tea. Polly might have even ordered her a cup already. She also had to use the necessary.

Why were her feet not moving?

A throng clamored out of a stagecoach behind them, and Thea took a step closer to Grace, who looked at her with those steady brown eyes, as rich and dark as the strong tea she was missing out on.

She absolutely would *not* offer to walk around the square with Grace, as much as she wanted to protect her from the rabble. It was best to take time away from her. Thea was going inside that inn.

Now.

Any minute.

"Would you care to walk with me?" Grace asked, and Thea's resolve blew away like a dandelion puff.

"Of course." She cupped Grace's elbow and led her away from the crowd. "Has anyone ever told you that you have the most kissable of elbows?" she asked, taking the outside of the sidewalk to protect Grace from any kicked-up muck from the passing horses.

Grace blinked up at her. "No one has kissable elbows."

"You do," Thea insisted. It might have been because it was the one part of her body that she could touch in public that wasn't covered up, but that bare elbow was driving her to distraction. "If no one has ever bothered to examine such a perfect part of you, then I suppose it must remain a secret between us."

"Has anyone ever told you that you are an incorrigible flirt?" Grace asked her, but she didn't shake her hand away.

"They certainly have. I hope the standard of my flirtation meets with your approval."

"Thea, we *can't.*" Her voice was barely above a whisper.

"What can't we do?"

"You know well what I mean. We cannot draw such attention to ourselves."

"No one knows us on the road. There will be no talk if we're discreet. Why deny ourselves what we both want?"

"It's not who I am," Grace said finally, fidgeting with her reticule. "I wasn't *myself* that night."

Thea had heard such things before. It never failed to infuriate her. Women who had been willing enough to go to her bed, but when she chanced to meet them again, they claimed that they couldn't have enjoyed such a thing as sapphic love. Women who protested that it was the sway of Thea's seduction that had compelled them, and not their own desires. They were *proper* women. *Good* women. *Dutiful* women, looking for a husband and not a lover. Especially not an unnatural sort of lover.

"Then I wonder who I lay with two nights ago?" Thea snapped. "Was it not you, if you don't lay claim to the legs that have obsessed me since last I saw them?"

Grace looked into her eyes. "That night was an exception. I don't engage in such behavior casually."

"But you have done this before, haven't you?" Thea felt a stab of guilt. If that had been her first time, then she had deserved more than Thea crawling out in the middle of the night.

"Yes. But not like this. I knew those women. I had *relationships* with them. It was…refined. Sensible."

They stopped walking and stood beneath the eave of an inn. A draft horse was standing to their right, and there was a haphazard pile of trunks and bags waiting to be thrown into one of the stagecoaches to their left.

No one paid the slightest bit of attention to them, however close they stood together.

There was that word again. *Sensible.* Grace had known her for a scant forty-eight hours and already recognized that Thea was good enough to travel with, good enough for one romp, but not for anything else.

Thea leaned forward so close that their bonnet brims overlapped, and she could see the tawny flecks in Grace's wide brown eyes. "You didn't seem refined when you were moaning my name."

Grace's lips fell open and Thea felt a surge of satisfaction. She wasn't as immune to flirtation as she claimed.

"We never did discuss the forfeit," Thea murmured.

"I beg your pardon?"

"You lost the game of bowls. Dreadful performance, even with my help. Now, I wonder what forfeit I shall claim." She stared into her eyes. "A kiss, perhaps?"

Grace jerked back. "That cannot happen again, Miss Martin." Her tone was sharp, every inch of her a frosty chaperone brandishing admonishments like a sword.

Miss Martin now, was she? She backed away, her hands up. "Don't worry, Miss Linfield. I don't sleep with unwilling women. There are plenty enough around."

"We have enough to worry about without an affair between us. Our journey began today and already I fear that we are too late."

"We will catch up with my hell-begotten brother and your unwise charge," Thea promised through clenched teeth.

"How can you know for sure?"

Defeat was not an option. Not when she had the opportunity to win Westhill Grange. "If they do say their vows before we arrive, I shall convince them to leave all memory of it in Scotland." She shrugged. "If no one except for us knows that a marriage occurred, and if we all promise to say nothing about it, did it really happen in the eyes of society?"

Grace gasped. "Those vows are *sacred*."

"It is but words spoken over an anvil."

"Mr. Charles Martin would be the worst of cads if he didn't stand by his word!" Grace cried. "I would never be party to such deception. Marriage is a sacrament that must be respected. It's a commitment, Miss Martin. Those words have *value*. They have *honor*. And any who speak them must be held accountable."

Grace strode back to the coach a step ahead of Thea, almost vibrating with offense.

Thea watched Grace's pert backside as she stepped into the coach. This trip to Scotland was sure to feel as long as Anthony's voyages to the Americas. There were plenty of dangers to be had along the road, but unslaked lust was a peril she had never expected.

"We are coming up to Swanley, where we will stop for the night," Mr. Robinson announced.

Thea and Polly cheered.

Grace's heart sank. "Please, could we go a little farther?"

Her hips and knees were sore from the constant jostle of the coach. She was convinced her very hair ached. She was so exhausted on the first day that she couldn't fathom how she was going to last all the way to Scotland when they had not yet even reached London.

But she felt quivery at the thought of failing Lady Harriet.

"Miss Linfield, the horses can't keep going at this pace." Mr. Robinson's tone was gentle but firm.

"Then we shall change horses again," she insisted. "What if they have continued straight through the night, and we have lost even more time?"

Thea frowned. "I doubt Charles would bother. Is Lady Edith the sort who would put her comforts aside?"

She doubted it. Edie was as pampered as any debutante ever had been. Grace saw the fatigue not only on Thea's face, but on Mr. Robinson's and Polly's as well. She couldn't dictate the journey. Companions never did. "Of course you are right," she said, pasting a smile on her face. "Do let's stop for the night."

The inn was cramped, noisy, and had its share of cobwebs in the eaves, but Grace forgave the establishment its multitude of sins as soon as the aroma of roast beef wafted over her.

The innkeeper sucked his teeth when he saw them. "You're not a minute too late," he boomed. "I've got two rooms left, one for the gent and one for the ladies. Plenty of space for the maid in the attic."

Grace should have insisted on traveling all night after all. She should march outside, hitch up a fresh pair of horses, and go on by herself if need be.

Anything to avoid the temptation of having Thea Martin in her bed.

All night long.

Again.

Chapter Nine

Grace refused to look at Thea, afraid she would see the same desire on her face that she had seen that morning when they had stopped to switch the horses. Grace had almost given in and kissed her then and there, on a public road filled with God only knew who. It had been decidedly unlike her.

"How fortunate we are that there is a room for us," Thea said. "We shall be quite cozy."

It was common enough to share a room on the road with a traveling companion or a family member. Grace and Edie had shared a bed during their journey from Manchester to London, and then from London to Inverley and had thought nothing of it.

The flame that burned between herself and Thea was something else entirely.

Thea tossed her bonnet onto the bed once the innkeeper showed them to their room. Polly had come with them to help Thea unpack her belongings. "I'm so glad that we are finished for the day. I cannot wait to sit down and have a proper meal."

The bed seemed impossibly narrow for the two of them. They were in tight quarters indeed. Grace frowned down at the beribboned straw bonnet and snatched it up, hanging it on the wall hook where it belonged. Thea didn't seem to notice as she dropped her shawl onto the bed too.

"Are you not starved, Miss Linfield?"

Grace picked up the shawl and folded it into fourths before placing it on top of the dresser. "I suppose I wouldn't mind dinner," she said, defaulting to a genteel disregard for one's physical condition while praying that her stomach wouldn't rumble. In truth, she could eat a whole wheel of cheese and a loaf of bread if given half a chance. What was it about the road that made one so hungry?

"You don't have to put away my things," Thea said. "You aren't a maid."

The word froze her in her tracks.

"Not even I am so invested in tidying after Thea, and I *am* her maid," Polly said cheekily. "That would be a full-time task unto itself."

"I like things to be orderly," Grace said, forcing her voice to stay calm.

There were plenty of other things in the room that she wanted to fix. The painting on the wall wasn't straight. The bottom dresser drawer was open half an inch. Their baggage had been dumped in a most inconvenient place, blocking the path to the folding screen where the chamber pot and wash basin were hidden.

Grace said nothing further and touched nothing else in the room. That was the first rule of companionship. To be agreeable, even when one felt most disagreeable indeed.

"Shall we go to dinner?" she asked, folding her hands in front of her.

They made for an unusual table. An earl's son, a gentlewoman, a lady's companion, and a maid, for Thea insisted that Polly sit with them instead of in the kitchens with the servants. It was a boisterous enough inn that it didn't matter who was where or indeed, who they were.

Grace had always been settled into a particular segment of society. Not a lady, not a servant. Not a relative, not a friend. Here at this table, she felt startlingly like an equal. It gave her the same unsettled feeling that she had when looking at the crooked painting and the open drawer.

She remained quiet for most of dinner, as platters of fried sole with mustard and roasted rabbit with root vegetables were briskly served and taken away. Listening to the easy flow of conversation among her party, Grace was envious of their comfort with one another. She drank plenty of wine, as Mr. Robinson insisted that everyone's cup be filled anytime he spied that a scant half-inch had disappeared.

The air was thick with tension as Grace and Thea returned to their room alone some hours later.

"I shan't bring up the forfeit again as it made you uncomfortable," Thea said, toeing off her shoes, "but I am happy to be of service if ever you change your mind on bedroom matters."

If Thea had sat next to her on the bed and murmured the words in her ear, or if she had looked at her the way she had in the coach yard that morning, then Grace thought she would have fallen right into her arms, her resolve as thin as her cotton shift and as easily removed.

This matter-of-fact offer was as surprising as it was tempting, but decline it she must.

"It is for the best that we do not engage in nocturnal activities together." Grace tried to sound as prim as she could.

Instead of wrinkling her nose at her prudishness, Thea grinned at her. "Then let us tuck ourselves into bed, as we have another long day ahead tomorrow."

Grace picked up her portmanteau to retrieve her toiletries.

"Even your luggage is plain," Thea said with interest, looking at the sturdy brown leather.

"Whyever wouldn't it be?" Then Grace blinked as she saw Thea lift her carpet bag, embroidered with bright threads that were highly impractical for travel. "Are you not worried that yours will become dirty along the journey?"

"Oh, I don't care much if it does. Something well used isn't less beautiful, and I have an eye for pretty things."

Thea disappeared behind the folding screen. Grace could hear the rustle of fabric as her dress dropped to the floor. After a moment, she busied herself by changing out of her own dress at the same time, to keep herself from imagining Thea in the nude.

"I hope we make better progress once we start along the Great North Road," Grace said, folding her dress and placing it in the dresser. She set out a fresh shift and stays for tomorrow.

She sat on the bed and brushed her hair until it crackled, then bound it into a thin plait. She found her tin of lavender cream and rubbed it into her face and hands. The scent always calmed her. She had long relied on routines that she could take from job to job to make her feel at home wherever she was.

Thea was still behind the screen. "We will pass through London tomorrow, and as far as St. Neots if we're lucky."

Grace wondered where Edie was now. She didn't want to say anything negative about Mr. Charles Martin to Thea, as he was her brother and presumably not *entirely* a villain, but she knew nothing of his character. Could he protect Edie? Or had she been left in some out-of-the-way inn, with no money and no knowledge of how to return to London or Inverley? As a man, and a wealthy one at that, Charles could hire a horse at any point and ride away unscathed, but Edie would be in danger until Grace caught up to her. She felt sick at the thought. The threat on the road was not always from brigands.

Grace slipped under the sheets, relieved that they smelled fresh, and watched Thea emerge from behind the screen. Her shift was thin enough to hint at the curves of her body, with a little frill edged with lace at the hem that Grace hadn't expected. It was sweet.

"Shall we divide the bed with a pillow?" Thea asked, her hands on her hips as she studied the bed.

Grace was touched that she had thought about it. "I don't think it's necessary."

"Good. You know, I do hope you are admiring my shift, because I don't wear one to bed for just anyone. Usually I sleep naked."

Grace laughed despite her best intentions as Thea blew out the candle and got into bed beside her. There was something about her that made it impossible not to like her.

They settled into a comfortable sort of quiet, despite the distant noise from the taproom where travelers were still drinking and laughing. The leaves outside rustled in the breeze, and Thea's breathing became deep and regular, and Grace relaxed into sleep.

Thea had thought that once they were past London that the journey would be easier. But while the first day had sped by in a blur of anxiety, the second day plodded along in tedium. Each mile on the road felt like ten.

They exhausted themselves all morning talking about where Charles and Lady Edith might be now and where they may have stopped along the way. No one at the London inn where the Inverley mail coach stopped remembered seeing anyone who matched Lady Edith's or Charles's description.

Polly was eager to bet a shilling that they had made it all the way to Grantham already, which was pure nonsense and only served to agitate Grace. Anthony gave a reasoned argument for them still being within a day's reach, and Thea was inclined to believe him.

"It was good luck that you found Lady Edith's letter. They won't realize that we are on their trail or that we know where they are headed, so they may not be in such a hurry," Thea told Grace, attempting to soothe. "Charles would have thought the plan to be a good deal cleverer than it is. But he loves nothing more than doing three things at once to avoid boredom, and he is almost professional in his ability to get himself into a scrape. He will either make a mistake, or slow his party down with some sort of buffoonery."

"His character does not sound at all reassuring to the good name of my charge."

"If they are going to Scotland, then I have no doubt that he intends to be honorable."

"*If* they are going to Scotland?" Grace's voice bordered on shrill.

"I didn't mean to cast aspersions. Of course that's where they are going. We saw it in the letter. Unless Lady Edith has convinced him otherwise since they have been on the road, but we have no evidence of such a thing." Feckless as Charles was, Thea was still surprised that he had chosen to elope on such short acquaintance.

"She is a kind sweet girl who doesn't get into trouble." Grace was composed, but her eyes darted away for an instant.

Thea was intrigued. Did Grace know more about Lady Edith's intentions than she was letting on? "Except running away with a man she barely knows right before her engagement to his brother, of course," she said.

Grace remained quiet and restrained her glares at the reticule in her lap instead of at Thea.

There was nothing else to do now but stare out the window and make their way through the basket of breads and pastries that Anthony had purchased at the previous stage for luncheon.

Thea and Anthony were sitting backward, and Grace and Polly were sitting across from them. Thea wondered if she could suggest for Grace to sit beside her instead of across from her. But which was worse—gazing at her all day, knowing that she didn't wish for her advances and yet being inexplicably afire to give them to her? Or sitting beside her, their thighs and arms brushing against each other's while the coach bumped over a rock, or pressing together in a most indecent manner during a sharp turn and—

Thea sighed and peeked inside the basket.

"I finished the last of the orange cake," Polly said. "It was that good, too. Mr. Robinson, you could not have chosen a better bakery at which to cast your custom. Can we return there on our way back?"

"I am ever your servant, Miss Polly," he said, touching his gloved hand to the brim of his hat, and she grinned at him.

Thea picked up a blueberry scone and nibbled a corner. Delightful as it was, it could only hold her attention for so long, its pleasures diminishing as the carriage wheels rolled on and on. The tedium had her looking again at Grace, by far the most intriguing attraction in the carriage.

At some point would Grace realize that there was little point to deny themselves the pleasures that they both so clearly wanted?

"Miss Linfield, would you care for a pastry?" Anthony asked, rapping his knuckles on the basket between him and Thea.

"I would indeed," she said, smiling at him as she selected a plain bun.

"Are you a Puritan?" Polly asked, her eyes bright with curiosity. "That's the dullest looking one of the lot. I cannot even believe Mr. Robinson included it in the basket. It's not *worthy*."

Grace tore off a piece and popped it in her mouth. "This is lovely. I don't care much for sweets."

There were crumbs on the cushioned bench after they had finished, and Grace brushed them into her linen napkin. She shook the napkin out the window to dispense of the evidence of their lunch and tucked the basket beneath the seat.

"I wasn't yet done with that bite of scone," Polly said mournfully.

"Then I shall buy you another at our next stop if you're still hungry." Grace sounded as unforgiving as any governess.

"Are you so opposed to disorder that you cannot bear even a crumb to be out of place in your presence?" Thea asked.

"I am aware that not everything can be put in its place." Her tone was calm but there was a twitch of her lips as she added, "Nor *everyone*, either."

Thea grinned slowly. So she was having *some* effect on Miss Prim-and Proper today, was she?

"Were you Lady Edith's governess before becoming her companion?" Anthony asked.

"No, I was hired by her mother before the Season began." Grace didn't offer anything further.

Thea wondered if she didn't wish to talk about it. "Where were you employed before?"

"I was a companion to an agreeable widow for some years in Manchester. She remarried and had no more need of me."

"And before that?"

"To go back too far would perhaps hint at my age, which is a disagreeable topic," Grace said with a smile. "I was a governess for years before I became a companion. Children are wonderful, but I prefer the companionship of adults."

"I am sure you must have some hair-raising stories about your time as a governess." Thea winced. "I am sorry to say that they suffered from unfortunate circumstances on occasion at Martin House."

"I was lucky to be placed in good households with well-regarded families."

"You never lost your temper? I shouldn't have blamed you," Anthony said. "I put a mouse in the bed of my governess once, on a dare from my older brother."

"Never," Grace said placidly. "I have always had the support of my superiors, and the children I taught were angelic. I have had an uneventful career."

There was nothing to her conversation but platitudes. Her conversation was polite but so reserved that Thea couldn't tell what she thought of her positions, but it wasn't possible that Grace had been perfect all the time. *No one* was.

Thea yearned to disrupt her calm and find out what lay beneath. Perhaps because it didn't add up to the Grace that she had held in her bed. They hadn't talked much the night that they had made love, but Grace had seemed passionately and vibrantly alive. The woman on the bench across from her now was like a doll, or an actor. It was all facade—nothing real. Daytime Grace could not be less like nighttime Grace.

"I cannot imagine such an existence," Thea said. "I have been courting mischief for what feels like my whole life."

It had once been true, though the most trouble she was in these days would be with creditors if she couldn't convince her parents to continue to support her. But Grace didn't need to know that. Everyone in Inverley thought of Thea as a bad seed, and Grace would have to think the same if Thea wished to keep her current life private.

The idea of telling any of her family about her botany made her flinch. That was hers, and hers alone.

All in all, it was a disappointing day. There would be nothing to do besides talk for hours on end until they reached Scotland. To discover that her traveling companion was to be polite and pleasant without even the smallest anecdote to share? Thea thought she would have better discourse from the horses. She was grateful that Polly and Anthony kept up a steady stream of conversation at least.

And yet Grace must have opinions in her somewhere. Any woman who dared to slip between another woman's sheets had to be someone of strong convictions, or she would never have taken the risk. So why was Grace acting as if she were accompanying an elderly dowager to church instead of chasing scandal with a known reprobate all the way to Scotland?

CHAPTER TEN

By the fifth day, Grace wondered if it was possible to expire from the exhaustion of travel. Although the journey consisted of nothing more strenuous than sitting, with the opportunity to stretch her legs when they switched out the horses for fresh ones, by nightfall she felt as if she had walked every one of the miles that they had covered.

Mr. Robinson rode ahead on a rented horse for hours each day, and Polly spent much of her time curled up in the corner of the seat, napping. Thea, on the other hand, was not a restful traveling companion. If there was a loose thread in a cushion, she was pulling at it. If there was a book at hand, she was sighing as she flipped the pages. When there was silence, she was drumming her fingers against the carriage wall.

But there wasn't much silence to be had because most of all Thea wanted to *talk*. She spoke of the weather and the clouds in the sky and the venison at last night's dinner. She talked of books she had read and the daily news that they were able to glean from other travelers at the inns they stopped at.

What they didn't speak of much was the reason they were on the road, to avoid arguments about Edie or Mr. Martin. Instead, they conversed as social acquaintances trapped in an endless afternoon visit. Grace was careful not to talk too deeply of her past, worried about revealing too much. As a result, she was embarrassed that her contributions included nothing more stimulating than her preference for apples instead of strawberries, and that she had never tried pineapple despite it being all the rage.

She was already in enough danger with Lady Harriet keeping her secrets. She didn't need to spread them even more thinly among strangers.

So she made sure that a smile was always hovering on her lips, and that she nodded at regular intervals to show her engagement. It was a guise that had always worked well over the years in the presence of employers, and it was all she could do to protect herself now when she felt overcome with fear and worry. But the pretense exhausted her as much as the travel did.

She listened as Mr. Robinson and Thea talked about London before he went outside again for another stage on the horse. Not for the first time, she wondered at the nature of their friendship. Whatever its basis, it sounded like they had a good life. A complete one—filled with friends and doing what one wished.

"If we were in London right now, I might be preparing for a soiree instead of traveling through—where did Anthony say we were now? Somewhere in North Yorkshire?" Thea sighed as she looked out the window. "Or perhaps I would be getting dressed for an evening at the theatre."

"If you were in London, you would be hard at work," Polly said, looking at her askance.

Thea frowned at her and she fell silent. Grace wondered what kind of work Thea engaged in. It must be nothing more pressing than planning her dinner party menus.

"I have been known to host soirees that go all night and leave friends staggering home at dawn. I once had an ice sculpture at the table that looked like a particularly intimate part of a lady's body, and it was much admired."

"Why?" Grace stared.

"Whyever not? Should not our bodies be celebrated instead of hidden away?"

"I don't recall this sculpture," Polly said, a curious look on her face.

"It was before you joined the household. I was quite wild in the years after my London debut. Uncultivated. *Unrefined.*" There was a tight smile on her face as she said the word.

"I enjoyed many evenings at the theatre with Lady Edith during the Season," Grace said, trying to veer the conversation toward something rather less intimate. "I particularly enjoy Shakespeare."

"I'm more partial to a farce," Thea said. "I like the ones where the wife turns her husband's life upside down. Especially if there is a revenge plot. Those are always good fun."

Her life in London sounded infinitely more interesting than Grace's experience there. Thea could choose which plays to see. Which eating establishments to frequent. Which nights to go out, which to stay at home, and what to serve on her table. The audacity of having such an ice sculpture at the table! It was all very shocking.

And, if she could admit it to herself—enticing.

If only Grace had the opportunity to live that kind of life instead of accompanying others through theirs. She would snatch it up and never look back.

"Did you have many opportunities to enjoy the theatre in Manchester?"

Grace didn't wish to talk about Manchester. "It is a city with the usual sort of enjoyments."

"Did you go to any of them? Would you recommend any of their stages?"

"My acquaintances all reckon the entertainments there to be as fine as any to be found in such a city."

She could tell that Thea was annoyed with her answers. She was too. She yearned to stray into more personal territory. She wanted to ask Thea more questions about her life and her friends. Most of all, she wanted to know about Thea's previous relationships with other women. But Grace didn't dare, for to ask would open herself up to the same scrutiny.

Grace's resolve was tested that night when they stopped at an inn and she again had to share a bed with Thea. No matter how many times she had repeated to herself that she was *not* to engage in an affair, she couldn't help but sigh as Thea came out from behind the screen in her adorable frilled and beribboned shift, her golden hair unbound and flowing over her shoulders. She seemed unconcerned that her nipples were puckered under the thin cotton fabric.

She had never had sex outside of a relationship before she met bold and outrageous Thea, who was far from an appropriate romantic partner. There could be no future in it, especially with Grace's uncertainty about where she would be next employed. But that wasn't the only reason she had stayed away, and it was weighing heavy on her.

Grace frowned down at her lavender face cream and scooped up too much in her fluster. "We must be more alert tomorrow. I am worried we will miss an important sign regarding their whereabouts. Isn't it strange that we have heard no news of them?"

Thea laughed. "What exactly do you think you will miss? Lady Edith hanging out of a stagecoach window and waving her petticoats from afar, hoping someone will rescue her? The letter you found indicated that she is going of her own accord. There is nothing to see here except the grand outdoors, and nothing to investigate unless we are in a town and can talk to the innkeepers. I am not surprised that we have seen no trace of them. There must be hundreds of passengers traveling each month along the Great North Road. Which innkeeper has the talent to remember them all?"

"Edie may have gone willingly, but she would never have thought of such a thing on her own," she said flatly. She knew how much pressure Edie was under from Lady Harriet. "It must have been Charles who instigated it."

"Charles is young and foolish," Thea said. "I don't disagree that it was likely to be him. But if we can catch up and set it all to rights, then it's like it never happened."

"As long as Edie marries Mr. James Martin after all this is done, then it's like it never happened."

"Oh, I doubt James would have her now."

Grace froze. "He must," she insisted. "There is no other way. That's how all this will be smoothed over. Your family owes it to Edie."

"The goal is to return without scandal, nothing more."

"And that can only happen if Edie marries Mr. Martin upon her return!"

"No, there's no need for them to marry. She has not been compromised, because we are saying that we went to visit a sick aunt," Thea said. "We have been over this."

"Edie must marry." Goose bumps rose on her flesh. It had never crossed her mind that Edie might emerge from this situation without wedding *either brother*. A wedding must happen—or Edie would be ruined when her secret pregnancy was uncovered. "Mr. James Martin was going to offer for Edie. Everyone knew it."

"Had he made his intent clear?"

"Indeed he had. He said he was looking forward to Edie meeting you and Charles because there was to be a particular affinity amongst you all. He cannot back down. Edie will be ruined!"

Thea frowned. "If there was no proper declaration, then it will be forgotten by the time we return. I cannot imagine James wanting to marry someone who rushed off with his own brother. *He* would still know, even if we cover it up so that no one else knows. That can't be the basis of a happy marriage, surely?"

"It need not be happy. It only needs to be honorable. If he has a shred of honor, he will marry her. If not, he is as great a cad as his brother."

They got into the bed in icy silence, facing away from one another.

Grace yanked the cover to her chin and tried to clear her mind, but it was a long time before she could relax enough to sleep.

Thea woke in the dead of night to a foot connecting with her calf, and the sound of Grace's panicked breathing.

"What's wrong?" she asked, groggy, then heard a key scrabbling in their door.

"Someone is trying to enter our bedchamber!"

The door creaked open. Thea's heart leapt into her throat as she sat up, her first instinct to block Grace from any intruder.

"Sorry for waking you!" Polly whispered, giggling, bringing the scent of liquor with her.

"Get some rest, Polly," Thea said. "We must be up early tomorrow. Or, today, rather."

She stumbled over their baggage to the trundle bed and collapsed onto it without undressing, her soft snores soon filling the room.

Grace's breathing was still unsteady. Thea could see the whites of her eyes shining in the dark. She must have forgotten that Polly was in their room tonight due to lack of space at the inn, instead of in the attic with the other servants as she usually was. Thea reached out her arms, and Grace curled up against her, her head pillowed on her shoulder and her arm wrapped around her waist. Thea clasped her hands together, circling her in her arms, and gradually Grace's breathing slowed and her body relaxed.

Thea felt uncertain. When was the last time she had held someone in comfort? When was the last time she had wanted to? In fact, had she *ever* wanted to?

Grace felt as fragile as a bird beneath her hands, soft and delicate. Thea made sure her touch was gentle as she cradled her, not wanting her to wake. Perhaps she was as great a cad as either of her brothers, with the thoughts that ran through her mind.

But surprisingly, not all of them were illicit.

Their argument earlier faded into nothing as Thea lay there. The longer she thought about it, the more ashamed she was at how she had reacted. She hadn't thought of the repercussions that any of them would face upon their return to Inverley, so focused she had been on the reward of Westhill Grange for herself.

Even if they succeeded and the journey didn't end in scandal, it would be the ruin of their family on a personal level. How could James ever forgive Charles for absconding with his intended bride? What lay ahead for Lady Edith now that the summer was over and she had lost her chance at marriage? Rumors would indeed swirl around her if James's attentions had been marked for the past few weeks.

What would happen to Grace, who seemed so afraid of Lady Edith's mother? Would she be let go without a decent reference?

Thea was awake for a long time, her thoughts a jumble of confusion. She felt somehow responsible for Grace, having pulled her along on an ill-thought-out jaunt to chase after Charles. She wanted to take care of her. To protect her.

She never felt this way for anyone. People crossed paths with other people. That was life. Sometimes they begat friendships, sometimes something more, but people slipped in and out of her life with a cheerful regularity that she rather liked.

This felt entirely different.

Who was Grace? She didn't know her at all. All she knew was that she felt perfect here in her arms.

And to her shock, that scared her far more than the idea of failing their mission.

CHAPTER ELEVEN

For what felt like the two dozenth time in seven days, Grace launched into a description of Edie. "An inch or two shorter than myself, slender, dark hair, quite young, with a smattering of freckles. She carries a reticule made of bright blue cloth with pink flowers embroidered on it."

On cue, Thea chimed in about Charles. "Tall, gangly, exceedingly loud but dim-witted, bright blond hair and a laugh like a donkey."

It wasn't worth holding one's breath anymore. No one that they talked to over the entirety of their journey had recognized their descriptions. Grace didn't expect it to be any different now that they were near the Scottish border. She lay awake at nights worrying that Edie hadn't taken the stagecoach from London. Maybe Mr. Martin had begged a carriage from a friend. Maybe they were taking a different route. What if they had disguised themselves?

The innkeeper stroked his beard. "I remember a lad like that, I do."

Grace's attention snapped back to him. "You *do*?" She couldn't keep the shock from raising her voice so high that it squeaked.

"Yesterday he passed by. Must have been around six or seven in the evening. Said he was with his sister, but she kept more to the back of the group. But I remember the lad. He was in high spirits. Boasted he could win a round of darts in the amount of time it took for the boys to change the horses. And you know with a stagecoach like that, the lads are right fast. He did it, too. Three bull's–eye in two minutes, with time enough to spare to chug a tankard of ale. Never saw a marksman of his ilk."

Galvanized, Grace grabbed Thea's arm as soon as they were outside again. "Did you hear that? We are only half a day behind!"

It was just after eight in the morning. There was still a considerable gap, but it was far less than the twenty-four or more hours that she had feared they were behind. No matter how fast their horses went, or how many miles they traveled each day, there had been frequent interruptions on the journey. They routinely had to stop along the side of the road to allow the royal mail coaches to pass, and they had been slowed by rain and muddy roads.

But now, they still had a chance.

Her face must have showed her worry, because Thea put a hand on the low of her back. "We can make up the distance," she said.

Grace peeked up at her. "Perhaps we can go an extra stage tonight?"

Thea hesitated but nodded. "Yes, let's try to close up the gap as best we can."

Grace wanted to throw her arms around her. Had they been friends, she would have. But they weren't friends, even though they had been lovers. It was an odd sort of relationship. She had shared her bed, shared her food, and shared her space over the past few days, in the most intimate of circumstances. How was it possible that they had only met one week ago?

Grace was learning so much about Thea, even if it was dribs and drabs of information scattered through superficial conversation. She didn't seem to be as wild and thoughtless as Caroline had painted her as. Instead, she seemed carefree. Happy. With good friends in her life, which Grace envied.

Grace also couldn't ignore that Polly was Thea's maid and had been better treated during this journey than Grace often had been as a companion by her own employers. Thea never spoke harshly to her, and from the look of her oft-rumpled clothes and her simple hairstyles, she wasn't a demanding mistress. More than anything else, that spoke volumes of Thea's character.

Maybe Thea *could* be trusted.

The only real issue Grace had with Thea was her conviction that Edie didn't need to wed either of her brothers, but the more she thought on it, the more she rationalized that it wasn't Thea's decision to make. If

Mr. James Martin was a man of honor, he would offer for Edie. A young lady oughtn't be held responsible for the rash impulses of a rogue.

Grace wished she could convince herself to believe it. Deep down, she dreaded what she assumed was the truth of it—that Edie had been a more than willing participant in scandal.

Worse, she couldn't deny that the Martins simply had something about them that might inspire *anyone* to scandal.

Including herself.

Since the night that Thea had held her in her arms and calmed her when she had been terrified that someone was breaking into their room, Grace had felt that her feelings were developing in triple time. Every hour that now passed in the coach could have been a day, for all her heart could tell.

It was beyond foolish.

But there was so much to admire about Thea. She was rash but confident. She was impulsive but assertive. She was so positive that she was always right, and her conviction that things would work out for the best was infectious.

And then there was the indisputable fact that no one had ever taken care of her before. No one had *ever* held her like that.

Grace remained lost in her own thoughts all the way until early afternoon when Thea rapped on the roof of the coach to stop alongside the River Tyne.

Polly opened one eye. "Is a cup of tea imminent? Is that why we stopped?"

"Not tea," Thea announced, gathering up her satchel and opening the door. "Flowers."

Polly sighed and resettled herself.

Grace was puzzled as she watched Thea exit the coach and march into a neighboring field. Her instinct was to stay in the coach. The quiet, agreeable companion. But this was ludicrous. Stopping to look at flowers? They had no time to spare. Why, she could see Newcastle from across the river, so why stop now?

She took a deep breath. She had to remember that she wasn't employed by these people. She wasn't here as a companion. She was here as their *equal*. Grace wrenched the door open and followed Thea outside.

"This will only take a moment," Thea said, casting a cool stare at Grace.

Grace could tell that something of some importance was happening but couldn't figure out what on earth it could be. Thea was deep among the weeds, looking down at a group of yellow wildflowers. The gargle of the Tyne sounded beyond the flower patch. She had a thick notebook open and was scribbling in it as she gazed down at the flowers. Grace hadn't thought her to be a sentimental person, but she cut several blooms with a penknife and pressed them in her book.

Even if she *were* sentimental, this was an unlikely trip to wish for a souvenir to remember it by.

Unless, of course, she was as affected as Grace herself was.

Maybe their trip *did* mean something to Thea.

Maybe at any moment, she would confess that she wanted to spend more time together after they returned from Scotland.

Grace's heart leapt at the sight of those flowers disappearing betwixt the pages. She would have admonished any debutante under her care for such a silly feeling, based as it was on little to no evidence.

But if they weren't still in sight of the coach, she thought she might have been bold enough to lean in and give up her forfeit for a kiss.

"What are those flowers?" Grace asked instead.

"*Lysimachia vulgaris*," Thea said, closing the book and turning around to return to the coach.

"And what is *that*?"

"You may know it as yellow loosestrife."

"I know it not at all," Grace said. As she followed Thea, she glanced behind her at the cluster of flowers, their yellow petals with a burnt orange center open to the sun. "They certainly are pretty."

"Loosestrife is more than pretty. It is wonderfully useful. It can help stop bleeding, can soothe a sore throat, and even help close a wound. But it only grows in the south of England, not the north. I never thought to see it along the River Tyne. This is remarkable indeed—it's a rare sighting." Thea shook her head. "I wonder how it came to be growing here?"

Grace wasn't sure why anyone should care.

The patch of loosestrife was but a dozen meters from the coach, but the terrain was uneven and the underbrush was thick. Grace was starting to fret about the brambles that were catching in her stockings when she lost her footing.

Unladylike curses flew through her mind, and some of them out of her mouth, as she fell hard. Her right hip and shoulder ached, but it was nothing compared to the awful throbbing pain in her ankle. She worried she might cast up her accounts right there in the weeds, mortifying herself in front of Thea.

"Grace! Are you hurt? Grace, can you hear me?"

She opened her eyes to see Thea crouched beside her, her bonnet flung to the side and her hand on her shoulder. Her eyes were wide and her brow was furrowed. Grace realized that Thea must have been repeating herself for some time.

Grace struggled to smile. "I am quite all right," she said, which was an outright fib. "I will be right as rain as soon as we are back in that coach."

The constant refrain from her childhood pounded in her mind as loud as the blood roaring in her ears. *Do not be an inconvenience. Do not be a bother. Only you can help yourself.* She must remain independent. She must.

"I should like to examine your ankle first. That was a nasty fall."

The thought of anything touching her ankle dizzied her. "No, thank you," she managed to say.

Thea frowned. "I am afraid I must insist."

"That was a real bruiser," Polly called out from inside the coach. "Best let her take a look, Miss Linfield!"

Mr. Robinson was standing over her as well, his horse tethered to a tree. Grace blinked. How had he moved so fast? Had she lost consciousness for a moment?

"I agree with Thea," he said.

"Then I acquiesce. But there is not much the matter, I am sure." Sick with worry, she willed it to be so.

Thea slid her shoe from her foot. Her hands were cool on her leg as she pulled her stocking down. Covered in brambles, Grace noticed, just as she had suspected. She didn't want to think of the cost of replacing them. Then she saw her ankle, swollen thrice its normal size, and wished rather heartily that Polly was the kind of maid who carried smelling salts with her.

Thea's touch was gentle, but the roaring fiery ache increased as she moved her ankle in all directions. "Your foot does not appear to be broken, but we must get you to a physician. We need to change the horses at Newcastle anyway, so we will stop there until someone can see to you."

"No!" she cried, and tried to sit up. "We must continue. We must not give up the miles that we worked so hard to gain!"

Thea took the penknife that she had used on the loosestrife and hoisted her own skirts up, then cut a strip from her linen chemise. She wrapped it around Grace's ankle and foot, firm enough to stabilize the joint. "That should help for now," she announced, "but you will have to lean on me and Anthony to get back in the coach."

Grace quailed for a moment at the thought of putting weight on her foot, but there was no choice. She gripped their hands as they pulled her up, and she managed to hobble her way between them to the coach. It was a relief to sit on the plump cushions, her leg propped up beside her, but she wished she could lie down.

As the shock wore off and pain settled deep within the bone, Grace realized with alarm that all her good nature had been left behind with the blasted loosestrife. She was in a fouler temper than she had been in years. It took the last of her energy to close her eyes so her companions would think her asleep. She dared not risk what might come out of her mouth otherwise.

Blackmail.

Her past.

The way she felt when she looked too long at Thea's lips.

Secrets, all of them, to be kept close to the heart.

CHAPTER TWELVE

Thea was sure that the time spent in racing across the bridge to Newcastle could have won wagers. Anthony had thundered off ahead of them on his horse, vowing to find a physician to tend to Grace.

Grace rested against the seat with her eyes closed. She remained as calm as she had been when taking tea at their last stop. But her face was tense with pain, and she swallowed hard whenever the coach hit a hole along the road.

Thea had been surprised to hear Grace swear enough to make a sailor blush upon taking the fall, but then again, she had been a good deal less vociferous than Thea would have been in the same situation. She shuddered as she remembered the awful sound of Grace hitting the ground.

As soon as they disembarked at the inn, Thea ordered a room for Grace to await the physician.

Grace was a good deal paler after hopping to the room, leaning on Thea and Polly the whole way. "We cannot stay longer than necessary," she insisted as she lay down on the bed. "We have only been four hours on the road today!"

Thea gave Polly a ha'penny to fetch barley water from the kitchens.

"I do *not* need barley water! What I need is to get back in the carriage!" It came out as a wail, and so unlike Grace's usual composure that Thea was alarmed.

She sat beside her on the bed and pressed her hand to Grace's forehead. There was no sign of fever, and when she unwrapped the makeshift bandage, she was relieved to find it not much changed. "We cannot go anywhere until you are capable," she said, trying to gentle her tone.

"I am *always* capable," Grace snapped. "This is nothing." Her chest heaved, and her eyes were bright and hard.

"I am sure you are, darling, but the body has its limits."

She stopped short. Had she just called Grace *darling*?

Grace struggled to sit half upright on her elbows. "You know how important this is."

"Of course I do," she said. "But I refuse to leave you here in Newcastle among strangers, and we cannot risk increasing your injury before seeing a physician."

Delaying in Newcastle would be the wrack and ruin of their plans. Bitter disappointment lodged in her throat. She was going to lose her chance at Westhill Grange. No acreage to plant an orchard if she wanted to. No lawns for the vast gardens that she yearned to grow. Instead she would continue to tend to her single camellia shrub in her tiny back garden. The loosestrife sighting had reminded Thea of the botanical study to which she had given so much of her time, money, and energy. What if she could no longer afford to maintain her plants?

At the thought of it, Thea felt sick enough to wish for a cup of barley water of her own.

"You have no idea what I face if I return in disgrace." Two bright red spots had appeared on Grace's cheeks, and her eyes were glassy.

Alarm pulsed through her. "Are you in some sort of danger?"

"I will never work again if Lady Harriet is disappointed." She trembled, and her eyes welled with tears. "I am not who you think I am."

Before she could explain, the physician arrived, harried and sweaty. Anthony marched him into the room as if he had pulled the man from whatever duties he had been performing and hauled him directly to the inn.

"Miss Linfield has twisted her ankle," Thea said, gesturing toward Grace. "Do you have anything that could help her? We must be on the road as soon as possible."

He tsked as he poked and prodded Grace's ankle, turning it this way and that.

"Enough now," Thea said sharply, noticing Grace grimace as she gripped the sheet with such force that her knuckles were white. "It cannot be much different from a hundred such sprains. What can be done, sir?"

"Rest," he said with a shrug. "A bandage to prevent the ligaments from further strain. That ankle is swelling fast and could do with leeches."

"No leeches!" Grace cried out.

Thea nodded. "No leeches then. And for the pain?"

"I've laudanum enough if you have coin to spare for it."

"No laudanum," Grace snapped.

"She will change her mind soon enough," the physician said, dismissing her. "Two drops every few hours should do the trick."

"*No.*"

Thea frowned. "If she doesn't want it, I will not force her."

The physician glared at Grace. "Who would you rather trust—your friend, or a trained doctor?" he demanded.

Without hesitation, Grace replied, "Miss Martin, a thousand times over."

"Have you any goldenrod?" Thea asked.

"Those folk cures are unreliable," he scoffed. "Are you one of those botanaphiles?"

Anger surged through her with enough force that she took a step toward the man. "I am a *botanist*, thank you very much," she snapped. "I daresay I know a good deal more about herbs and plants than you do, sir. I insist on powdered goldenrod to arrest the inflammation, and willow bark for pain relief. If you haven't any, then perhaps you would be good enough to direct me to the nearest apothecary?"

He packed up his satchel with alacrity and gave her directions. "If you must do more harm than good, then I wish you Godspeed on your errand, madam. Now, my fee is ten shillings."

Thea spluttered a protest—the man had been next to useless—but Anthony dropped the coins in his palm and dismissed him.

"I can go to the apothecary," Anthony said. "Tell me again what you need?"

"I will go myself," Thea announced.

"Stay," Grace murmured. "Please."

Oh. Grace wanted her to stay. Her chest felt funny, and she gave Anthony instructions to pick up chamomile as well as the goldenrod and willow bark. Clearly, she needed something to soothe her nerves after the excitement of the afternoon.

Polly went downstairs for tea, promising to bring up fresh barley water for Grace as she hadn't touched the first glass, and Thea and Grace were alone.

"I ache like the devil." Grace scowled at Thea from the bed. "I dislike it immensely."

"Have you changed your mind about the laudanum?"

"I have not. But I am in sore need of distraction."

"I certainly don't wish to contribute to any additional sores. Please do tell me how I could best distract you."

Thea wanted to ask about Lady Harriet, but she didn't want to upset Grace. What had she meant that she was not who she appeared? Then again, wasn't Thea also not who she appeared? She had taken refuge in a facet of herself that she hadn't been in years. She didn't hold such parties anymore. She didn't even associate with those so-called friends now. But she found herself cultivating her image as carefully as she did her plants, encouraging the showy parts of her life and pruning away what wasn't useful. Like honesty.

"Come here, please," Grace said, her eyes imploring.

Thea sat down.

"Closer."

She moved forward an inch, almost touching Grace's knee.

"Lie with me," she whispered. "Please."

Thea gently arranged herself on the bed, careful not to jostle the mattress more than necessary. She slid one arm under Grace's head and placed her other hand on her waist. She was well rewarded when Grace sighed and nestled close.

"Tell me about botany," Grace said, her voice muffled against Thea's breast.

Thea froze. She didn't talk about botany to anyone outside her network of florists, collectors, and scholars, and others of a scientific mind. She *never* talked about it to anyone who could bring tales back to Inverley—or to her parents.

"Who doesn't enjoy flowers?" Thea asked.

Grace's eyes narrowed as she tilted her head up to look at her. "When I was a governess, I taught primers on botany. I encouraged my students to illustrate plants and leaves in as much detail as possible. I am well aware of the general popularity of flowers. *You*, however, seem to enjoy them a good deal more than most."

Gone was the quiet companion of the traveling coach. In her place was a sharp, fretful woman who wasn't afraid to speak her mind, and whom Thea found she liked quite a bit more.

Thea considered deflecting again. But Grace looked so uncomfortable, her fingers twisting in the coverlets and her ankle propped up on the plumpest pillow that Thea had begged from the innkeeper.

If helping meant speaking of botany, then so be it.

Thea took a deep breath. "Everything comes from the muck, you know. Nothing more than seed and dirt and water. But from such humble origins can grow the most beautiful flowers you have ever seen in your life. Leaves as delicate and intricate as you cannot imagine if you've never had the pleasure of looking at them through a microscope. Petals as vibrant and glorious as a sunrise. Perfection emerging from almost nothing." The plants she studied were as perfect as nature intended them to be. As perfect as she wasn't, but at least she could make perfection if she could never live it herself.

Grace's face relaxed into a smile. "I should have realized you are scientific."

"Oh?" An odd sort of glow warmed her chest. "No one ever thinks so. Those who know my reputation expect me to act like the reprobate of the Martin family, from hearing old stories of the ruined debutante of fifteen years ago."

"And if they don't know you by reputation?"

"Then they see my face and the way I fill out an evening dress and they think I am available for a rather good time of nothing particularly serious." Thea heard the trace of bitterness in her voice and wished she could take back the words.

"You are curious," Grace said. "Determined. You are unafraid of your own conclusions, and you are earnestly looking for the right thing to do."

Earnest? No one ever thought it of her. Grace must still be in the throes of pain and unable to think clearly. But she tucked the compliment close to her heart.

"It is noble of you to chase your brother to save your family's name."

The warmth disappeared. "Nothing could be further from the truth." Thea stroked Grace's shoulder, careful not to jostle her. She couldn't see Grace's face at this angle, and it made it easier to talk of intimate things. It was different from their conversations in the coach each day, where she spoke of whatever was on her mind, none of it personal. "I almost feel like I am on this journey to spite my parents. To prove that they are wrong about me. Moreover, I made them promise to gift me with a minor estate that otherwise will go to Charles, and which I told them he no longer deserved. So you see, I am selfish in the extreme." She sighed. "I am as selfish as my family thinks of me, no matter how hard I am trying to portray a different picture to them."

"If they think there is anything wrong about you, then I am pleased to inform you that they are incorrect. You are *magnificent*, Dorothea Martin." Grace took a deep breath. "Forgive me. The pain has me talking of things I ought not say."

"We shared a bed. Is sharing confidences so different from being intimate?"

But as soon as she said it, Thea knew that it was. Oh, it *was*.

In bed, she had felt passion and desire and satisfaction.

But now, she felt *seen*. More naked than she had been without clothes.

To her surprise, Grace looked fitful. "Our being intimate is how all of this started." She scowled up at her.

"Two women engaging in sexual intercourse is not so great a sin to set off such a chain of events." Thea shifted away from her.

"Of course not." Grace swallowed. "But when I met you in the parlor, looking for pins—that was the first time I had left Edie unchaperoned for such a long time in the ballroom. When I had returned, she was already dancing with a new partner. I had thought to be back long before the first dance had ended, you see."

"Ladies dance." Thea shrugged. "That is the entire purpose of a ball, is it not?"

"Yes, and after each set, they return to their mama or sister or chaperone or companion." Grace fidgeted, moving her ankle with a wince. "But I wasn't there. I was with *you*. When I returned, I didn't recognize the man she was dancing with—nor did I recognize him at breakfast the next morning, when Edie so anxiously insisted that we go early to table—but I was introduced to him when we went lawn bowling. It was Mr. Charles Martin. If not for a packet of pins, Edie wouldn't have danced with him. She had been supposed to dance with Mr. Allbright. I remember she had all her dances booked for the evening. I would have *never* let her snub one gentleman to dance with another."

Thea shook her head. "Lady Edith and Charles may be ninnies, but they are ninnies who made their own decisions. If she hadn't danced with him that night, she still would have met him at breakfast. They might have eloped a day or two later, but if it's a case of love at first sight, then they would have found their way."

"Do you think so? I have been so worried that I let my own passions distract me. Remember that night in my bedchamber? Edie knocked on my door, but I didn't answer because we were together. I could have talked to her then and prevented this whole situation!"

After all these days in the carriage and all these nights along the road together, Grace was finally saying something meaningful. Thea wondered if it was due to the pain loosening her tongue and if she would regret her words tomorrow.

"Don't worry," Thea said, and cupped her cheek. "We are not responsible for other people's actions. You may feel as if you were because you were Edie's companion, but that does not absolve her from her own choices."

"There were thirteen pins in the packet that night," Grace whispered. "I should have paid attention."

She was superstitious, was she? Thea was learning a great deal about Grace today.

"Thirteen pins or not, darling, the die was cast when they saw each other. You cannot control what they feel."

Polly bustled in with the barley water. "Here you are, Miss Linfield! Now, drink this one up, please. The kitchen maid will be rather put out if she needs to work to make yet another and you not even benefiting from the labor."

Grace took an obedient sip. "Thank you, Polly."

"We are staying the night in Newcastle," Thea said, waiting for another outburst from Grace.

She surprised her by nodding. "I fear you may be right." Her face crumpled. "I am so sorry. This is all my fault. I am holding us all up."

"I'm glad to have an evening away from the road," Polly announced. "Are we not all sick and tired of traveling?"

"Polly is right," Thea said. "We should be grateful for the rest. And you need the time to heal, Grace."

For the first time in three nights, Thea and Grace each had a room to themselves. Thea relaxed in her bedchamber after worrying all evening about Grace, making sure she swallowed every drop of willow bark tea and goldenrod tincture.

She had insisted that Grace be housed in the best room the inn had to offer, wanting to give her comfort and privacy to heal. Her own bed was surely among the worst, with sagging ropes beneath a mattress that boasted more lumps than the poorly strained barley water.

Maybe she should hire a horse for a leg or two of the journey tomorrow. Sitting in the carriage, next to an enticing woman who she had no chance with…it was getting unbearable.

Now she was not only physically attracted, but something inside her yearned to comfort her. To soothe her.

This was getting too close.

She never showed fear to anyone. Not when her parents had threatened to cut her off. Not when she had ruined herself. In fact, she had laughed in the face of societal and parental displeasure.

It would be easier if Grace saw her as a rogue, a cad, a ne'er–do–well who wanted nothing more than to get her naked again.

And she *did* want that.

But she was becoming afraid of this yearning to hold Grace's hand and stroke her hair and to give up kingdoms to protect her. Lay her best cloak over a puddle lest she wet her slippers.

Thea worried that she wasn't good enough to even kiss one of those slippers.

Her heart ached.

Charles had a lot to answer for when she found him, because this trip was proving to be a thousand times more difficult than she had ever bargained for.

CHAPTER THIRTEEN

No one had ever had such regard for Grace's physical well being before, let alone a group of people who were anxious for her comfort. The next day, Polly brought her a flask of hot water at every stop so that she may make her medicinal tea. Mr. Robinson told her lively stories of his travels when he gauged her to be in the mood to be distracted and insisted that she call him Anthony. Thea tucked a shawl around her like a blanket, which was rather too warm, but she refused to pull it off because it held the weight and comfort of affection. That was too rare in Grace's life to discard lightly.

Grace pulled her bonnet down to hide the tear or two that fell down her cheeks and told herself she could always blame it on the pain if anyone asked. But no one did. They respected her privacy too much. She was embarrassed by the solicitous behavior, but also gratified.

Oh, how she wanted this for herself. A scrap of affection. A sliver of kindness. To relax under someone else's care, to feel that the world would not end if she did not fend for herself.

Grace had woken exhausted. Worries had raced through her mind as she tossed and turned all night. Alone in her room, she heard every creak in the floorboards, every murmur from someone walking in the hall, every burst of raucous laughter from the taproom. She cast her mind over the events of the day, anything that she should have noticed that could have foretold her injury so that she may have tried to prevent it. But there had been no salt spilled at the table. No sow had crossed the path of the carriage. There had not even been any magpies about, which she had often considered the most common harbingers of ill fortune. She resolved to put one of her stockings on inside out the next morning, to help reverse the bad luck that she seemed to be under.

It had taken hours to find a comfortable enough position for her throbbing ankle.

But what she worried about was that there was but one place that felt comfortable now, and that was the space next to wherever Thea was.

How had one woman become so important to her?

Thea had held her, and soothed her, and tended to her ankle so thoroughly that were it in her power to do so, it felt as if she would sternly forbid any further harm to befall her. Grace didn't feel like an inconvenience, wasting everyone's time if she wasn't being useful.

She felt nurtured.

She had trusted Thea with absolute confidence for her physical well-being, even when she had been scared and unable to think straight.

This was all a good deal more terrifying than the threat of not catching up to Edie and Mr. Martin.

Grace allowed herself the indulgence of a daydream, an illusion that what they had could last forever. If they were successful on the journey, then Lady Harriet would help her find good employment in London. She could spend her half-day off with Thea. On Sundays after church, they could find a few hours of pleasure together before she must resume her duties.

That thought was depressing. How could she ever condense her feelings for Thea into a scant few hours per week?

Well. If a relationship in London was impossible, then Grace needed to make sure that they make the most of their journey here together now. She wanted to soak up every drop of attention and laughter and happiness that she could. They would never have so much time together again. They may never even *see* each other again, given that Grace couldn't guarantee that she would indeed be stationed in London.

She looked at Thea, remembering those lips on her breast, those hands skimming her hips. That hand on her mouth.

Her mouth went dry thinking about it.

Thea wouldn't want anything to do with her after this trip anyway. She had a dashing life in London, filled with entertainment and friends. She wouldn't have time for Grace, not even for a few hours a week.

The thought hurt.

But then maybe it was an even better reason to indulge again. If this was all they would ever have together…her heart clutched. Well, if it was, then she should plan. There would be time enough for lovemaking in Scotland after they found Edie and Mr. Martin. Surely they would all wish to rest for a day or two before making the journey back to England.

All she had to do was make it to Scotland and stop a wedding, and then she could indulge. She could *celebrate*.

She couldn't wait.

Thea purchased clothes from a stableboy at the next stage and donned trousers to ride astride with Anthony for a few hours, uncaring that she had never done such a thing before. She hadn't expected to want to ride and hadn't packed her riding costume, but eight days in the coach had proven to be her limit.

"How are things progressing between you and the lovely Miss Linfield?" Anthony asked her.

She sighed. "I like her, Anthony. I cannot deny it."

"How fortunate you are to have someone with whom to pass the tedium of the journey. Well planned indeed."

"The lady is unwell. And besides, even if she were in fine fettle, she does not return my affections in such a manner," she said, scowling.

He looked at her. "Are *you* unwell? You have never had trouble engaging in affections."

"I am hale and hearty, but indeed I have been rebuffed."

Anthony was right. She never faced trouble with finding a willing bed partner. Granted, there hadn't been as many of them in recent years as in her younger days. She had embellished her reputation to impress Grace.

But Grace would never have a chance to find out. She would return from Scotland with not much more knowledge of Thea than her own parents had. Minimal, and damning. The idea didn't sit so well with her.

Curious, Grace had said about her. *Determined. Earnest.* She shifted in her seat at the thought, uncomfortable with such kind words.

"I'm impressed," Anthony said.

"Why is that?"

"The lady has caught your attention, and she didn't even need beauty to snare you. You're not able to move on from her."

"No one can move on, can we? We're stuck on this blasted trip to find my blasted brother. Besides, she is respectable. And more than that—I respect her." She frowned. "And she isn't plain! She's *refined*."

"She is no beauty."

"She has her own kind," Thea insisted. "You just have to get to know her." The longer she knew her, the dearer her face became to her.

"Entranced, are you?"

He was teasing. She knew because of the warmth in his voice. But still, it rattled her.

"I'm nothing of the sort. Yes, I find her intriguing. And sweet. I like her manners, and her voice." She caught herself before she could list *everything* about her. Those lips. Even those elbows. "But I won't see her again after this. She'll have another job to go to, and I'll be back in London. After another week, this will be over."

It would be a *relief* when it was over. It couldn't happen a moment too soon. Her plants could only survive the housemaid's attentions for so long. That was the life she needed to return to, without the distractions of a quiet-voiced mild-mannered secretly-feisty lady's companion.

"It happens," Anthony agreed. "I've been close as brothers to some of the sailors and scientists on some of my trips. Some of them stay that way, and others…well, life is different when one returns. It's never the same." His tone was wistful.

Thea didn't want to admit it, but she was relieved to be back in the carriage at the next stage. Her thighs were sore after the ride, though it was a nice relief from the bone jangling aches that the carriage provided in abundance.

She was worried about the confessions that spilled from her lips when she was around Grace. Grace was such a good listener, so calm and quiet and encouraging, like cool water on her face after a long hot day.

She couldn't afford any more emotion.

She wanted oblivion.

They had lost so much time in Newcastle yesterday that it felt impossible that they would ever catch up. Thea almost thought it better to turn around now and wait for Charles at an inn on the way back to

London. The ache in her legs was nothing compared to the well of pain in her heart, the loss of everything looming before her. Wild, bitter hurt raged inside, and it was hard to restrain.

When she returned to Inverley, it would not be to take possession of Westhill Grange. She would be hard-pressed to keep her Chelsea townhouse without her allowance to pay the rents.

She wouldn't even have the pleasure of companionship. Anthony would sail away. Grace would be employed elsewhere. Her other friends, much as she had played them up to Grace during the journey, had proved fair-weather indeed after she had started dedicating her time to botany. She still had her professional network, florists and gardeners and scientists that she loved to invite for dinner and talk of plants, but how could she host them with no money? She wouldn't even have her plants to console her, as she would no longer afford their upkeep.

Once she was in the carriage again, Thea pulled out the bottle of brandy that she had purchased at the last stage, thinking it might help Grace's ankle if she was tired of willow bark.

This was the rebellious streak that had Thea in trouble so often when she was young. She could hear her mother's voice as plain as if she was there in the coach with them. Accusing her of corrupting sweet Miss Linfield. Of being a terrible example to her maid. Of being a hoyden, riding with Anthony earlier instead of sitting inside the coach like a decorous lady.

She smiled her way past the echoes of memory and held up the bottle, the amber liquor sparkling in the bright sunlight. "Would anyone be interested in a mid-afternoon tipple?"

Polly wrinkled her nose. "What is that?"

"The best brandy I could purchase at the last stage. A dubious claim from a town boasting of no more than five hundred souls, but it was the best that the inn had to offer." She'd had to pay through the nose for the bottle. Even mediocre spirits seemed hard to come by in a place as remote as this.

"None for me, thank you. I would have been happy to take a little wine, but I suppose your choice was limited."

"Miss Linfield?"

There was an adorable little crease between Grace's brows as she stared at the bottle. "Brandy? At half past three in the afternoon?"

"What better time than now? We have hours more on the road today. What else is one to do? Besides, a stiff drink will help the ache in your ankle."

She hesitated, then squared her shoulders. "Then yes, I would like some."

Thea unstoppered the bottle and offered it to her.

"There is no glass?" Grace squeaked.

She hadn't thought this through. Embarrassment washed over her. What had she been thinking? Grace was refined, and fastidious. She was a woman who liked linen napkins when only eating a plain bun, where Thea had often hastily eaten meals in the middle of her plants in the conservatory.

"I suppose I am to remain alone in my vices." Thea took a swig of brandy. The taste was no better than she had expected, but warmth spread down her throat with the promise that it would help her forget.

She took another drink. If only she were alone right now. She could curl up on the bench, drink to her heart's content, howl out her frustration and pain in a good bout of tears, and sleep for the rest of the day to escape the fear of the future that roiled around in her belly.

Then she saw a gloved hand out of the corner of her eye.

"May I have the bottle?"

Miss Prim-and-Proper sat there, her back as straight as a ruler, her hand outstretched, and…a smile on her face?

Thea's heart felt a little lighter. "I do apologize for our straightened circumstances," she said, handing her the brandy. "I know you are unaccustomed to them."

A shadow crossed her face. "I am not so unfamiliar." She tipped the bottle up and pressed her lips to it and took as delicate and elegant a sip as Thea could imagine, her throat working as she swallowed.

The brandy wasn't going to help her forget Grace at all.

The rest of the afternoon passed in an unexpectedly delightful way with Grace by her side, drinking and laughing so hard that her sides ached.

"Whoever sees a bird must drink!" Thea exclaimed, one eye shut as she pointed out the window.

"You only bought one bottle," Grace said. "I think we would run through it rather quickly, as I see five birds in the sky right now."

"Well then, what's your suggestion?"

"Perhaps a sip at every cottage we pass?"

"Then we shall be parched!" she cried. "I know—any time anyone mentions Lady Edith or Charles. They are quite forbidden conversation today. I've had enough of fretting about them."

With the brandy fast depleting, the terms were settled on flocks of sheep, with stern warnings given about declaring anything so meagre as three sheep a flock.

This was the most relaxed Grace had appeared since the night they had spent as lovers in Inverley. Thea had forgotten how she looked when she laughed in pleasure, and how a little crinkle appeared by her eyes when her smile changed to a genuine grin.

"You are a sight to be seen," Thea told her, unable to find the words to express herself properly through the brandy-induced haze.

"Those are kind words considering you have seen me at my worst," Grace said, nose in the air. "I am unused to revealing that I even *have* a worst side. Now that I am feeling much better, I still am not presenting myself at my best, in my thrice-worn dress."

"I find you charming," Thea said quietly.

Grace leaned against her. "Is it charming that I am unable to keep myself upright?"

Thea shifted to move her arm behind her so that Grace might rest her head on her shoulder. "Yes, it is. You may lean against me all you wish. You are nursing an injury."

"I may as well nurse this bottle to handle it." She took a sip and sighed. "I cannot believe all the time we have wasted on my ankle. We've been on the road eight days now, and we're still in England! We shall arrive in Gretna and the smithy shall tell us that he wed them three days ago."

"No speaking of Mr. Martin and Lady Edith," Polly piped up. "Drink up."

Grace sipped the brandy. "It's awful to think that we are now so close, but further than ever from success."

"We gave it a valiant effort though," Thea said. She saluted her. "It was an honor to serve with you in the pursuit of reputation."

"Sheep!" Polly cried in excitement, and took the bottle.

Grace then downed the rest of it. "I can be wild when I wish to be," she told Thea.

Thea snorted. "You have dipped your smallest toe into the waters of rebellion and claim to be going for a swim," she said, then she softened. "You are not wild at all. And you don't have to be. You are lovely as you are."

CHAPTER FOURTEEN

Grace lay awake half the night after they arrived at the inn in Carlisle. Thea slept beside her, sharing her bed for the first time in two nights. She inhaled, catching the intoxicating orange scent of Thea's soap. It was now as familiar and soothing as the smell of her own lavender lotion.

Her mind was still spinning with drink, and she could barely feel the throb in her ankle.

Gretna Green would be in sight by tomorrow morning.

Tomorrow, for better or for worse, her life would change. She would know whether they had succeeded, or whether they had failed.

They had traveled later tonight than had been wise, inspired by the full moon and in high spirits from the brandy. It was almost impossible to imagine that they would close the distance now, but there was always a sliver a hope. At least, that's what Thea said, and Grace couldn't help but believe in her.

She didn't understand why she felt so melancholy.

Was it because the journey was almost over?

She had never been on such an adventure in all her life.

Eight days was all that had passed. She knew that to some people, like Thea, this might be but one more week of a life lived for their own pursuits. To Grace, it was an incredible amount of time out of the ordinary. There had been worry and stress and fear, but she also hadn't given one lesson, or poured one cup of tea except for herself, or worried about the appearance of obedience and gratitude.

It would all end tomorrow.

Either they would stop Edie and Mr. Martin or they wouldn't, but either way the course of her life would be decided and the independence she had experienced over the past week would be over. As much as she looked for clues as to where her luck would land, she couldn't seem to find anything helpful.

She lay there in silence, wanting to toss and turn and sob into the pillows, but she resisted. She couldn't wake Thea. Not when she had been so kind, so thoughtful, so caring.

Despite her efforts, Thea stirred and turned toward her. Bleary-eyed, she gazed at Grace. "You are awake," she murmured.

The moonlight silvered her hair and face and reminded Grace of how they had met in the parlor in Martin House. "I cannot sleep. I'm sorry for waking you."

"Don't be." Thea shifted, and tugged Grace over so she was flush against her body, with Thea's arms around her. "I can hear you worrying from over there. I'd best hold you if that's the only way you will sleep, for tomorrow is a day of reckoning."

Grace felt as if she might melt as she nestled closer. "Actually, I think I'm ready for you to claim your forfeit."

She would return to real life tomorrow. Back to responsibility. She would travel back to Inverley with Edie, and Charles would go with Thea.

Tonight was her chance to bid farewell to her brief interlude. Later, she could blame it on the drink, or blame it on the moon, but she would take her moment now. She had thought she could wait until Scotland, but she didn't want to make love in the throes of failure. She wanted to embrace the memory of lovemaking while she still had hope, however slim, of success.

"You make me feel such things as I have never felt before," Grace whispered. "You conjure up such desire in me."

To her surprise, Thea moved away. "With my scandalous ways, I coax moans of desire from you that you would never dare utter if you had your senses about you? It isn't that way," she said fiercely. "We are equally responsible for our actions, Grace. Whatever desires you have for women, whatever feelings you have for me specifically—those come from *you*."

She was too surprised to reply.

Thea sighed. "I have had many lovers, Grace. Some have been wonderful, and some have insisted that they are good decent women who would never in their life have even conceived of such a thing as making love with another woman, if not for my undo influence."

"I am not one of those women," Grace said quietly. "I kissed another girl when I was fifteen years old, and was roundly slapped for my efforts. You were not my first lover, Thea. I am so sorry if I gave you the impression that I don't desire you for who you are. I certainly do."

Thea cupped her face and kissed her, and Grace felt boneless under her touch. She had wanted this since that first night together. She had thought about it when she watched Thea sip her tea in the mornings, her full lips resting on the china cup, and she had fantasized about it a thousand times during the restless nights that had plagued her on the journey.

The heat of her mouth, the soft press of her tongue, felt better than any memory.

Thea pulled away, smoothing her thumb over Grace's lips. "Now, let us sleep. We can talk about it more once we are in Scotland."

"Not now?"

She grinned. "Not now. Not when I am too soused with brandy to do anything properly. You deserve better, darling. Wait for it, and I shall make it well worth your while."

Grace shivered as she curled under the covers and felt Thea's arms settle around her. She couldn't wait for Scotland.

The innkeeper at the neighboring establishment nodded at them the next morning before they started the day's travels. "Aye, the stagecoach broke an axel and was stopped here all yesterday. They couldn't get started until an hour ago. I saw the pair you're describing. They were right anxious to be on their way to Gretna."

They were only an *hour* behind?

They hadn't investigated the area last night, as they had arrived at their own inn late and weaving on their feet from drink, but now Thea cursed herself for ever having purchased that brandy. If not for that, they might have caught Charles and Lady Edith yesterday while they were still in England and unable to wed.

"An hour is nothing," Anthony said, clapping a hand on her shoulders. "We can make the time up if the horses are fresh. We can catch up with them."

"This is marvelous!" Thea cried, and explained to Grace once they were settled in the coach again. "We've done it." She pictured her parents' faces when she sauntered back into Inverley, with an unmarried Charles in tow.

"Not yet," Grace said. She looked paler than she had when she twisted her ankle. "Anything might happen. Why, our own axel may break!"

"It won't." Jubilation coursed through her, more potent that yesterday's brandy. "We're almost there."

Westhill Grange was once more in her grasp. Nothing could stop her now.

"Even one minute could be too late," Grace said quietly, staring down at her lap.

Thea felt a renewed motivation. She wanted this. Not just for her own sake, but she wanted it for Grace. She wanted to give her that relief, ease her strain. They would get to Gretna.

No matter what.

Thea was exuberant when the village of Gretna Green came into view. The carriage wheels roared their way round and round, clattering out the sounds of victory to her ears. The horseshoes struck the cobblestones like swords clashing. She was certain that they hadn't been so loud coming into any other town along the way. Lady Edith and Charles surely must hear them. Why, the whole town must hear them.

Thea almost tumbled out the door before the coach had stopped in front of the smithy, the horses whinnying and snorting. She gripped Grace's arm to support her while they walked up to the door, Grace limping but refusing to be left behind.

A man came outside, wiping his hands on his leather apron. "Looking for new horseshoes?" he asked cheerfully. "I can set you up, right as rain."

"We're looking for a young couple who have come here to elope," Thea blurted out. "My brother is tall, blond—"

Grace was just as eager for news. "My charge has black hair and freckles—"

"Laughs like a donkey—"

"Reticule with big flowers—"

The smithy laughed and held up his hands. "Ladies, slow down! No need to rush your words. There hasn't been anyone in town today looking for marriage."

Thea blinked. "No one?"

"No one."

"What about yesterday?"

They had been told that a broken axel had stopped the stagecoach, but what if Charles and Lady Edith had abandoned it and found another way into Gretna? Folks might have a kind disposition to help a young couple eager to marry.

"No one came through yesterday, either."

Grace looked ready to collapse with relief. "We aren't too late!"

And yet, there was no sign of them.

"Is there perhaps another smithy?" Thea asked, frowning.

"It's a small village, miss. I'm telling you now, Angus hasn't seen anyone either. I would know if any stagecoach passed, loud as they are when they rumble on through. But if you do see anyone looking to wed, be sure to send them over to me." He puffed out his chest. "William Campbell's the name. I've better rates than Angus has, and that's a promise."

Thea helped Grace back into the coach.

"No luck?" Anthony asked.

"Yes and no," Thea said, frowning. "Somehow we must have overtaken them, if they have not yet arrived. But where are they?"

"They are *definitely* on their way to Gretna Green," Grace insisted. "It's famous. If Edie can't have a big wedding, then at least she would want a romantic one that she could sigh about with all her friends."

"Perhaps she wrote it in her letter to throw us off the scent," Anthony said. "She may well have written Gretna if she thought you would follow, and then planned for the other side of Scotland."

"But the innkeeper in Carlisle saw them!"

"What if it was a blind, and they hied in the opposite direction?"

Thea felt deflated. If they were somewhere else…then it was all over. "Let's rent rooms here for the night," she said. "There's still a chance that they will come through today."

Grace nodded but looked forlorn.

The innkeeper confirmed what the Mr. Campbell had said—no one had passed through in the past few days.

Grace and Thea sat in their room together, quiet, knees almost touching.

Thea bumped her shoulder against hers. "Until we know for sure that we have failed, there is still hope."

"I'm trying to believe it."

But her voice quavered. Her hands, neatly folded in her lap, trembled.

Thea tucked a strand of Grace's hair behind her ear, then stroked her cheek. "No matter what happens, I am glad for the journey. I know it has been difficult, but it's also been a grand adventure."

That startled a laugh from Grace. "Has it been? I rather thought it has been a grand nuisance. Adventures are meant to be at least somewhat amusing."

"Has none of this been entertaining for you?" Thea tipped her chin up and pressed a firm kiss on her lips.

"My ankle begs of me to say a few words on its behalf. There may have been moments of amusement, but it has not been so *very* entertaining."

Thea was delighted. Grace's face was serious, the shadows dark under her eyes, with lines of strain on her brow. And yet, it was clearly a rare moment of levity for her. There was wry humor in her eyes and in the press of her lips as she struggled to suppress a smile. Though all might be lost, Thea felt as if she were truly getting to know her. Perhaps traveling so far north had tipped her life upside down, because the trip seemed worth it just for this one moment of fellowship with Grace.

Then she heard the unmistakable clattering of an approaching carriage, and her heart leapt into her throat.

Grace gasped. "Could it be…?"

They leapt to their feet in unison and scrambled down the stairs, Grace hopping on one leg, their bonnets and gloves still strewn across the bed.

Outside, Charles stood by a large stagecoach, helping Lady Edith down.

They locked eyes.

Then Charles whooped and ran.

Chapter Fifteen

Grace's heart pounded as she watched Edie scamper off with Mr. Martin.

"They're going to the smithy!" Thea cried, jolting Grace out of her shock. "Quick, we must follow them!"

Grace's ankle hurt too much to put much pressure on it, but she hopped as best she could while Thea helped her across the cobblestones to the smithy, which was well within sight of the inn. She thought Mr. Martin could have outpaced them all, but thankfully, Edie was of a delicate constitution and wasn't all that much faster than Grace.

They reached the smithy at the same time.

Edie clutched Mr. Martin's arm as Mr. Campbell came out. "Please, sir, would you do us the honor of wedding us?"

He nodded at Thea and Grace. "This the pair you were looking for, eh?"

Grace nodded. "Yes. We do not agree with their marriage."

His face softened as he looked at Edie, tears brimming in her eyes. "The wee lass looks in a mighty rush to be wedded."

"She cannot," Grace said. "Edie, come with me now. Your mother won't approve."

"But I love him, sir," she said, staring up at the smithy with wide eyes that could melt iron better than his forge.

"And I love her." Mr. Martin put a hand on Edie's shoulder and drew her close.

"Hell and blazes, Charles, be reasonable," Thea snapped. "Call this off and we can all escape scandal."

"I've every intention of making this an honorable union!" cried Mr. Martin. "After so many nights on the road together, it shall cause a far greater scandal if we *don't* wed, you know." He looked indignant that Thea would suggest any such thing.

"We told everyone in Inverley that we traveled with you to visit Lady Edith's sick aunt. No one will be the wiser—as long as we leave this instant and return home together." Thea reached out her hand. "Please, Charles. Think of Mother and Father."

Mr. Campbell stroked his beard. "You love one another?" he asked Edie.

"Of course." She beamed at him.

"There's no *real* objection here?"

"None," she declared. "They want me to wed another, but I cannot! Not when I love my Charlie."

"This is preposterous," Grace exclaimed. "Her mother is expecting her to marry this man's brother!"

"Let's get inside and see if we can settle this," Mr. Campbell said, and ushered them through the door.

Grace blinked as they stepped out of the sunlight and into a large, whitewashed room with rough hewn wooden beams that crossed the ceiling. A desk and a pair of chairs took up half the room for business affairs, and she bit her lip as she saw a sturdy wrought iron anvil prominently featured in the other half.

"Please, Mr. Campbell, please may we be married over the anvil, like in the tales?" Edie sighed with happiness.

"Edie, you cannot be serious." Grace was nonplussed. In all her imaginings of this moment, it had never occurred to her that Edie would be determined to continue after being caught.

"I have never been more so." Edie looked around the room, sparse in decoration. "I know this isn't a detailed ceremony, but is there anything we could do to make it a little more…elegant?"

"There is a fee to getting married," Mr. Campbell said. "Fifteen pounds. Nothing extra included."

"Anything for my darling." Mr. Martin was besotted, a sunny grin on his face as he took Edie's arm in his.

Grace was shocked at the cost. Why, it was three times the cost of a special licence, all for the privilege to elope!

Mr. Campbell shrugged. "We do have some bits and bobs if you've a mind to gussy things up a bit." He rummaged through a drawer and came up with a bright blue length of ribbon. "You could be handfasted in a trice, in the old manner."

A woman came bustling through the front door. "Oh! Another young couple? This is our third this week. You've come to the right place." She beamed at them. "I am Mrs. Campbell, and there's nothing I love more than a wedding."

"There is no marriage to be had here," Thea protested. "That is my brother, and he is not marrying this woman!"

"Have you been taken against your will, lass?" She shot a dark look at Charles. "We've cleavers on the premises for the likes of him, if that's the truth of it."

Edie gasped. "No, indeed not! I love Charlie."

"Then there can be no objection, can there? Love rules all in Gretna. Come along now, my husband has horseshoes to make for the vicar and a latch to mend for the butcher today, so let's not dally."

"We can leave immediately," Grace said, "if Lady Edith and Mr. Martin will give up their foolish scheme."

"I would like a pink ribbon, if you have one," Edie announced, fluttering her lashes. "Perhaps I could pick some flowers from the meadow? You won't mind a little delay, would you, Charlie? What is a few more minutes when we have spent so many days on the journey?"

He shook his head.

Edie sailed out the door, and Grace followed her.

"What are you doing?" Grace cried as soon as they were alone. "Edie, you must listen to me. You must return home."

There was an abundance of flowers beside the smithy, sporting cheerful blue and pink petals that Grace thought Thea would recognize. Edie started plucking them by the handful. "Beautiful," she declared. Then she sighed. "Grace, I must marry Charles."

"Your mother will be furious. What about Mr. James Martin? I thought you had reached some sort of agreement."

"James is horrid," she said flatly. "I was going to marry him to please Mama, but it was foolish of me. Charles is who I must marry."

"But why?"

"Do you still not understand?" Her face was shining. "Charles was my lover in London. He is the father of my unborn babe. I have been waiting and waiting all summer for him to return home—he never knew that I was with child. Mama insisted that we leave ever so quickly from London. It was the feat of the Season for me to have begged an invitation to Martin House for the summer with no one being the wiser!" Edie smiled, her eyes twinkling.

Grace had never seen her so happy before. Not in Manchester, with the stress of the London Season before her. Not in London, with the pressure from her mother bearing on her for months. She shook her head, still trying to piece it all together. "I hadn't even realized that you knew who it was—you never mentioned a name."

Guilt overwhelmed her, her skin crawling as if she were caught in cobwebs. Guarding a young lady's innocence was of utmost importance when chaperoning, and she had failed in her duty. She thought she had watched Edie's every move during her Season as if she were the only person in all of London, but she hadn't been careful enough. There had been no portends of such a disaster, nothing to warn her that her life was in danger of falling apart. Grace still remembered how the shock had felt like a stab in her back when Edie had confessed to her.

It could have so easily been the ruin of them both.

The worst of it was that it still could be.

Grace felt a flash of anger. They had been so close to covering up the scandal if Mr. James Martin had only made his proposal early enough. But now Edie had compounded it by this madcap flight to Scotland.

If Charles was truly the father, then what business did Grace have in coming between their union? He would be making right by the woman he had compromised. If she had known his name and caught him in London, wasn't a marriage between them exactly what she would have tried to accomplish to save Edie's reputation? On the other hand, Charles was a younger son. Lady Harriet had greater expectations for her daughter.

She swallowed hard. Where did she owe her loyalty? To her employer, under threat of blackmail? Or to her half-cousin, who was looking at her with such wide eyes, one hand filled with wedding flowers and the other pressed to her belly?

Grace entered the smithy behind Edie. It was hard to make eye contact with Thea, but she simply shook her head in exasperation, jerking her head toward Charles. She must not have had any luck in dissuading him.

Mr. Campbell picked up a pale pink ribbon and wound it round Edie's hand, then scowled down at it. "Can't tie a ribbon to save my life," he muttered, holding the rest of the length in his hand.

Mrs. Campbell tsked and grabbed a yellow ribbon from the drawer. "It's that easy, it is," she said, then drew closer to Grace and Thea. "Apologies for my husband, we started up this wedding business recently, you know. But I swear, we perform the ceremony as right and tight as anyone can—and at a *much* better rate than Angus across town! Ladies, may I demonstrate?" She didn't wait for an answer, but wound the ribbon round Grace's wrist, crossed the palm of her hand, then wrapped it around Thea's palm and wrist. "Like that, William. Easy as can be."

The ribbon felt warm around Grace's hand as Mrs. Campbell continued to wrap the ribbon before making a neat bow. Her skin tingled beneath the satin. Why did being bound together somehow feel more intimate than sharing a bed?

"Edie, listen to me," Grace said, steeling her spine. She could not fail when there was so much at stake. Even with the babe. Even with the rightful father standing right there. "There is still time to call off this wedding. I swear I will help you find a way out of this, if that's what you're worried about."

She felt sick. What was the right of it in this situation? Could Mr. Martin provide for Edie the way his brother could? Would the scandal of their elopement ruin her for the rest of her life?

"What's the next bit?" Charles asked Mr. Campbell, looking at the scraggly bow that dangled between himself and Edie.

"Charles, there is no next bit," Thea said. "Come to your senses."

Mr. Campbell hesitated, his brow furrowed as he gazed at Thea.

Mrs. Campbell tsked again. "Fifteen pounds," she hissed at him. "Come on, then, the next bit! 'Are you both of marriageable age?'" She glared at Thea and Grace. "Let's show them how it's done, then."

"Yes, we are of age," Charles said.

"I want a ring!" Edie declared.

Grace felt a surge of hope. Why was she delaying so much if she claimed to wish to wed Mr. Martin so badly? "There are no rings here," she said soothingly. "Let us go back to Carlisle. We can shop and we can talk, and—"

"Of course we've rings here!" Mr. Campbell boomed. "You think a blacksmith has no rings to be had? Pah! Forged my fair share of gold and silver in the past. No rings. What falderol."

He opened a drawer and grabbed a fistful of rings. While Edie perused them, he plucked one from his palm and gave it to his wife. "Show her! No rings indeed."

"I didn't mean to disparage your work, sir," Grace said, flushing.

Mrs. Campbell picked up Grace's left hand, still wrapped with ribbon, and shoved it on her finger. "Isn't it beautiful? Very fine indeed. My William does good work."

Grace blinked down at the ring. It was a perfect fit. Plain gold, bright as sunshine. Her breath caught as she stared at it.

Mrs. Campbell slid another gold ring on Thea's finger. "You take a good look at that, now," she insisted. "Isn't it lovely?"

Distracted, Grace almost missed Mr. Campbell ask Edie and Mr. Martin again if they were of marriageable age.

"Good question," Mrs. Campbell said loudly. "Are you ladies of marriageable age?"

"Yes," she whispered, straining to hear Edie and Mr. Martin. Was Mrs. Campbell trying to distract them from what her husband was doing?

"Of course we are," Thea snapped. "Do we look young to you? We're spinsters."

"Spinsters, are you? Why, so you're free and willing to marry, are you then?"

"Of course," Thea repeated, impatience on her face.

"I suppose we are," said Grace, "but why do you ask?"

"Why, so you can come back and be wedded proper. Remember us! Smithy Campbell of Gretna Green!" She beamed at them. "We do a good trade in spinsters up here, looking for a little adventure. Now you can recommend us to your friends at home. You did all the steps, and now you know what it's like to be married."

Married.

Grace met Thea's eyes. Her pulse picked up, and the hair on the back of her neck stood up. *Married.* The ribbon around their hands could have been around her throat, for she felt too choked to breathe.

"And are you both free to marry?" Mr. Campbell boomed at Edie and Mr. Martin.

This was it then.

Grace clutched her end of the ribbon, the ring biting into her finger—odd how it fit so perfectly on the finger that she had sworn would never see a ring—and waited. She reached out with her other hand and clutched Thea's, taking comfort in the warmth of her touch.

"Yes!" Edie cried. "We are free!"

"Yes," Mr. Martin said.

Grace's heart was going to burst from her chest.

Mr. Campbell grinned at them. "You are well and truly wedded!" He struck his hammer on the anvil so hard that sparks flew. "Congratulations!"

"Fifteen pounds, and a guinea for the rings," Mrs. Campbell chirped. "I won't charge for the ribbon."

Grinning, Mr. Martin dug into his pockets.

Mrs. Campbell turned to Grace and Thea. "You too," she said cheerfully. "Fifteen pounds and a guinea."

"Fifteen pounds!" Thea cried. "For what?"

"And a guinea," she said patiently. "Why, you went through the ceremony too."

"This is *outrageous*—"

"You have the rings," Mrs. Campbell pointed out. "You did all the steps. Even the extra bit with the ribbon. You took time out of our day. Fifteen pounds' worth, to be precise."

"Unorthodox, this is, Mary," Mr. Campbell said, scratching his head. "Charging two ladies for a ceremony. Maybe we ought to charge for the rings only. Or maybe offer half price. On account of there being no man, you know."

"I don't want the ring," Thea said, and tossed hers onto the table.

Grace tugged at hers, but it wouldn't budge. "Oh dear. Mine is stuck."

"They should be charged what it's worth," Mrs. Campbell said firmly. She leaned close to her husband. "Angus down the road wouldn't turn away good business, I can tell you that."

Mr. Campbell snorted, then banged his hammer on the anvil again. "So be it. There you go, lasses, another ceremony completed."

Mrs. Campbell held out her hand. "Now, fifteen pounds, if you please. Plus the guinea. Keep the ring, dear, for when you do it for real next time." She pressed the ring back into Thea's palm. "As a keepsake."

Mr. Martin couldn't stop laughing. "I would pay the fee just to see the look on your face, Thea," he gasped, and thrust a fistful of coins at Mr. Campbell. "There you are, money for the both of us. That's good fun, that is."

It didn't feel like good fun to Grace.

She stumbled after Thea, still bound with the ribbon, her ankle protesting the movement, as they followed Edie and Mr. Martin outside.

Edie was radiant, clutching her bouquet to her chest with her untethered hand. "Was that not terribly romantic?" she cried. "It was perfect. I cannot wait to tell my friends."

Mr. Martin was still laughing. "I can't wait to tell mine that my sister was at the wedding, and she was charged for the ceremony too!"

Thea shoved him. "You are a boor to mock marriage like that," she snapped at him.

Grace rubbed her thumb against the smooth gold of the ring. "It is no laughing matter," she said quietly. "We are all in a good deal of trouble now."

Edie shook her head. "I am a woman grown and must make my own decisions. Mama must understand. I have everything I could possibly want." She looked at Mr. Martin. "We succeeded."

And Grace had failed.

What would become of her now?

CHAPTER SIXTEEN

It was nearing dusk, and the raucous celebration from the inn's taproom wafted into Thea's room through the open window. It seemed to have been ongoing since Charles had entered with his beaming bride and shouted that he would purchase a whole barrel of ale if there were folks enough to drink it. His jubilation was clear, as was Lady Edith's. Thea had told him she would speak with him the next morning and had spent the rest of the day walking through the quiet village streets to clear her head. She had returned half an hour ago to find dinner in progress, which she decided against joining in favor of the peace and quiet of an empty bedchamber.

They had lost.

Eight days of worry and stress and aches and pains had gotten her nowhere, and now she faced another week on a return journey so that she may confess all to her parents and end up with nothing.

Despite what she had said to Grace earlier in the journey, she would never be able to convince Charles that he wasn't truly wedded to Lady Edith if only he would agree to keep everything quiet. Not when he had cried it aloud so the whole of Gretna Green could hear.

But also because it wasn't the right thing to do.

She had flouted society's stuffy rules in the past. But what harm had it done anyone to take a lover when she pleased, or to entertain friends in her own home at any hour of the night? It didn't mean that she had no moral code, though this would have been its greatest test. She would have done a great many things to secure Westhill Grange.

Grace had been right that night. If Charles abandoned Lady Edith after the ceremony, he truly *would* be a cad of the first water.

The thought gave her an uncomfortable feeling.

For Thea, too, had spoken words over the anvil this morning, and she couldn't deny that they had sparked something within her.

She had looked over at Grace, tall and pale with the morning sun streaming over her brown hair, her eyes wide and worried, with a ring on her finger and a pretty yellow ribbon binding her to Thea—and a voice deep inside had whispered *mine*.

Mine.

Of course, it had been loud inside the smithy with so many people talking at once. She couldn't be sure what she had heard.

There was no denying how she had felt, though. Staring at Grace while the world tipped on its axis and Charles married Lady Edith, she had felt...*whole*. This person had believed in her. Trusted in her. Even in their mutual defeat, Grace stood next to her and clung to her hand instead of fleeing and leaving her behind to reap what she had sowed.

No one had ever stayed before.

Instead of a spark, Thea worried that it was a seed that had been planted inside. A seed, nurtured carefully enough, could grow into something unexpected. Something grand.

Something, however, that she had no desire to examine or measure. She didn't want to assign nomenclature to it, to breathe it to life along with a name. Best to leave such a discovery deep under the soil.

Her failures, after all, were visible for all to see and couldn't be ignored. They were as sharp as a thorn and as bitter as arrowroot.

She had promised Grace that they would succeed in stopping the elopement. She had sworn to her parents that she would bring Charles back, scandal-free. She had failed their expectations.

It was overwhelming and embarrassing. She had almost asked the innkeeper for a room of her own tonight instead of sharing with Grace, but then realized she could not justify any extra expense. Every farthing in her reticule would need to go toward survival now, for she could not count on her parents to help her.

They were so insistent that she settle down, and she had been so insistent on showing them that she had changed. She should have known that she could never have won their approval with a wild goose chase.

Grace opened the door, letting in the noise for a moment along with her lovely, wholesome self. The ache that Thea felt in her heart at the sight of her was almost alarming, and she contrived to hide it. "Is dinner finished already?"

"Yes." Grace held up a napkin. "I brought you a meat pasty and a slice of currant cake. I wasn't sure what you would like."

"That is kind of you, but I find I have no appetite."

She put the napkin on the table and came to sit beside Thea on the bed. "Perhaps you have an appetite for something else?" she asked shyly.

She laughed. "That sounds more like something I might say."

"A week in a carriage with you has done me a world of good," Grace said, her eyes shining. "Perhaps it is no bad thing for me to become a little more like you."

"By all means, follow in my example if you wish to be a beacon of failure."

Grace took her hand. "We might not have succeeded, but you have been wonderful this whole journey. You have been brave, and strong. You are the most amazing woman I have ever met."

The praise gave Thea an uncomfortable feeling in her belly. "You are sweet," she said quietly and trailed her fingers up Grace's arm. "And truly lovely."

Grace smiled before leaning in and kissing her. Her lips tasted like wine and spice. "I want to be with you tonight. We have waited long enough, haven't we?"

"I certainly don't think I can wait much longer." Thea grinned. "And with all the noise from downstairs, we won't need to be so quiet."

"I don't mind quiet," Grace said. "I don't want to talk anymore. I don't want to think." She pressed Thea's hand against her breast. "I want to *feel*."

That was something Thea could whole-heartedly embrace.

Thea pulled Grace to her feet and kissed her, enjoying the press of her body against her own as much as she enjoyed the teasing play of her lips and tongue on her mouth. Ah, but Grace was sweet. So sweet that she wanted all of her, now, and not just a taste. She moved her hands down her body, unlacing here and unbuttoning there, until the gown slipped to the floor and left Grace in her stays and chemise.

"A delight to the eye," Thea murmured, looking at the slight swell of Grace's breasts beneath the stays that lifted them up, as if they were offered to her. She could see her nipples were already puckered as they strained against the fabric. The evening light that came in through the window made the bedchamber warm and cozy, a touch of amber and rose on everything she looked at, as the sky gradually darkened to deep lavender. Grace's long face with its customarily serious look was transformed in the dusk to true beauty, her skin luminous, her eyes glowing.

Mine.

Hell and blazes.

Well, Thea could make it true for one night, at least. She kissed the curve of Grace's breast above the ivory cotton, then tugged the stays down with her teeth to bare her nipple, and lave it with her tongue. Grace gasped and threaded her fingers through Thea's hair. Thea grinned. The lady liked that, did she? She could give her more. She unlaced her stays and they joined her gown on the floor, and her shift followed. Impatient, she tugged at her own clothing and tossed it away, then toppled Grace to the bed. Grace gave a little shriek as she fell, her eyes huge and her lips parted.

"I didn't mean to harm your ankle," Thea said with a guilty start.

"You didn't. But I have other parts of me that are in dire need of tending."

Thea laughed. It seemed the way to get under Grace's surface was to get her under the covers, where she was willing to peel back the layers of her prim and proper disposition and reveal the wanton woman who lived beneath.

"I am happy to be of service."

Thea wanted to spend an hour on her breasts, licking and teasing and sucking, learning every inch of them, but she was too impatient to touch Grace where she desperately wanted to. She moved her hand lower, stroking her between her thighs where she was already wet, and Thea felt as victorious as if this had been the true goal of the journey.

Grace nipped her shoulder, and Thea almost climaxed.

"I liked your hand on my mouth," she whispered, burying her head against Thea's neck. "I don't know why, but I liked it. I hope you don't mind."

"You can bite wherever you like, darling. I don't mind at all."

The way Grace moved under her was almost more than Thea could handle. Her hips ground against Thea's fingers as she twisted her body in search of release, and though she grasped Thea's back with both arms, she was constantly shifting, restless with need. Thea loved it. She felt both her own desire and Grace's, in an intimate embrace where she could hear Grace's every little sigh and whimper and gasp, along with the rush of blood that Thea felt roaring in her ears.

Grace bit her shoulder again, gently enough, but Thea felt the fierce need and desire in the action, and she reveled in it. It was what she loved most about plants. They thrust up from the ground, greedy for sunshine and water, perfect and whole in their unfettered and earthly yearning for survival. That was what Grace felt like underneath her as she shattered and cried out. Perfect and whole and fresh and free.

Mine.

Thea rolled over, her heart pounding. She hadn't caught her breath before Grace rolled her over and pressed eager kisses along her jaw and neck, so tender that she thrilled inside at being handled with such care.

Grace was a more measured and deliberate woman than Thea was, and Thea appreciated the nuances as she took her time about touching and kissing and squeezing. Her center ached and she knew it was slick and ready enough that she wouldn't take half a moment to explode with the barest touch. But Grace wasn't in a rush, and Thea somehow found the untapped reserves not to beg.

She lost herself in a haze of pleasure as Grace found all of her sweetest spots. The juncture of her jaw and neck, just below her ear. The whisper of breath on her nipples after they had been thoroughly sucked. The gentlest of pressure on her thighs to nudge her into just the right position as Grace's fingers entered her at long last.

Thea kissed her, her hands on both of Grace's shoulders as she moved and bucked, plundering her mouth with her tongue with all the urgency that she had felt building in her for days. Finally, she found her release, shuddering and gasping until she lay limp in Grace's arms in the bed.

She knew she hadn't given Grace the leisurely lovemaking that she deserved, but she hoped she had at least given her a night to remember. It was certainly etched into her own mind forever.

"I wouldn't mind talking now," Grace said, blinking up at her some time later.

Talking was both the last thing Thea wanted, and the *only* thing she wanted. She needed to unburden herself. She propped herself up on one elbow and gazed down at Grace. She wanted to trust her.

In fact, she was starting to worry that she needed to.

And she had no idea what that could mean for either of them.

CHAPTER SEVENTEEN

In the aftermath of lovemaking, with night falling outside and a thick blanket pulled up to her shoulders, Grace felt like anything was possible. This journey had been incredible. It had also been frustrating, painful, and ultimately disastrous, but she had experienced things she had never felt before. She had felt free, in a curious way. More importantly, she felt that she was an equal member of their party, with the same standing as Thea. She was not a lady's companion while she was in Scotland.

If only she could keep this feeling forever.

But Inverley loomed in her thoughts, with Lady Harriet awaiting news of her daughter. Ruination was all she had to look forward to, so for now she clutched the feeling of freedom to her bosom. She would wrench every moment that remained to her that she could. No more hiding away. No more fear. She had to be brave enough to face her future head on.

Thea cupped her cheek in her hand. "You stayed," she said. "My parents didn't stay when they discovered I'd been with my first lover when I was eighteen. The lover didn't stay when he discovered I had no intentions of marrying him and giving him my dowry. Many of my friends proved fair-weather indeed, flitting away when I stopped hosting raucous parties and buying brandy and fancy ices. It hurt, to be left."

"You have friends. Anthony. Polly." Grace had envied their friendship for days, watching the easy exchange among them.

"Yes," Thea acknowledged. "I have friends now, who stay with me and beside me. But not like you. Not a gently bred woman, refined and mannered. Anthony is a devil-may-care rogue, and Polly is my maid." Her smile was wry.

"And I am the natural-born daughter of a butler," Grace said. Her heart felt light as she said the words aloud for the first time.

Thea stared. "No. What?"

"Yes. Lady Harriet is blackmailing me about it."

"Blackmail!"

It wasn't funny, and yet Grace couldn't help but laugh at the look of astonishment on Thea's face. "In fact, Lady Harriet is my aunt. My mother is her sister, and I am the product of an affair with her butler."

"How on earth did you become a companion?" Thea was sitting up in bed now, the blanket pooled around her waist. Her eyes were wide. "This rivals any of my own most scandalous behavior, you know."

Indeed Grace did know. The single most important credential of being a lady's companion was her good breeding. A companion came from the gentry—never, ever, *ever* from service. The very idea threatened the social structure.

Her existence among the gentry, while she raised and educated their children and guided their young daughters through society, would be seen as a slap in the face of anyone of good character. She would be seen as the lowest sort of charlatan. And yet, what had she done wrong? Her educational services had been exemplary, and she took her role as chaperone and companion seriously. No one had come to harm.

Except the night that Edie had slipped away and compromised herself. That hardly had been Grace's fault, but she couldn't help but feel guilty. Her face grew hot at the memory of the one true failure in her unblemished employment history. If she had only been more observant and stopped Edie's misdeeds before they happened, she could have prevented a good deal of trouble.

Grace sat up. "I played a long game to get out of my circumstances. As you may imagine, it wasn't easy. At first, I had no greater aspirations than to become a housekeeper. But as I grew older and noticed the slights against me, and the way I was hidden away by both of my parents and denied any significant opportunity to better myself, I knew I had to rely on myself. And my aspirations grew."

"What did you do?"

Thea looked engrossed, and it made it easier for Grace to continue. "I decided that I am as equally the daughter of a gentlewoman as I am the daughter of a butler, for all that neither truly loved me. Why should I be bound to service because of who my father is? Why could I not reach as high as my mother had? I belong to the gentry the same as my legitimate half-sister, Sarah. But I didn't sound like her. I didn't behave like she did."

"You certainly do now. I have often thought that you look every inch a lady."

The thought warmed her. "I appreciate that. I worked hard enough for it. I befriended my sister—in secret, of course. I learned her accent, her manners, and applied myself as much to her lessons as she did, earning my education alongside her. At fifteen, it became more difficult, because my father put me to work as a housemaid. But I stayed up at nights, begging the nubs of candles from the housekeeper so that I could keep up with Sarah's studies."

"You are remarkable. You became a maid in your *own mother's house*?"

"She was unkind," Grace acknowledged. "And thoughtless. She truly paid me no mind when she saw me working, which would have broken my heart if it hadn't already been hardened against her years earlier."

"This is shocking. Grace, I had no idea." Thea took her hand and squeezed it.

"No one knows. That is the entire point. Only myself and my family."

Now that she had started the whole sorry story, Grace was unable to stop. The words kept pouring out of her. She trusted Thea, more than she had ever trusted anyone with her secrets.

"When I was seventeen, as soon as I thought I was old enough to make it credible, I lied about my age and my background to the employment agency in Manchester. I secured a position as a governess. I forged letters of reference, of course, but I didn't need to rely on them for long because I made sure to excel at my employment. I was employed by three wealthy families over the course of seven years. Finally, I was able to become a lady's companion, as the qualifications were much the same. By then I had enough proper references from families with sterling reputations in Manchester society. That was as high as I thought I could reach, and I was content. It's respectable employment—and a dashed sight easier than life as a housemaid."

"However did Lady Harriet become involved?"

"Moving in society as a lady's companion, no matter how limited, brought its own dangers. I tried to stay in positions with the elderly to keep me out of view, but even they wish to attend the theatre and the assembly rooms on occasion. It brought me to my aunt's attention." Grace sighed. "I look rather like my mother, I'm told. It didn't take much investigation on her part to discover the ruse."

"And yet she took you into her own employ?"

"Yes. She threatened to expose my roots to the employment agency, and all the families I had worked with, if I didn't help launch Edie into London society. Who better to brush the dust of a Manchester coal mine away from one's fortune but an accomplished liar who also happened to be almost-family?"

Thea nodded. "Ah. Were they new money?"

"Yes, my mother and Lady Harriet were daughters of a man who owned a great many mines. Lady Harriet married an earl who mysteriously passed away not long after she bore Edie, leaving them quite the fortune—but no opportunity to teach her the manners of the upper class. There were plenty of lessons for both myself and Edie, but she was a good learner and I helped her a great deal." She felt proud, thinking of Edie's success in London. She had done wonderfully well and had even danced at Almack's. "One year of heartache, to coax Edie into better and more refined manners without *ever* letting it slip that we were cousins, and Lady Harriet promised me that my next position could be companion to a dowager countess. Or even a duchess." Grace sighed, thinking of it. "I never quite believed that she had that sort of reach, but I did believe that I would have my pick of opportunities once Edie married. And now she has gone and married the wrong man."

"You ought to have told them to go to hell," Thea said. "Using you and threatening you? Her own *niece*? It's beyond the pale."

"Maybe I wanted to be needed," Grace said softly. "As much as I needed to belong. But of course I never did belong with any of them. There is not much opportunity for familial affection when blackmail is part of the picture."

"Does Lady Edith truly not know?" Thea asked.

"She knows nothing. She thinks of me as a former governess and companion from her hometown."

"What about your half-sister? Did she not recognize you?"

"Sarah would have—if she had been in London. But she was older than I was and married an American during her first Season. Our mother went with her, and they have lived in New York for the past ten years."

Thea shook her head. "This is incredible. Oh, Grace. I don't know what to say."

Grace felt better than she had in years. "There is no more to say. It was enough that you listened to me, as long as the tale was. I've never told anyone, you know."

"Then I am grateful to be the one to receive your confidences." Thea's eyes were warm.

"Now, let us sleep," Grace said. "We have even more to discuss tomorrow." She certainly would need the rest. Instead of the past, tomorrow would be the start of talking about the uncertainty of the future.

After spending a second night in Gretna, they began the journey back to Inverley.

Grace couldn't seem to get settled. She asked Thea to wrap her ankle, then to unwrap it. She propped it up beside her, then on the seat across. She leaned into the corner of the coach, then the middle, then contemplated the floor. She blamed it on the sprain, telling her traveling companions that it was still aching—which it was, but it was much better than it had been.

It was her mind that wouldn't ease.

She fretted and fussed so much that Polly resorted to traveling outside during the next stage, sitting beside the driver. She cited the need for fresh air, but Grace was ashamed that Polly was likely tired of hearing her complain. Or she was being kind and trying to allow Grace more space to be more comfortable.

Now she was alone with Thea, who knew all of her secrets. That, more than anything, was the cause of her discomfort. She trusted Thea, but she had never in her life told her story to anyone. She felt exposed, though also oddly light. It had been good to talk about it.

Cold reality was settling over her. She had toiled for most of her life to improve her situation, and one dreadful woman was going to unravel every hour and every year of effort with a few choice words to a few choice people.

It wasn't fair.

Edie and Mr. Martin had insisted on traveling back to Inverley on the next available stagecoach again, claiming it had been the grandest adventure of their lives. Given that Anthony didn't have the room in his own coach to accommodate them, they had to trust that they would meet up at the same stages along the way home. But Mr. Martin seemed delighted to have Edie as a wife and was evidently looking forward to claiming her as such in front of his family, so Grace was no longer worried that he would behave dishonorably along the road.

"I dread returning," Grace told Thea, her eyes on the fields that they passed, flush with sheep. If only they had that bottle of brandy again and could drink whenever they saw a flock. She needed it now more than she had needed it then.

"Must you return to Inverley?" Thea gazed at her intently.

"What do you mean?"

"Well, we are making a great many stops through England. We could leave you almost anywhere you might like."

Grace shook her head. "I have no money. No credentials that I can rely on. No family to claim me. How could I make my living, alone in a new city? If I venture back to Manchester or London, where the employment companies know me, and where I could contact my previous employers, I shall be ruined straightaway. Those will be the first places Lady Harriet would go to discredit me. I am ruined, whether I face her or not."

"Maybe you could be something other than a companion," Thea suggested.

"I have no other skills than a governess or a companion. I will *not* consider service again," she added. "I refuse to be a housemaid for the rest of my life." The idea of returning to her roots was too dispiriting to contemplate.

"Do you know much about botany?" Thea asked, a smile on her face.

Grace drew herself up. "I know enough. I taught the basics to my students when I was a governess. I know how plants are categorized, and the way they reproduce."

"Do you know about seed dispersal theories, or anything about soil nutrients?"

"Well. No. But I can learn." Could Thea be offering her employment?

"It is no matter. I find I have no need of an assistant," Thea said, but she still had a thoughtful look on her face that Grace couldn't quite read. "Polly is excellent in that regard."

She tried to swallow her disappointment but felt close to tears.

"Could you guess what I am most in need of?"

Grace was too tired to play games. "I cannot fathom."

Thea leaned forward. "In fact, I think I am most in need of a wife."

CHAPTER EIGHTEEN

Grace couldn't have heard her properly. "A *wife*?"

She still wore the gold ring from the ceremony. It had proved impossible to remove, though she had tried with soap, tallow, and oil. There was something comforting about it. The ring felt as if it belonged on her finger. She had tried not to tell herself that it was a sign.

"Why should we not consider ourselves married in truth, if not in law?" Thea's eyes were shining.

Grace finally found her voice. "Because we are women."

"Why should that be held against us? What is it about the words and ceremony that would not be valid to any who went through it?" Thea counted off her fingers. "We were in Scotland. We were of age. We even consummated the marriage with a wedding night. All that is left is the *willingness* to be wed. I know I am willing. Are you?"

The scenery rumbled by, exactly as it looked when they had traveled in the opposite direction on their pell-mell pace to Scotland. But everything was upside down now. Everything was different.

"But we are *women*," Grace repeated faintly.

Thea shrugged. "We had rings. There was a handfasting. Mr. Campbell struck the anvil. We even paid the fee. Or Charles did, anyway. What does being women have to do with anything, in the face of all this other evidence?"

Grace couldn't understand it. "Why do you even want a wife? A husband could give you money, protection. Maybe title or a land. Security."

"Because I don't want a man. I want a woman. In fact, I want *you*."

"But for how long?" Grace said. "If we take this seriously"—her mind reeled at the idea—"then I would be loyal for our whole lives. Forgive me, but you are…impetuous. You are impulsive. How can I know that you won't become bored with me?"

"Those words are binding," Thea said, and her brow lowered over her eyes.

"And yet you would have persuaded Edie and Mr. Martin to forget them."

"That was not well done of me."

"How do I know I can trust you?"

"As a wife?" Thea looked at her, and Grace felt the thrill of it shoot through her body. "I believe I have proved that you can trust me to take care of your wifely needs."

"There are needs outside of bedroom matters." Was she truly discussing this, as if it were an option? Grace's mind was racing.

Thea glanced around them and leaned forward. "We are outside the bedroom right now," she said, her voice dropping to a husky murmur. "Shall I prove to you that those needs can be serviced anywhere my wife desires?"

She slid onto the bench beside Grace and draped one arm behind her, resting it against the edge of the seat. "I promise to be considerate of your ankle."

Grace squeaked in indignation. "Here?"

"Perhaps you are looking for additional proof of our compatibility." Thea stroked her upper arm with the back of her gloved fingers, then dropped her hand to cup her elbow. "Here are those troublesome elbows of yours," she said, and leaned down to press a kiss against the inner crease of her elbow. "I cannot resist them. You would do well to put me out of my misery by consenting to be shackled to me."

"According to you, we are already shackled."

"Indeed we are."

For a moment, Grace felt giddy. Was it possible that she could have this? Security? Flirtation when she wanted it? She imagined a life where she no longer had to work, and her mind went dizzy with all the possibilities.

Then Thea lifted up her skirts, and her mind went dizzy for all new reasons.

"We *cannot*," Grace gasped. "Polly and the driver will hear us!"

Thea stroked her, and she bit back a moan. "Those wheels are thunderous. No one can hear us."

"Anthony could look in the window at any moment."

But instead of the idea filling her with horror, Grace was delighted that Thea was coaxing such pleasure from her. In broad daylight, no less. She had never done such a thing in her life, let alone in a carriage along a public road! She wriggled on the bench, allowing Thea to slip a finger inside her, and she gasped. Perhaps they had ended up traveling farther north even than Scotland, for surely this was approaching heaven.

"No one will look at you," Thea promised her. "Except, of course, for me."

Thea dropped to her knees on the floor of the carriage, and before Grace could comprehend exactly what her intent was, she angled herself between her thighs and kissed the curls hidden there.

Then Grace could no longer think at all, for Thea's warm mouth was on her center, her tongue stroking her, her lips kissing her in the most intimate of places, in a manner that had always made Grace blush to even fantasize about. She must be blushing now, for Thea's lips and tongue were far more skilled than her clumsy imaginings had been.

She thrust her hands into Thea's hair, dislodging her hair pins, and was distantly aware of the clink they made as they fell against the floor. "Thea!"

Thea moved her head enough to look up at her, her eyes dark with pleasure. "I *love* it when you say my name."

Then she leaned in again and Grace fell back against the bench, writhing with pleasure. This was the most wanton she had ever felt in her life. Her head rested against the back of the seat and she could see the brilliant blue sky outside, with flashes of green trees and fields blurring her vision. It was the most amazing feeling to be so connected with nature amidst such pleasure. Her toes curled inside her shoes and her thighs trembled as Thea continued to move her mouth against her center, heat building up inside her. Her stomach dipped as they went over a rut in the road, and Thea eased a finger inside her as she kissed and stroked.

Just as it became too much to bear, Thea changed pace to match the steady rhythm of the carriage wheels, and touched her tongue to her most sensitive place, and Grace fell apart in waves of pleasure, riding it until the last vestige of ecstasy had been wrung from her.

Thea eased up from the floor and sat across from her, a little smile on her lips. "Was that not a convincing argument toward matrimony? No one could deny that you look the part of a blushing bride right now."

How amazing it would be to have such intimate experiences all the time.

Without the worry of having to find employment again. And again. And again.

Stability. A life of her own.

A *wife* of her own.

It was too much to dream of.

"What are you getting out of this?" Grace asked, trying to focus her mind. It wasn't her experience that someone would offer something without expecting something in return.

"A helpmeet for the rest of my days," Thea said promptly. "I have no interest in household matters. I would greatly prefer to focus on my plants. I don't speak of botany to many people, but it is my life's passion." She glanced down at Grace's lap, where her legs were still spread and her skirts on her thighs. "Although I do have other passions."

Grace pulled down her gown, her face aflame. "I don't wish to be a companion," she said. "I would expect to be your equal in the household." She felt bold as brass saying such a thing.

"Of course. Though I don't have a grand household," Thea said. "Your situation in the house wouldn't be questioned by the staff, but on the other hand, the staff is not used to being managed. I am not able to offer you luxury." For the first time, she looked anxious, as if she hadn't been afraid until now that Grace might say no.

The fact warmed her. It was a sign that Thea really wanted this. Wanted *her*. "I don't need luxury," Grace said, feeling unaccountably shy. "I like to be useful." She swallowed. "I found a horseshoe in Gretna Green."

"A horseshoe?" Thea looked perplexed.

"It's good luck," she said. She patted the reticule beside her. She still had the penny from when she had picked it up in Inverley, which seemed like years ago, and now she had a heavy iron horseshoe. "Perhaps this was all meant to be."

Thea's lips twitched. "Did you perchance find such a thing outside of Smithy Campbell's? Where he perhaps often forges such things?"

Grace sniffed. "It does not matter the provenance of such a sign. I found it, and luck has followed."

"Do you truly believe such things?"

"Yes," she said firmly. "And I shall not be made fun of in my own house by my own wife."

"Then will you marry me?" Thea asked. "It may not be accurate in the strictest of legal terms. And I'm afraid we cannot breathe a word of it to anyone, except in the very strictest of confidences. But will you be my bride, to live with me until the end of our days?"

Grace hesitated, then leapt into her arms, knocking her sore ankle against the seat and not even caring. "Yes."

Everything was indeed backward, but it felt like life had never made more sense. How many could say that they had accepted a marriage proposal, two days after the ceremony and the wedding night?

Grace was the luckiest woman in England.

In the end, they didn't return to Inverley.

It had already been the longest journey of Thea's life. She discovered a newfound appreciation for Anthony's stamina, given that his voyages were measured in months instead of mere weeks. Another day on the road to Inverley would be a recipe for heartache.

Thea could imagine what would have happened if she and Grace had followed Charles and Lady Edith to Martin House. Mother and Father would be so disappointed that they would hardly deign to talk to her. The scandal would be swept under the rug as best as it could be, Charles would be celebrated as the first of their children to marry, and they would clutch Lady Edith to their bosom almost as readily as if she had wed James.

Even if Thea had wanted to celebrate Charles's nuptials in Inverley, there was still Lady Harriet to contend with. Grace shook with fear when she spoke of her, and that alone was reason enough for Thea to insist that Charles and Lady Edith go on without them.

Their families were free to vent their spleens as much as they wished without Thea and Grace having to endure it.

Moreover, Thea didn't want anything to mar her newfound happiness. The more she thought about it, the more pleased she was with the idea of a wife. She flirted with Grace through countless counties on the way back to London and was delighted when Grace agreed to share a room each night at the inns. The world had changed when they had stood over the anvil together, and her whole perspective had changed with it.

Something inside her felt different since the moment that ribbon had twisted around her wrist. Something warm and tender, to be protected. The feeling was only a bud, not yet in bloom, but what she did know was that it was a miracle beyond measure to have won the hand of such a thoroughly *good* woman. She could never have courted someone like Grace otherwise. She was far better than Thea deserved, and she was determined that Grace would never realize what a poor bargain she had made.

It felt scandalous in the best possible way to arrive in Chelsea with a *wife*, though it was a pity that she could never announce Grace as such.

"This is Miss Grace Linfield," she told the household staff, which consisted of a housekeeper, a cook, two maids, and Polly. "She is a dear friend of mine and is to be treated without exception as if she owns this house."

That would please Grace. Most women she knew loved overseeing domestic arrangements.

Thea did not. She looked forward to the end of fussing with the housekeeper over the weekly marketing and determining which repairs to the old townhouse could no longer be put off. No more meal planning and economizing and handling issues with the servants. She would be free to lose herself in blissful contemplation in the conservatory.

The rush of emotion she felt upon walking into the conservatory for the first time in over three weeks choked her. It was a chaotic spread of leaf and flower, pot and vase, exactly as she had left it. There were her dear chrysanthemums and sweet begonias. Her orange tree was heavy with fruit. Her notebooks were sprawled on the table from the last time she had been here. The plants, with the exception of a sad violet that had never looked too healthy to begin with, were thriving.

With her heart in her throat, she stepped into the garden to check on the camellia bush. It was the longest she had left it since planting it outside seven years ago. It looked healthy enough, its glossy variegated leaves unchanged except that they seemed a little thinner than usual, with a few that had fallen off to lay forlornly on the soil below. She questioned the maid who had taken care of it and was relieved that her instructions had been well followed while she was gone.

With any luck, she could nurse it back to health, and this would be the winter that it bloomed.

Thea had meant only to check that everything had survived her absence, but there was so much to examine. Flowers had bloomed, leaves had unfurled, and some plants had grown by six or more inches. By the time she lifted her head again from her notebook, it was dusk and Grace was scowling at her from the door.

"How long have you been there?" Thea asked, dropping her pencil.

"Not long. I have been busy reviewing everything with your housekeeper." She had her hands folded in front of her and her tone was pleasant, but her lips were thin and her eyes were narrowed.

"Is the house to your liking?"

"I like it well enough."

Thea's parents had agreed to lease a modest establishment for her in Chelsea, with the stipulation that their scandalous daughter be housed far from the Martins' own townhouse in Mayfair. It suited Thea because it was close to some of London's finest nurseries and the Chelsea Physic Garden. But the house was neither grand nor fashionable. It was three stories tall, narrow and economical, with standard enough rooms for the usual activities as sipping one's tea, eating one's dinner, and laying one's head on one's pillow.

The best part of the whole house was right here in the conservatory, but Grace hadn't even glanced at its wonders before glaring at her.

"Well, it's your house now," Thea pointed out. "You may make any improvements that you see fit."

Grace twisted her ring, then sat down on the stool across from Thea. "I would have liked your company. Your thoughts on the house and the neighborhood. Your observations, from the leak in the attic to the loose step at the front door. *You*—the person I am to share this house with. Not the housekeeper."

"I thought it best for you to make your own impressions. But I admit I lost track of time. Perhaps I could make it up to you?"

"How?" Grace asked, crossing her arms on her chest.

She nudged Grace's ankle with her foot. "I rather doubt that you received an adequate tour of my bedchamber."

She was delighted to see a shy smile spread across Grace's face.

Thea chased Grace up the stairs and into her bed, where she took pleasure in showing her the finer points of each corner of the mattress and demonstrating the plumpness of her feather pillows and sprawling her across every thread of her fine linen sheets.

This new development in her life was the best thing that could have happened to her.

What she hadn't told Grace was that she had posted a letter to her parents the day after she had proposed to her. It had dawned on her that she may have failed to bring Charles home unwed, and she would never hold the deed to Westhill Grange, but she *had* managed to fulfill her duty to her parents by marrying. Albeit in secret, and to another woman. However, her parents didn't need to know the details.

Thea wrote that witnessing dear Charles and Lady Edith's nuptials had renewed her faith in a settled life. Therefore, she told them that she had chosen to employ Grace as a lady's companion, and trusted that her parents would understand that this was as settled a life as marriage would be, and they didn't even have to give up her dowry to do it. In conclusion, she trusted that Father would continue to furnish her allowance.

What her parents would never know was that Thea's situation, virtuous as it may appear to them, was the most scandalous thing Thea had ever done in her life.

Grace knew nothing about her financial arrangements, as Thea had never told her that she lived on an allowance from Father, or that her parents had threatened to cut her off. Thea felt honor-bound to keep her from worrying about it, given that her bride was inclined to fret.

Thea looked at Grace, sleeping as easily in her arms as if they had been married for years instead of a sennight. She prayed that her financial gamble would work and that within the month she would receive a letter flush with bank notes, her pin money restored in full. But no matter what, she knew she would do anything in her power to keep such a woman.

After all, a wife like Grace was lovely indeed to have and to hold.

She was a woman worthy of forever.

CHAPTER NINETEEN

By the end of September, Grace wasn't sure that she had made such a fine bargain.

From the day she had turned fifteen and started working as a housemaid, she had been accustomed to adapting her life to best serve others. It was strange to glide into Thea's house and act as if it were her own. For all her lies to advance her positions over the years, she had never once bargained on becoming the mistress of a house herself.

Every day, Grace half-expected to pack up her worldly belongings, which Thea had arranged to be sent from Inverley, and go in search of employment. She applied so much lavender cream to soothe herself at nights that she had to purchase a new tin a month earlier than expected. She brushed her hair with her old ivory-toothed comb so often that her scalp tingled. She rubbed the lucky penny that she had picked up in Inverley until it had a shiny spot.

What was the legitimacy of her position in this house? What real rights did she have as a wife to another woman? No one except the most intimate of friends could ever know of their union, and even then Grace wasn't sure how many would recognize it as a true marriage.

It had been all well and good to accept Thea's proposal in the coach with the threat of Lady Harriet pressing down on her. She had been swept up in a web of romance and adventure, infatuated with the woman who had taken care of her along the road like a bold and dashing heroine, and who made love to her like her wildest fantasies.

But the truth was that the only thing that bound them together was their own word.

It was a big risk to take, having borne witness to Thea's impulses and humors along the way to Scotland. Was her word as flimsy as the ribbon that had tied them together for the handfasting, and which had been so easily slipped off after the deed was done? Would Grace be disposed of after the novelty of keeping a wife wore thin?

The relationship between herself and her employers had been well-established when she worked as governess and companion, and the tasks were defined and straightforward. Although the positions had been respectable and secure, she had always worried about the length of each new employment, as temporary as most of the positions naturally were. And yet, she could rely on her work ethic to ensure success where possible. There was something comforting and reliable in earning one's livelihood.

A wife should be a secure position for life, and one that should not be discarded lightly. But could she trust Thea to treat her as such for a lifetime? What was she contributing to earn her place here?

Grace reasoned that if she could prove her value, then she could convince Thea to keep her in her household regardless of what her stature in it became. There was plenty enough work involved in running a household, after all, and Thea seemed disinclined to involve herself in it much once Grace moved in.

There had been no discussion of adding a servant to the house to care for Grace, and she was too worried about contributing an additional expense to bring it up herself. She consoled herself by noticing that Polly hardly did her share for Thea in the capacity as a lady's maid, spending more of her time fetching and carrying plants and cuttings or sending off correspondence on Thea's behalf, compared to curling her hair or ironing her shifts. It was no matter. Grace was used to doing for herself.

It was an odd house, all in all. Silks and muslins were overstuffed in the chest of drawers in the bedchamber, and the chairs in the dining room were each individually lovely but none of them matched each other. It suited Thea, somehow, for though it wasn't well cared for, it was comfortable. The only room that looked new was the conservatory, which housed a cheerful chaos of flowers and greenery and a fresh earthy smell that was of no singular type of flower but was somehow the sum of the best of them. Even the conservatory, however, was a jumbled mess of plant cuttings and tools and discarded slippers that had been toed under the table where the maid forgot to tidy.

Looking through the expenditures, Grace discovered Thea spent a shocking amount on household affairs. Candles, linens, sugar, bread—all of it was more than Grace would have expected for a small household. She asked the housekeeper for the ledger detailing the previous year's expenses and wasn't surprised to find it much the same. Thea was carelessly extravagant, yet hadn't troubled herself much to make necessary repairs to the house itself. There was plenty that Grace could do to improve the household economy.

Grace gave the ledgers back to the housekeeper. "Thank you, Mrs. Fernsby. Everything seems to be documented."

"I am pleased it met your expectations." She bobbed a curtsy and replaced the books on the shelf.

Mrs. Fernsby was younger than Grace would have expected for a housekeeper and had an air of fashion that Thea couldn't have instilled in the staff given her own rumpled appearance. She wore her hair in short curls, and her frock was the newest style. Although she did whatever Grace asked of her, her attitude lacked warmth or sincerity.

"Have you worked for Miss Martin for long?"

"Two years. It has always been an unusual household, Miss Linfield," Mrs. Fernsby said. "But perhaps never more so than now."

Grace forced her breathing to even out. Had she somehow guessed that Grace was no better than she was? Had Lady Harriet spread her secrets already? A housekeeper would be affronted to take orders from a former housemaid. "Oh? What is so unusual about things now?"

Mrs. Fernsby's face soured like spoilt milk. "You know perfectly well."

"I'm afraid I don't."

"I've seen plenty of your kind around this house, putting on airs that you assuredly do not deserve. Did you think we don't notice when there is only one set of sheets to wash, miss? Shameful, is what this is."

Each syllable pierced her mind where the words would rest until the middle of the night when they would rise to haunt her. She had to remember that she was here as Thea's equal, as neither a servant nor a companion. "Notice what you will, Mrs. Fernsby. But I recommend keeping your opinion to yourself."

She strode up the stairs to Thea's bedchamber to compose herself.

The room that they shared was small but functional. There was a comfortable armchair with faded upholstery in front of the window, a fine oak dresser with a chip in the center of the first drawer, and a well-worn rag rug on Thea's side of the bed. There was little ornamentation, as if Thea couldn't be bothered to decorate. A pair of gloves had been tossed on the dresser, and the rug was crooked on the floor. Fresh towels—an abundance of them—were stacked in an uneven pile next to the washstand.

Grace's chest felt tight, as if she had been running. It didn't improve until she had straightened the rug, rearranged the towels, and tucked the gloves back into the dresser. Everything was where it belonged now.

Except, of course, for her.

She didn't want to talk to Thea about Mrs. Fernsby. She had been granted authority over the house, but what right did she have to reprimand its inhabitants? Thea had known them for far longer than she knew Grace. Would she listen to Grace if the household rallied against her?

She went to bed that night with her head full of numbers and lists and worries and fears. She was more than happy enough to curl up beside Thea and find respite in their shared pleasure beneath the sheets. Lovemaking as a married woman was sweet in its constancy. It was wonderful to have the leisure to explore one another without the threat of time running out, either because when she had been employed she had only had so many free hours in a week, or because the hour was growing late and she had never dared spend an entire night with another woman. It was no less sensual for being routine, and she delighted in it.

She propped her head on Thea's shoulder. "I want to do more to contribute," she said, Mrs. Fernsby's words echoing through her mind. The staff's realization of the nature of her relationship with Thea had been swifter than she had expected, though she should have known that the servants would be the first to notice anything out of the ordinary. All she could hope for was that they would be discreet.

But what had she meant by *airs*? Lady Harriet couldn't have written to anyone so quickly, could she? And yet it was no secret that she had been a lady's companion in her previous other households and yet not in this one, as Thea never addressed her as such. Perhaps Mrs. Fernsby didn't care to take instruction from a companion. To strengthen her position, Grace needed to gain a better foothold in the household.

Otherwise, she would always be at risk, and she couldn't bear the stress of it. It was impossible to relax when the threat of discovery remained high.

"You contribute plenty. The rabbit we had tonight was a blasted sight better than anything the cook had come up with before."

Grace poked her shoulder. "You never noticed what was on your plate because you were too busy with your plants. Now you notice because you have a wife to dine with. No, I wish to do something beyond the necessities."

"Do what you wish," Thea said, kissing her forehead. "Take a sitting room and refurnish it if it would help you feel more at home. This house is yours."

Grace twisted the ring on her finger. She would much rather the house was *theirs*. She wouldn't quibble, though. In so many ways, this new life was beyond her wildest dreams. She should be grateful enough that there was space in the house for her in any capacity.

Thea scowled down at the shoots of the blue ginger plant that she had planted the night before she had left for Inverley. Though it was more accurate to say that she was looking at what was left of the shoots.

She could hear Grace humming in the front parlor. It didn't matter if she was speaking to a servant, or walking down a hallway, or writing a letter—Thea felt wildly aware of every scratch of Grace's pen and every step of her slippered foot.

The conservatory had been her sanctuary. It had been her favorite part of the house. Until Grace moved in.

Four weeks had passed since their return to London, and Thea had noticed distressing changes in her routine. She finished experiments early so that she might wander over and press a kiss against Grace's neck and talk with her about her day. When she reviewed her notes from the previous day's study, she saw that she had drawn a little heart in the corner of the page.

It was most unlike her.

And the worst of it was that the plants were suffering, and Thea felt certain it was because of her reduced attention to their care.

The camellia in the back garden looked peaky. It was drooping and its leaves were yellowing, and she wasn't sure what to do. She had been so positive that this would be the plant that would finally bloom outdoors after so many years of trying to propagate camellia shrubs, but what if this was the end of that dream? She would have to check with the head gardener at the Chelsea Physic Garden in case he had any suggestions for her.

Most of the blue ginger seeds that she planted from the ones that Anthony had brought back weren't growing. It was a much higher rate of failure than usual. She poked at the soil in the clay pot, finding shrivelled roots and evidence of rot.

Thea had cultivated hundreds of plants with care through the years, doting in particular on her beloved orange tree, and the dozens of camellias that she had donated to other botanists after she finished studying them and they outgrew the space allotted in her house. There was only one camellia that she was currently trying to nurture outside, but she liked to grow the shrubs in pots and study their growth indoors so she could analyze better ways to nurture them outside.

But what she loved best of all was growing new life from next to nothing. Fresh buds, new leaves, and petals unfurling for the first time never failed to delight her.

There should have been a blanket of greenery in the little dirt-smeared pots that were scattered across the table. Instead, it was barren and empty.

Her work these days was proving difficult.

Much like her life.

Marriage had clear benefits—not least of which was an enthusiastic bed partner—but it was challenging. It was difficult to adjust to another person in her house. She had wanted a helpmeet, but it was far more distracting than she had thought. She never noticed the servants as they bustled about, so why was she constantly noticing Grace?

Perhaps it was because having someone at home all the time with her put her own moods and inclinations in stark contrast. Grace was as serene and calm as she had been in the carriage. Her sweetness had attracted Thea before, where now it terrified her. What was Thea to *do* with such a person in her life? She had never measured up as a daughter or a lover, so how had she ever thought she could manage a *wife*?

Her impulses had gotten her in trouble before, but the consequences had never felt like the sinking feeling she was experiencing now.

The best news of the past month had been the arrival of bank notes from Inverley. Her allowance, at last. Thea didn't like accepting money from her parents while they thought of Grace as nothing more than a companion, but at least Grace would never know the lengths she took to protect them financially. She reasoned that as long as *she* knew that Grace wasn't a companion, it wasn't so unusual a situation. Plenty of parents supported their children. How was this any different from her brothers' inheritances?

Thea shoved herself away from the table with enough force that one of her pots smashed against the floor. One more headache. She instructed a maid to set it to rights and to discard whatever had been inside the pot, not even bothering to check which plant it was.

Thea stood for a moment in the hallway, Grace's humming floating over her like a soothing blanket that she wanted to claw away. But she needed to wash up after spending hours with the plants, so she passed the parlor and spared Grace a nod in passing before going up the stairs to their bedchamber. She knew the towels would be piled high by the washstand as per her standing request to the maids, waiting for her to wash up after working. Cakes of soap were always at the ready to scrub away soil, sap, and grime.

Thea pushed open the bedchamber door, then swore as she walked straight into an armchair that hadn't been there that morning, her right foot banging against the carved wooden leg.

"Are you all right?" Grace called up the stairs.

The bright pain in her toe faded to an ache. "I'm fine."

Grace came up and stood beside her, peering around the room. "I thought I would try something different."

The dresser had been shoved up against the wall next to the window, and the chair was near the doorway now. The rug that had been beside the bed was now in front of it.

"This is the third new arrangement this month," Thea said, struggling to keep her tone neutral. "It looks nice."

She hated it. Grace fussed so much with the furniture that the room never felt like hers anymore.

"I see you have added some dried violets." Thea nodded at the cluster tied to the vanity mirror with a yellow satin ribbon tied into a bow. She didn't keep flowers in the bedchamber, as she suspected the maids would be too lazy to sweep away the fallen petals. She'd never had a firm enough hand with them. But maybe Grace had improved things with the staff. "If I had known you wanted flowers, I could have brought up my wax begonia. It's a pretty shade of pink that I think you would like. I cultivated it from seeds that Anthony brought me from Brazil two years ago. Have you ever seen one before?"

"But this way it's no trouble." Grace beamed at her. "You can save your cultivating for your conservatory."

"The beauty of growing a plant is in its maintenance. Trouble is part of the joy," Thea said, then wanted to kick her toe into the chair again when she saw Grace's face fall.

"I would be happy to see your begonia here instead of the violets," Grace said, her voice wooden.

Thea plunged her hands into the basin and scrubbed them clean, trying to rinse away her ill temper at the same time. There must be something she could do to lift Grace's spirits again. She hated to see her unhappy. "Would you care to accompany me on a walk?"

Grace smiled. "I would love to. I shall fetch my bonnet and be ready in a trice."

The Chelsea Physic Garden was a brisk quarter-hour walk from her townhouse. They entered the garden through a wrought iron fence in a brick wall covered with ivy. A few acres of land sprawled in front of them, a mix of trees and flowers and herb gardens in a cheerful jumble.

"This is one of my favorite places in all of London," Thea said. "It shows to better advantage in the spring and summer, but there are still a great many plants to appeal to the eye in all seasons. Many of them are medicinal in nature."

"How interesting. Can anyone enter here? I don't see anyone else walking around."

"Oh no, it's not open to the public. I do a lot of work with the gardeners here, and have donated many plants to them, so they welcome me. I have also given them plenty of seeds for their exchange scheme, which sends out seeds to many different countries and welcomes their seeds in return. Botanists around the world benefit from such a program." She liked to think of the seeds she had harvested from her conservatory being grown and studied in France, or China, or Italy.

"We haven't had much occasion to be out of the house together since we came to London," Grace said. "This is lovely." She tucked her hand into the crook of Thea's elbow.

A wife like Grace deserved dinners at the finest eating establishments, evenings at the playhouse, and walks to Gunter's for an ice on nice afternoons like this, instead of accompanying Thea on an errand. She felt like a churl. She hadn't even thought about enjoying the city together, so focused she had been on her botany.

Oh, why had she thought it would be easy to invite someone to live with her? She had spent more time deciding on plants to purchase than she had in contemplating whether to bring Grace home as her bride.

"I suppose you've noticed that my lifestyle is not quite what I claimed it to be on our journey." Thea had hosted a dinner in the past month for some of her botanical colleagues, and Anthony had dropped by any number of times for tea. But it wasn't like the dinners she used to host with the naughty ice sculptures and ne'er–do–well friends, when she was still feeling her way through her rebellious years. "I apologize. I should have said something before I proposed." It was one more thing she hadn't thought of, so caught up she had been in the magic of the moment.

"I had thought your life a touch more social, full of friends and dinner parties and plays." Grace's voice was wistful. "Though a sedate life is more than enough for me."

"I've been sorely neglecting you, haven't I?"

"I wouldn't say I feel neglected. There has been plenty of *other* sorts of attention." Grace's smile was a little shy. Thea had noticed that this sort of teasing was still new to her, and it pleased her every time she tried to flirt.

"Rest assured there will always be plenty of that."

"Then we have all we need for a happy union."

"But we haven't talked about what you might like to do in London together, have we?" Thea asked. "I suppose I thought we found out all there was to know about each other during those long days in the carriage. But I daresay I don't know if you would prefer the Royal Menagerie to the British Museum."

"A month isn't much time to learn all about another person. We could know each other for a dozen years and still have plenty to discover."

The thought of Grace being by her side for so long was like sunshine after a long rain, encouraging her heart to bloom with happiness. "Is that so? Why, I suppose that means we ought to begin our investigation of each other, if we have years to get a heads up on. I am yours to discover, darling. Be as thorough as you wish."

"As we are here in a garden, I admit to growing curiouser every day about your love for botany. Why is it so important to you?"

This was one of the loveliest things about Grace. She was interested. She *listened.* Thea looked at her face, so serious and peaceful, and felt the last trace of her bad mood drift away.

"I felt like a failure during my London Season. I hated everything to do with being a debutante—it was dull, and I didn't care much for anyone I was introduced to. Nothing about the experience was satisfying. It seemed as if society was reduced to the same room of people no matter which events I attended, all trying to impress one another."

"It can be a bore," Grace agreed. "I went to many such events with Edie."

"And so many people were mean spirited for no good reason. People like my brother James." She shook her head. "I didn't think twice before I ruined myself with a man who I later realized was only attracted to me for my dowry. I had fancied myself in love, and meanwhile he had planned for us to be caught *in flagrante delicto* so that my parents would force us to wed."

"That's terrible." Grace squeezed her arm. "I am so sorry. It must have been humiliating."

"It was. It was more humiliating when he refused to stay with me, after I told him in no uncertain terms that I didn't intend to marry anyone. I lost both him and my parents, and I decided that I would pursue a life of pleasure with anyone I was attracted to. Men, women. I had a good deal of fun with a good many people, and years later I discovered botany through a series of scientific lectures hosted by a library. Plants take time and effort and care to look after. It was soothing to me, and I found I enjoyed the peace it brought me. I liked dedicating my life to study and experimentation, which I had never dreamt I would be interested in. But growing new things from the ruins appealed to me, I suppose."

"What a fascinating idea. We are all looking to grow new leaves in our life from time to time, I suppose." Grace smiled. "I like that idea."

Grace didn't just listen. She *understood*.

Thea laughed. "But it doesn't always work like that. Sometimes the experiments themselves end up in ruins, and one learns from those experiences too. Today, for example, I discovered that none of my blue ginger has grown, and now I shall have to try to understand the reason. And my camellia is looking the worse for wear, and I cannot figure out the problem with that either."

"Is that why you were in a beastly mood this afternoon?"

"Well—yes. I'm sorry, Grace. It's important to me, and when it doesn't go right, it feels like everything in the whole world is wrong." She stumbled over her words, unused to expressing them.

"Is that how you felt when your family cast you off?" Grace asked softly. "As if fixing one important thing could somehow maybe fix everything else too, all at once?"

Thea flinched. That was exactly what she had thought. If she could grow the right plant, find enough success, join a respectable scientific society, then she would have empirical proof of her worth. Those milestones came with standards of success that she could point to and say that she had achieved them, so therefore she deserved her standing in scientific circles.

It was much less nebulous than familial love or societal respect.

"The head gardener should be working over there," she said, pointing to a greenhouse as if the question hadn't bothered her one whit. "Come, let me introduce you, and he can show off his collection of herbs."

She would prefer to show Grace every last plant in the greenhouse than talk about her fractured family for even one moment longer.

CHAPTER TWENTY

Grace recognized the handwriting on the letter that the maid presented to her. She had exchanged letters with Caroline and Arabella already, explaining her new situation in London as Thea's wife, and had also written to Maeve before Maeve had settled in London herself.

This was the only other letter that she had received, and it was the one that she had dreaded since their return.

It was difficult to find the nerve to open it. Each time she went to crack the seal, she flinched away from the task. After fussing over the placement of the chairs in the parlor, she felt calm enough to read it. The contents of the letter would not change whether she read them or not, so it was best to be as informed as the letter-writer.

Grace slid the paper open and forced herself to read every word from her aunt.

Lady Harriet was still in Inverley, ensconced for the time being with Edie and Mr. Martin at Westhill Grange. Grace spared a moment to think of poor Edie, a newlywed with her overbearing mother in her house. It wasn't a fate worse than marriage to James, but it wasn't a comfortable beginning to married life.

Lady Harriet had decided to write to the employment agencies so that no poor innocent young ladies would be caught under the misguided influences of one Miss Grace Linfield ever again, given the scandalous circumstances that her own daughter had found herself in. Any word from Grace to *anyone* about any pre-marital impropriety between Edie and Mr. Martin, and Lady Harriet would not hesitate to reveal the truth about Grace's humble origins.

In conclusion, she hoped Grace was keeping well as a friend of Miss Martin's, and that she would not deign to show her face anywhere near Edie or Inverley.

Grace stared at the letter.

Lady Harriet clearly thought her new station with Thea was a meagre position indeed and wanted to be sure that she couldn't escape it.

A wave of relief washed over her. At least this meant that the blackmail was over. Grace would never cause Edie harm by gossiping about her, which meant she was safe from further repercussions from Lady Harriet. Lady Harriet didn't seem to have exposed the roots of her personal history, merely highlighting that Grace had been a terrible companion to have allowed her charge to run wild and free to Scotland. It was damning enough for the employment agencies to turn up their nose at her.

If Grace didn't associate with anyone from the agencies, then maybe no one in her new life would ever know of her soiled reputation as a lady's companion. Thea didn't bother to mingle with the rungs of society where Grace had worked. The horseshoe that she had hung in the bedchamber above their bed had proved its luck again.

On the other hand, it meant that she had no alternative livelihood if her marriage didn't work out as she hoped it would. But she trusted Thea. She wasn't looking for a way out. The ring on her finger caught the light and she remembered how the satin ribbon felt, tying them together.

Grace didn't want to leave, but it was worrisome to know that there was no other choice in the matter. In a way, it was as if she was trapped here in Chelsea, without any other means to earn her survival.

She *liked* Thea, she reminded herself. She wanted to give this a chance.

Truly, the worst part of the letter was that Lady Harriet had made it clear that she was never to see Edie again. That hurt more than she expected. She had never thought it likely that she would see Edie after her wedding, no matter who she married. Grace had always been prepared to move her life forward, onward to the next employment.

Gretna Green had changed everything. The journey had shown her how much she cared for Edie, and how much she wished she could claim the relation—*any* relation. It was lonely, always relying on herself and no one else.

She would have liked to talk to Edie as equals. As cousins. How was she faring as a married woman? Was she having an easy pregnancy? Was she as happy as she had appeared in Gretna Green? Or had she found new bumps in her journey, as Grace had since her arrival in London?

She would have to count on news from her friends in Inverley. As meagre as it would be, it was all she could hope for.

Grace hid the letter among her sewing and went downstairs to have luncheon with Thea.

"You must be feeling better," Thea remarked. She took a sip of tea and flipped the page of the scientific newspaper that she arranged to be delivered to the house on Mondays.

"Oh? I haven't been feeling poorly." It wasn't quite the truth, but Grace thought it passable enough.

"You used to jump at the sound of the door knocker, but these days you sit as cool as you please when the milkman drops off a fresh jug."

Had her nerves been so transparent over the past few months? Grace stiffened. "It is difficult to settle back into city life after a sojourn in the country, is it not?"

It was the type of thing she would have said to any employer, slipping back into the pretense that she was like them. That they could trust her. Be comfortable around her. The truth was that she had always lived in cities. Inverley had been the first countryside jaunt of her life.

Grace had indeed been dreading each knock at the door, terrified that it would reveal Lady Harriet. She was afraid that every piece of mail that crossed her desk in the morning room would be filled with admonitions from previous employers, having discovered the extent of her lies.

Now that the letter had indeed arrived, it raised fresh worry.

Even though Thea knew about her past, she realized that the truth could still ruin her life even if she wasn't in search of employment. It would affect her standing in her own household. A maid-turned-mistress was a topsy-turvy world indeed. It would also affect how people thought of Thea, if they knew that the woman she lived with was nothing more than a butler's illegitimate daughter. How would she be able to make any friends among her peers?

"It's been ages since we were in Inverley, though I suppose it is difficult to readjust," Thea said. "Not that I bother much with the country."

She gave a sniff of disdain, but was that a hint of wistfulness in her voice? Grace hesitated, having seen before how Thea shied away from talking about her family, but they were *wives*. It wasn't overstepping her place to voice her support. "I know how much you had wanted Westhill Grange," she said. "I wish you could have realized your dream."

"Well. I wish it too." She cleared her throat and turned another page, and Grace saw the paper tremble along with her hand.

"What would you have done with it, had you won it?"

Her face spasmed, and Grace didn't think she would answer. Finally, she shoved the paper aside and looked into Grace's eyes, her face intense. "It would have been magnificent. I would have transformed the grounds."

"Pleasure gardens?"

"A *botanical* garden," Thea corrected her. "For the seaside visitors. It would have been wonderful. The Grange has acres of land. I would have the room to grow a whole row of camellias if I wanted. Fir trees from the Americas would line the perimeter. I would have beds of flowers in all the brightest colors, and a gravel path meandering around so one could walk where one pleased. There would be a garden of herbal plants and flowers, and Polly could make remedies and simples for the local apothecary to keep in his shop. She likes that sort of thing and rarely gets to practice. I would like to talk to people about where the plants come from and how to cultivate them in different environments and give people the pleasure to see things that most of them would never be able to travel to see."

Her face was dreamy, and Grace didn't think she had ever seen her look so...soft.

"It sounds beautiful." She yearned to visit Inverley again, and to revisit the friends she had made there. But if Lady Harriet was there and had forbidden her to see Edie, then it was for the best that Thea was estranged from her family. The thought made her sad for them both.

Thea's face shadowed and she grabbed the newspaper again. "It's not meant to be, is it? Though if it were, I suppose I would be more likely to take my inspiration from Sir Francis Dashwood and create a suggestive hill in the middle of the garden, with shrubs at the base surrounding a round door and give it the lascivious name of Venus's Parlor. That would shock the people of Inverley, would it not?" She smiled and winked at Grace, though it seemed forced.

Grace laughed because she knew that Thea wanted her to, but her heart ached for the evident pain in her voice. "I suppose it would."

After breakfast, Grace went to visit Maeve, who had recently arrived in London. She had spent the last two years with her mother traveling from Ireland and across England in search of cures for her mother's ailments. Maeve had written to her to let her know her address in London for the few weeks they would be there before adjourning to Bath for the winter.

During the hackney ride from Chelsea to Mayfair, Grace thought about Thea's dreams for a botanical garden. She wanted her own dreams, she realized. Something to be passionate about. Something to work at. Not something to dig her hands into and soil her arms up to the elbows, as Thea liked to do, but *something*.

She couldn't live in fear for the rest of her life, nervous to venture forth and meet new people who may have heard about her from Lady Harriet. The letter today proved that she should be safe enough now.

"Grace, it is wonderful to see you again." Maeve embraced her and then ushered her into the apartment at the edge of Mayfair.

Grace looked around at the rooms that the Balfours were renting. Maeve always looked exquisite, and she perched herself on an armchair as elegant as any fashion plate. Silk cascaded over her body like a waterfall, and rubies and gold dangled from her ears. But the room was small, the furnishings adequate but antiquated. Maeve was the brightest spot in it.

The rooms that Maeve and Mrs. Balfour had rented in Inverley had been similar. Grace remembered the heavy scent of lily perfume from the previous tenants that had never faded, and the lace crochet and floral brocade that covered every surface. Maeve had claimed that such accommodations were the best they could find with such a last-minute decision to venture to Inverley, as all the finer places had already been rented to the fashionables that descended on the seaside town in the summer.

But looking at the sitting room in London, Grace wasn't so sure that was the reason.

Maeve demanded to hear all about Thea the instant the tea setting was brought out and the maid waved away.

"It's better than anything I've experienced before," Grace said, clutching her cup of tea. It felt so *good* to talk about it in person instead of brief mentions in letters, where she had to be careful not to write too much in case other eyes glimpsed the missive. "Thea is wonderful. She is strong, brave, and kind. And funny." She smiled. "I had relationships before—one with the companion from the establishment next door to where I worked in Manchester, and one with a woman who ran a boarding house—and I don't think I laughed so much in those relationships combined than I have with Thea in two months."

Maeve reclined into the armchair, her eyes heavenward. "May the Lord give me the strength to resist jealousy, for I know it to be a sin."

"My life isn't perfect."

"Do tell."

"The bedroom is the only place I feel that we communicate," Grace confessed. "When our conversation turns too serious, Thea brushes it away with a joke or an innuendo or we end up in bed. I want to learn so much more about her, but it's difficult at times." She smiled. "Thea keeps an odd little plant called a cactus that reminds me of her. It has tiny spikes all over that prick if you if you get too close. But there's a beautiful flower at the top, once you get past the pricks."

Maeve sighed. "I must work even harder not to be jealous in the face of such untold luxury as having a woman to prick you every single night if you wish it."

"Maeve! That's the type of thing Thea would say to me if I was trying to express something heartfelt. It does not help matters to make a trivial remark." She frowned down at her teacup.

Maeve stirred her tea. "I apologize, but flippancy doesn't mean insincerity. I was as heartfelt when I spoke as you were. Despite the humor, I really am envious. I've never had a real relationship, you know. I've had kisses in the dark, and I am no green maiden ignorant at the idea of other intimacies, but my lovers have been few and far between and didn't have much to offer after the night was done."

Grace hadn't thought of it that way. Perhaps Thea didn't mean to dismiss a conversation when she spoke like that. Was it possible that Grace worried too much? Maybe it was a matter of them enjoying different conversational styles.

"I meant what I said," Maeve continued. "It's extraordinary to be in the situation you are in. *Married*, Grace!" She sounded impressed. "I had never even dreamt of such a thing."

"I do know how lucky I am to be with someone without fear of judgment."

"Has there truly been none?" Maeve looked skeptical.

"The household staff is not too pleased with my presence."

Despite her youth, Mrs. Fernsby looked down her nose at her each chance that she got, and each time she did, Grace felt like a fifteen-year-old housemaid again. She felt guilty even now, sitting in Maeve's parlor taking tea as if there was nothing else in the world more important, when she knew perfectly well that at this very moment in Chelsea there was a pile of linens in the kitchen that had not been ironed in two days by either of the maids.

But she was no longer a housemaid.

She was no longer employed at all.

She was free to have friends and pursue her life.

If only she believed that it could last forever.

Grace sighed.

"There is something else the matter," Maeve said. "It does not take much intuition to see that you are unhappy."

"I am not unhappy. Truly, I am not," she said, swatting Maeve's arm when she made a face at her. "But perhaps I could be *happier*. I simply feel like I should be doing more." She struggled to put it into words. "None of this is what I expected, you know. I never planned on a life where I wasn't employed."

"What is it you wish to do?"

"I haven't any idea."

"Why do you wish to do anything at all, then?" Maeve studied her over the rim of her teacup. "Personally, I am quite fond of not doing much. My mother may call me lazy all she wishes, but I think it is a wise conservation of energy to read all afternoon when one has half a chance."

"Thea is so occupied with her botanical studies. I suppose I feel lonely in comparison."

"Do you want your own occupation? Or is it that you want to spend more time with *her*?"

That was such a good question that Grace couldn't quite resolve it. Was she envious that Thea had a passion, or was she envious that Thea's passions seemed more directed toward her conservatory than to her wife? Maybe they didn't need to talk more, and maybe she didn't need to do more. They did enjoy intimacies together that were better than anything Grace could have ever imagined. Maybe that was the key to their happiness.

Maybe it was time to remind Thea that she could be more interesting than a plant.

CHAPTER TWENTY-ONE

M r. Yates, I am pleased to see you again." Thea smiled at him as she clipped another leaf from the plant in front of her. She enjoyed when people came to visit her conservatory.

Mr. Yates was a slim and dapper man in his forties who had made his fortune renting out nature to wealthy socialites. There were many who liked to have flowers and trees adorn their ballrooms for an evening at a time, wishing for something extravagant yet temporary to show off to guests. He also did a tidy business in contracting out plants for those who wanted a garden but didn't want the effort of maintaining it. His gardeners took care of the plants by the week and whisked them away at the end of the month.

"With the amount of mignonettes I have rented out this week, I wouldn't be surprised if I am permanently marked by their odor. At least it is inoffensive enough, if one likes spice. Though I do apologize if I have brought it with me." He sniffed his lace cuffs. "I don't think it has yet breeched my closets."

"It would save your bills on cologne if it did, and your valet the trouble of dabbing it on you."

He laughed. "Have you anything new that I could borrow for a few days? The pink of society favors novelty, and my gardens are sadly depleted at this time of year. People want geraniums and sweet briar, but I want to offer something special."

"Is the demand not slowed by it being autumn?"

"Yes, but there is always someone wanting something," he said with a shrug. "Not for the gardens, but for the events. There's always a party waiting to be hosted in London, is there not?"

She brushed the soil from her hands and went to the table near the windows beside the padded bench where she liked to read in the afternoons sometimes. "I have a quill-bloomed chrysanthemum, if this is to your fancy?"

Thea pointed to a clay pot on the corner of the table that sported three dozen blooms, the thin spiky petals vibrant orange and dark pink. The flowers were striking against the dark green leaves.

"It's not so much to my fancy as it must be to the Countess of Sinclair's fancy," Mr. Yates said, scrutinizing it. "She's wealthy as anything and is hosting a soiree that will fill my coffers for a month or more. I've already delivered two wagon loads of laurels and evergreen, and enough wax lights to make a ballroom bright enough to rival the sun. This chrysanthemum will be a nice addition as a table centerpiece. I will have my man bring over payment when he comes to pick it up."

The additional funds would be most welcome to her accounts. Although her allowance had been restored, Thea was realizing that while it may have been enough to keep one person housed in some comfort in Chelsea, it was not quite enough to support an additional person to the household.

Thea nodded. "I am happy to do business with you, as always." She hesitated. "If you have any additional needs, I hope you come to me first. I am happy to supply you with anything you might require. I could grow almost anything to your specifications."

"I will review my upcoming events, but I specialize in large volume for these types of parties, you know. People don't want one or two of a thing when a dozen would do as well, except in such situations where there is a special request as this."

Thea swallowed her disappointment. "Of course, I understand. Well, do keep me in mind." A thought occurred to her. "Would you happen to have any dried lavender? If you do, could your man bring some by when he comes to collect the chrysanthemum?"

"I would be happy to. By the way, where is Mr. Robinson spending his time these days?" he asked, trailing a finger over a large glossy leaf. "I would be most happy to see him again."

Anthony was well known among botanical circles for what he brought back from his travels. Thea was far from the only one who hired his crew to obtain seeds and cuttings. She grinned. "He is coming to dine with us tomorrow if you would like to join us. I would expect him to be pleased to see you as well."

He beamed. "I am delighted to accept. Until tomorrow, Miss Martin."

Grace entered the conservatory as he was leaving. "Are you still working?" she asked, closing the door behind her.

"Yes, I was repotting some plants when Mr. Yates came by."

"The conservatory is like your mistress. I am lonely." Grace folded her arms across her chest. "I don't understand why I'm jealous of a room, but I am! Maybe it's because you shut yourself away for so long, and I know so little of what you are doing. I want to share more of our life together, and sometimes…I feel like you don't."

"I don't wish for you to be lonely, but you must understand that botany is the key to my life. I can no longer give it up than learn to fly."

She sighed. "I would never wish for you to give up botany, but I wish for more balance. Is it not normal to find out our likes and dislikes, our habits and our beliefs, as we settle in together?" Grace took a deep breath. "I want this to be forever."

"So do I," Thea said quietly.

"It truly is beautiful in here."

"I know. I meant it to be."

"But nothing in it is as beautiful as you are."

Grace looked up at her, and Thea's heart stuttered. She had been called beautiful by many lovers and didn't think much of it. When Grace said it, it felt different. Warmer. Softer. Things she wasn't normally interested in, but when it came to Grace, she was interested in every experience she could get.

This was her bride. The fact warmed her more than the afternoon sunlight that heated the room through the glass windows. "You are the beautiful one," Thea said.

Grace laughed. "I know perfectly well I can lay no claim to beauty."

"But you can, you know." Thea walked over to her and tipped her chin up. "Your eyes are large, and the tawny flecks sparkle in the light. Your lips are the pink of a new rose." She brushed her thumb over her lips and was delighted when Grace touched the tip of her tongue to the pad of her thumb. "You look distinguished. Poised is what I thought of when I first saw you, you know." She didn't mention that she had also thought her almost plain when she had first seen her, for now she couldn't understand how she hadn't seen Grace's real loveliness.

"Poised is far from beauty."

"Then maybe I see you with more than just my eyes," Thea continued, and ran one finger down Grace's arm. "I see you with my whole body."

"Then perhaps you would like to take a closer look now?" Grace unbuttoned her gloves, one tiny button at a time, then slipped them from her hands.

"Anyone might come in."

"The servants have a half day today," Grace said, her eyelids half lowered.

Ah. Thea had forgotten. As soon as Grace had moved into the townhouse, she had happily relinquished all household duties and schedules to her.

"I have friends who may enter. You know I don't stand on ceremony here. Anyone might wish to visit the conservatory."

"Friends ought to knock when they find a door closed."

Thea grinned. "When I married you, I thought I was getting a decorous woman. Now look at you."

Grace unbuttoned her pelisse and shrugged it off her shoulders. "I do wish you would."

Sexual intimacy with Grace had proved to be more deeply satisfying than anything Thea had previously enjoyed, and she was always thrilled when Grace initiated the experience. This was the first time she had surprised her in a room that wasn't the bedchamber, but perhaps Grace was thinking of the excitement of their carriage encounters on the journey home from Scotland. Thea was happy to indulge her.

She turned Grace around and unlaced the back of her dress, then removed her stays and shift so she was bare in the afternoon sun. When Thea had planned out the conservatory with her architect, she had never dreamed that it would be used for leisurely lovemaking. But a nude woman amid the bright blooms and lush green leaves and golden sunlight turned out to be the perfect addition to the room.

"Here are those delightful elbows of yours again." Thea kissed the crook of her elbow.

Grace laughed. "I know your vision of beauty is skewed if you continue to think of such a thing as my elbows as attractive."

"They captivated me from the moment I saw them peeking out beyond your gloves in your traveling dress on the first day of that long journey to Scotland. I thought they would drive me to distraction. I am well pleased to have them within sight now." She traced a finger against the sharp bone. "Why not appreciate something unusual?"

"Because I have several more usual bits that require attention."

Thea bent her head and touched her tongue to Grace's nipple. "This kind of attention?"

Grace sighed with pleasure. "Exactly."

Thea took her time caressing and licking her breasts, entranced as always by her little gasps when she found a particularly sensitive spot. She then took off her own dress until they were both bare among the flowers, their sweet earthy scent mingling with Grace's lavender aroma, and nudged Grace toward the far wall.

"Face the windows and kneel on the bench," she murmured in Grace's ear.

Grace knelt.

"Part your knees more, darling."

The muscles in her thighs flexed as she shifted. Her back was straight as ever, her posture impeccable, her arms loose at her sides. She glanced back and met Thea's eyes, her serious face thoughtful. "Anything else?"

"Relax, and enjoy."

Thea spared one long admiring look at her narrow waist and long back before moving against her. Grace's bottom fit snugly against her pelvis, and Thea's breasts were pressed against Grace's back. She skimmed her hands up over Grace's hip and belly before stroking one hand between her thighs and the other hand against her breast, rolling her nipple gently between her finger and thumb. Grace reflexively moved backward, her bottom thrusting against Thea as she shifted to allow Thea to gain deeper access.

Thea could tell it was difficult for Grace to maintain her balance with her fingers pressing against her slick center and driving her toward her pleasure, but she held her in place with both hands firm on her body. "I will never let you go," she said, and Grace's wide eyes met hers over her shoulder. "Trust me."

"Always," she whispered, and then it became difficult for Thea because when Grace let go, it was always with abandon. Whenever they made love, Grace moved restlessly beneath her hands, always eager for pleasure, and delightfully responsive when she found it. She had to hold tight when Grace started to move her body on the bench at a quicker pace, grinding against Thea.

And then Thea gasped when Grace moved an arm between them and reached for Thea's center, her palm connecting with her clitoris, stroking her with fast, firm movements that matched the thrust of her body, both of them off center and struggling to hold their balance while also moving toward a wave of pleasure that threatened to crash over them both. When it hit her, Thea buried her head against Grace's back and cried out, her voice and Grace's mixing together, their bodies responding in unison as they found their release together.

It was a long time before they caught their breath again.

"I am vastly pleased to have had a new experiment in this conservatory," Thea told Grace, pressing a kiss against her collarbone. "Now I know how sturdy the furniture is."

Grace laughed. "I enjoyed participating in your study."

"I don't wish for you to feel jealous," she said. "I want you in my life, Grace. In here, too." It was difficult to imagine the space without her anymore. Thea gathered her in her arms. "You always have a place with me."

CHAPTER TWENTY-TWO

The next week, after visiting the Chelsea Physic Garden, Thea stopped short when she saw the conservatory.

It was beautiful.

Everything was somehow still in the right place, but it was better organized than it had ever been. Not a drop of spilled soil anywhere. No loose petals on the floor by the begonias. No errant snips of leaves or stems strewn on the table.

The leaf clippings were in a wood box near the door, instead of in the haphazard canvas bag shoved under the table. There was a new shelf where her notebooks and research books were stacked next to her work gloves, shears, and twine. Her pots had been carefully moved so that although they remained in their proper places—some in the sunlight, others in the shade—everything was more spaced out and looked more attractive.

The large windows had been meticulously cleaned, which meant that Grace had indeed encouraged the maids to do a proper job of it for once.

There were plenty of people in her botanical circles who cared about the work she did and who were interested in hearing about theories concerning plant growth. But no one cared like Grace did. Thea pressed a hand to her heart. Grace might not know much about plant properties, but she knew Thea, and had made sure to fix the space around her to be more useful, more elegant, and more appealing to look at.

Thea found Grace in the parlor, sewing a rent in a torn chemise.

"You are a marvel," Thea announced. She pulled Grace up and embraced her, burying her head into the crook of her neck. "You did so much work in the conservatory today. For me."

"I like organizing and putting things in their place. I told you I wanted to contribute to the household," Grace said, smiling. "Isn't that part of a wife's duties? To see to the comforts of her...well, her other wife?"

They went to the conservatory together, and Thea leaned against the doorway and watched as Grace swept about the room, pointing to things that she had adjusted. She was so elegant, each movement precise. Grace always did the right thing, and here she was doing something for *her*. It was touching.

Thea had felt guilty since bringing Grace to London, convinced that Grace would someday realize the poor bargain she had struck. She wouldn't blame Grace if she ever wanted to walk away.

"This was so kind of you."

It was an understatement. It was more than kind, it was *caring*. Grace was so efficient and so organized, and she had a talent for bringing an easy peace around her, for all that she worried and fretted about things. But if Grace valued her so much to have done this for her, then she must think their life was worth living together.

Maybe Thea could breathe a little easier.

"I also helped with the camellia," Grace announced, beaming.

Thea stepped back so abruptly that Grace stumbled. "You did *what*?" Her heart pounded and her voice came out as a croak.

"I have been watching how you take care of it, and I went out to add the mulch this morning."

Thea sailed out the conservatory to the garden, with Grace following.

"Have I done something wrong?" Grace's voice was high, and when Thea glanced behind her, she was twisting her wedding ring.

"It's good of you to want to help, but the camellia is important to me," Thea said, struggling for patience.

The mulch was piled high around the base of the shrub. Too high. Thea tsked. This wouldn't do at all. She grabbed a trowel and started removing the soil.

"I'm sorry," Grace said, and Thea realized with a start that she was still there.

"It's been seven years without a single flower. I need this to be the year that it blooms."

"I only wanted to help."

Thea blew out a sigh. "I know. There's no lasting harm." She rose to her feet and touched Grace's shoulder. "You didn't do anything irreparable. Do not worry." She got back down and continued to remove the new layer of soil and oak leaves, her preferred mixture for her garden, then frowned as she saw a flash of bright orange peeking through the dark soil. She picked up a piece. "Orange peel?"

"Yes. I saw that you mix the kitchen scraps in with the soil for the mulch, so I added my orange rinds from this morning. Should I not have done so?" Grace looked worried. "I am sorry if I have done anything to your shrub. I suppose I should have talked with you first, but I wanted to surprise you."

Thea turned the peel over in her hand. "I've never added citrus rind, but it's not a bad idea. We shall see if it can help the camellia."

"But you're removing the mulch."

"I won't remove all of it." Thea patted the soil with her trowel. "You were kind to help, but the camellia is a delicate plant and I've been working on it for a long time. The roots are shallow, and if they are too deep under the soil, the entire shrub will die."

"It seems to be doing well enough."

The leaves were still yellower than Thea would have liked, and some of the branches continued to droop. She had talked it over several times now with the head gardener of the Chelsea Physic Garden, but he hadn't had any suggestions for her, given that she refused to uproot it and bring it inside for the coming winter.

It was possible that changing the soil and adding more elements to the compost might help breathe new life into the shrub. Maybe experimenting was the right way to go. Change could often yield surprising results. She looked at Grace. It certainly had in her life.

"Have you ever seen a camellia in bloom? This one should flower any year now, but I have worried over it since I moved it from inside the house to the garden. No one in England has ever been able to grow one outside, you know."

"Does it not like the winter?" Grace guessed.

"It doesn't, but there's a great many other things it doesn't like also. I've grown camellias inside to study them and found they don't much like the morning sun. I've also tried growing them outside before, including transplanting fully flowered shrubs that I've purchased from the florists, but I've met up with all sorts of trouble. They don't do well in the wind, or with too much water. Their roots need lots of space and must be planted shallowly, which is why I am removing the excess mulch—I've had other camellias die due to root rot if they are planted too deep."

"Why focus on camellias, if they are so difficult to grow?" Grace's brow was furrowed. "You have so many other beautiful plants inside."

Thea laughed. "I suppose I don't like to be told that one cannot do something, and I have been told time and again by gardeners, florists, and other botanists that it is impossible for them to live outdoors in England's climate. They might be right. This shrub here is the closest I have come to success—and still it may never bloom. I have my hopes for this year, though, despite the yellowing leaves."

"It seems like an awful lot of work. Do camellias smell nice, at least?"

"They have no scent, but they would make a glorious addition to a garden. They're beautiful in bloom." She hesitated. "Also, if I am successful, it would mean the world to me. I'm known enough in certain circles, but this would be my entry to botanical fame. If it blooms in this garden, it will be the first to have done so, and it will disprove the many men who told me that it was too delicate to survive the elements."

"They are not useful, like the loosestrife?"

She remembered. Thea was touched. "No, but some things brighten a space by being lovely."

Like you, Thea wanted to add. Grace improved her life in every way just by *being*.

If only she knew what to make of that realization.

Grace looked up from her correspondence the next afternoon to see Thea enter the parlor with a paper-wrapped package the length of her arm.

"I brought this for you." Thea dumped it on the table where Grace was writing.

"Oh!" A present. How unexpected. She eased the paper away and saw a heap of dried lavender. "How wonderful." She bent and inhaled, the aroma sweet and soothing. It was a luxury to have so much of it.

"Maybe you would have preferred fresh flowers from the florist, or a potted plant from my conservatory." Thea sounded a little embarrassed. "But a friend brought these by today, as I thought you might like some to keep with your clothing. Or to hang by the mirror with the dried violets. I noticed your cream was scented with lavender, so you must like the scent."

"I do." Grace beamed at her. "I shall sew it into sachets and tuck them in the dresser drawers and the wardrobe. Oh, this is wonderful, Thea!"

She hugged her close, then saw Mrs. Fernsby pass by the parlor from the corner of her eye. She cleared her throat and stepped away. "Thank you."

Thea pressed a kiss to her cheek and whisked herself off to the conservatory.

It was so thoughtful of Thea, and she *did* prefer the dried lavender to a bouquet of fresh-cut flowers. This way she could keep her favored scent on her all day long, and moreover, she would be able to think of Thea whenever she noticed it on her clothes. An extra layer of comfort and kindness to wrap around herself.

She had been so worried that Thea had been upset about the camellia. Grace was being well taken care of, and she wanted to show her appreciation by taking care of things around Thea.

If only the words were easier to say.

It was difficult when Thea wouldn't tell her what was important and what wasn't. How could she know that the camellia was somehow more precious than the Queen's jewels, when Thea had never spoken of it? It stung, knowing that Thea was content to keep Grace well-occupied in the bedchamber, but never thought to share her botanical passions with her.

She stared at the corner where a crack bisected the plaster.

Thea was generous with money and gave her anything she asked for. But she wondered sometimes why the funds had not already been spent on necessary repairs. She had the sense that Thea didn't like to spend money on the necessary things, instead focusing on pleasures like fancy plants and fine dinners. It worried Grace. Where would they be if the house trespassed the border beyond comfortable disrepair into ruin?

She took a deep breath. A crack in the wall was not threatening. The issues she had been fixing up around the house as winter settled in had been superficial, with no hint of rot in the walls or vermin in the basement. She needed to stop relying on signs to prepare her for good luck or ill, for so much had happened in her life during the past few months that she could never be sure what to expect anymore, no matter how many pennies she spied on the ground or how many magpies gathered near the eaves in the evening.

Their townhouse was perfectly safe. She was sure of it.

But she did worry that her relationship with Thea was cracked, and she didn't know whether their foundation was solid enough to withstand it.

They had pledged themselves in marriage. But marriage was more than living together, more even than the intimacies they shared. At least she thought it should be. She wanted a deeper connection with Thea.

But could she risk saying so?

This marriage was all she had. Lady Harriet had made sure that Grace no longer had the option of finding employment if the relationship failed. If Thea didn't think of their union in the same way, if she wasn't willing to share her thoughts and interests with Grace, then maybe it was a sign that Thea was becoming bored. Grace worried that Thea, impulsive as she could be, might want to move onto something newer. Or someone more interesting.

With a start, she realized she was shredding a stem of the dried lavender into powder. She brushed the dust into her handkerchief and brought the lavender to the bedroom, where she kept her sewing. She would busy herself by starting on the sachets right away, so she could show Thea how much she appreciated her gesture.

She needed to focus on Thea's actions. She had brought her a gift, and Grace needed to remind herself that worrying about something wouldn't bring it to pass. She would simply have to ensure that she continued to fit into Thea's life. Grace was more than accomplished at such a thing. How many times had the ladies that employed her said that she was an ideal companion to pass the time with? She knew how to make herself agreeable.

She would make sure that this marriage worked.

CHAPTER TWENTY-THREE

Christmas Day dawned bright and cold. Grace would have liked to spend the afternoon in the house with a hot cup of tea, but Thea insisted that she ready herself for half past one o'clock.

"Where are we going?" Grace stared at her clothing, unsure what type of dress to wear.

"You shall see. Wear something warm, as we shall be out of doors," Thea called up to her from the parlor.

Several weeks had passed since Grace's mistake with the camellia and her resolution to mold herself more to Thea's lifestyle. She felt as if a new beginning had sprung up between them, a trust that was as tentative as it was fragile, etched into her life like frost on the windowpane. So although she thought wistfully of tea and biscuits by the fireplace, she wrapped a thick shawl around her shoulders over her wool pelisse and tugged a knitted cap onto her head.

Thea was bouncing on her heels by the door when she came down the stairs, a large wicker basket in her hand. Grace puzzled over where they were going as they left the townhouse, then bit back a sigh when she saw the entrance to the Chelsea Physic Garden. Of course, Thea wished to do something botanical. But whatever she wanted to do for Christmas, Grace would oblige her for the joy of seeing her pleasure.

"What a lovely surprise," Grace said, hoping she sounded more enthusiastic than she felt.

"Ah, you have no guesses yet, have you?"

"Are we to go on a tour?"

"No."

"Luncheon with the groundskeeper?"

"Wrong again, darling."

Thea led her to an uncultivated part of the garden where the grass was coated in icy frost that sparkled in the sunlight. "Here we are. Now guess again."

This was looking increasingly dire. "Are we *planting*?" Grace couldn't imagine digging into the half-frozen ground, but what else was there to do here?

"In December? Hardly. Have you no sense of tradition?" She pulled a ball from the basket with a flourish.

Grace burst into laughter. "Lawn bowling?"

"I finally figured out why you never bowled before. You never had your one-chance-a-year on Christmas Day to bowl with the servants as a child, because your father would have wanted to keep you out of sight if possible. Is that right? Now, as my wife, you can bowl anytime you wish—but I thought this might be something you might particularly enjoy today of all days."

The words warmed Grace all over, more effective than a hot cup of tea with a lap blanket tucked around her. Servants were forbidden to bowl except on Christmas, out of fear that all they would wish to do with their time otherwise would be to play instead of work. She had pressed her face to the windowpane on many a Christmas morning to watch the rest of the household servants—including her own father—make merry.

It had been miserable.

But today, the memory didn't hurt the way it usually did. Thea had plucked the sting from her heart by giving her new memories to latch onto. The old memories would never go away, but she was grateful that Thea had recognized the wound and had been thoughtful enough to find a way to soothe it.

Grace discovered that she was no better at lawn bowling than she had been in Inverley. She and Thea laughed as she attempted to skate the ball down the grass toward the jack, her fingers as frozen as the ground and her heart as light as the clouds. Thea fared rather better than she did, but the ground was not as flat as a proper bowling green ought to be, so she won by the smallest of margins.

"May I claim a kiss as forfeit?" Thea asked.

Thea was beautiful in the cold winter sun, her cheeks pink and soft puffs of air billowing in front of her as she breathed. Her hair shone like gold.

Grace glanced around, but the gardeners must have all been in their own homes for Christmas as she didn't see anyone. "Of course," she said, and leaned forward.

Thea's mouth was startlingly hot, her lips a welcome respite from the cold. Grace wrapped her arms tight around her neck, wanting to hold on to this moment. It was rare that she felt comfortable enough outside to touch more than Thea's hand or to take her arm, and she allowed herself the gift of indulging in the risk today. Thea had her hands on her waist, holding her steady, which Grace appreciated because she felt so light with happiness that she feared she could drift away amidst the sweetness of her kiss and the delicate touch of her tongue against the corner of her mouth.

Thea drew back but pressed another kiss to her forehead before she let go of her completely. "Your kisses are the sweetest currency I could imagine."

Grace felt absurdly pleased. "It is not much of a forfeit when the loser enjoys the prize as much as the winner."

She helped pack the balls back into the basket, but Thea insisted on carrying it back to the townhouse. "I am happy as ever to serve you," she said, with a wiggle of her brows that made Grace blush.

"This was wonderful," she said. "I appreciate that you arranged this for me. For us." She took a deep breath. She never spoke of her childhood, but maybe doing so would further lance her wounds. "I suppose you can imagine that life as a lady's companion was paradise compared to being a governess, and that being a governess was a luxury after having been a housemaid. Especially a housemaid employed in her own mother's house."

"It must have been so difficult to endure among your family." Thea's face was serious.

"It was humiliating." It hurt to speak of it, but Thea had never once made her feel anything less than equal. "My half-sister never questioned the situation. Sarah never thought how hard it would have been for me to dust the bannisters and clean the fireplaces during the day, then sneak into her rooms in the evening to study from her books. She thought it was the natural order of things that my father was a butler, so of course I was a maid. She had no issue with me as a person and considered me a friend of sorts, but also never thought twice about ringing me from my bed to fetch something for her when she had need of it."

Thea squeezed her hand. "It's good that you left that life behind as soon as you could. You should be proud of where you are now."

This was the hardest confession of all. "But how can I be, when I don't know *who* I am now? What part of my life is the truth?" She laughed. "Am I servant or gentry? Governess or companion or wife?"

"You are who you are. A sum of your past, but why should the past alone define you? Why should you carry your parentage around like an albatross around your neck?" Thea shrugged. "You are whatever you want to be, and whatever you are living, in this moment. You are Grace Linfield. My wife. And most important, you are *you*."

Like she had with her ankle, Thea knew how to soothe her wounds.

She was starting to worry that her heart was in danger.

January was cold and snowy, and Thea was content with quiet days at home. Grace had insisted on scouring every inch of the townhouse and sweeping all the soot out of the fireplaces on the last day of December, insisting that they needed to start the new year fresh and to wash away any bad luck from the previous year. Thea didn't believe in such things, but was happy enough to indulge her if it made Grace happy.

She loved to make Grace happy.

The freshly scrubbed conservatory was warmer than the rest of the townhouse as long as the sun was shining, but it was draughty from the multitude of windows where the cold air seeped in. Thea wrapped her hands around a cup of tea to warm them up before she began her work for the morning.

"Thea!"

Thea looked out the window at Grace, who was pointing at the camellia and practically dancing. She had left for her daily constitutional walk ten minutes ago, and Thea was surprised to see that she had not yet left the garden.

"Come outside!"

Alarm raced through her. Was there something wrong? Had the wind uprooted the shrub and exposed its roots? Had a branch broken off? She didn't bother grabbing her cloak, and yanked the door open and strode through the snow in her shoes.

"Whatever is the matter?" she asked, looking at the shrub. Its leaves were glossy and thick, there was no debris or broken branches at its base. She wasn't sure if she could attribute it to the orange rind in the mulch, which she had faithfully added as often as she could, but she had to admit that the camellia had not only recovered but it now looked better than it ever had.

"There!" Grace cried, pointing, and grabbed her arm. "Oh, look!"

Then Thea saw it.

One beautiful, perfect flower.

It was already a handspan wide, so Thea was baffled that she hadn't noticed it before. It hid deep among the variegated leaves, its ruffled petals bright red striped with patches of white. She cupped it, hardly daring to touch it and yet at the same time delighted to feel the soft and silky petals beneath her fingers.

"It bloomed," Thea whispered.

"It bloomed!" Grace cried. "You did it!"

"I did, didn't I?" She whooped and then scooped Grace up into her arms, swinging her round in a wide circle. The snow was cold around her ankles and the air was brisk, pinkening Grace's cheeks. But the sparkle in her eyes wasn't from the cold. It was pride.

"You believed in me," Thea said.

"Of course." Grace put a hand on her cheek. "Always."

Thea drew her close again. "It means everything."

The emotions running high overwhelmed her. She bent forward and touched the flower again, then examined the rest of the bush for buds that she had overlooked. There were five or six of them that she could see.

She burst into tears.

Grace grasped her hand. "It's beautiful, isn't it? You've done something marvelous."

"I shouldn't cry." Thea wiped her eyes with the back of her hand. "They are joyous tears, I promise you."

"I know."

The work she had done, the experiments that had failed, the bushes that had bloomed in her house but shriveled up outside—years of study and work and pruning and mulching and shade and sun—all of it had been worth it.

Camellia japonica variegata could indeed grow out of doors in England. She, Dorothea Elizabeth Martin, had proved it.

Another thrill raced through her.

"I can write papers about it now, and see if I can publish them," she told Grace. "I can write about my process and my discoveries. I could even petition to join the Horticultural Society."

"I am so happy for you."

"And you discovered the very first flower," she said. "It's a gift beyond measure. Thank you, Grace."

She beamed, and Thea kissed her in the dazzling sunlight, the wind whipping her hair loose from her chignon and her hands cold as she pressed Grace tight to her.

It was a perfect day, and it was made all the sweeter to have Grace share in the discovery with her.

❖

Grace tore open the letter from Caroline and Arabella. They had written to each other once a month since Grace had arrived in London, and she was grateful each time a letter arrived from a friend, as she had precious few of them.

It was always wonderful to hear from them and to read their news, laced with their love for one another. It warmed Grace's heart. They were living together in a little cottage by the seashore, and Arabella was busy with her paintings.

She scanned through the first page, then flipped it over to read the next, sagging with relief when she found the part she was looking for. Arabella had written that Edie was safely delivered of a healthy baby boy, and that all was well with her and Mr. Martin.

She wished she could write to Edie and congratulate her, but she would have to make do by writing back to Arabella and Caroline and hoping that at some point they would be able to pass along her greetings. She couldn't risk writing to Edie herself, not when Lady Harriet might still be staying in Inverley with them.

Her heart cracked. She had a new baby cousin, and she would never know him. Never have the chance to hold him or teach him. For all that Lady Harriet had wanted to take from her, this was by far the worst.

It was cruel to have had the companionship of family for such little time as she had been permitted to enjoy it, under the guise of employment. It wasn't fair that the chance of a relationship was snatched away from her. But Grace wouldn't do anything to jeopardize Edie's reputation.

Grace tucked the letter into a drawer and left the drawing room. She noticed Polly in the dining room, the table in front of her covered in papers and seed pods, and she paused.

"What are you doing, Polly?" she asked.

She blew the hair out of her face. "Seeing to Miss Martin's correspondence."

There were papers and pamphlets and piles of seeds and Grace's fingers itched to tidy it all up. "May I be of some help?"

Polly brightened. "Would you? I would be grateful. Miss Martin was insistent that all this go out in today's post, but I don't reckon I'll have time to hop to the post office before the mail coach goes out."

Grace sat beside her and picked up a hard brown pod the size and shape of a chestnut. Some of the ones scattered on the table had hard casings with cracks in them. "What are these?"

"Camellia seed pods. But the pods can't be sent through the post, they're too bulky. I need to crack open all these pods and get the little black seeds out. Those will fit nice in a letter."

Grace started cracking them open, separating the seeds into a pile. She scooped up the cracked pods into a clean rag to easier transport them to the kitchen with the rest of the scraps.

"But the camellia has only just flowered," Grace said. "There can be no seeds yet from the bush in the garden?"

"Oh no, these aren't from that plant. Miss Martin has grown many camellias over the years and donated most of them to the greenhouse at the Chelsea Physic Garden. These seeds are from those plants, but they're all related to the bush in the garden, so she wants to send the seeds across England and to ask other botanists to try growing them outside to replicate her own experiment."

JANE WALSH

"How fascinating." Pride welled up inside her. Thea had set out to accomplish her goal. Soon, many other botanists and gardeners and scientists would know that she had succeeded in growing the camellia, against all odds and against every expectation. It was exactly what she had wanted.

Polly gestured at the table. "There are about a dozen people to send them out to, and she's written detailed instructions to each one. She thinks there might be something special about the particular plant she's got that made it hardy enough to survive the outside."

Grace counted five seeds and tipped them into a paper sachet, like Polly showed her, and tucked it into one of the letters that Thea had penned, then set it aside. "I wouldn't mind helping more," she said idly. "This is most enjoyable."

Polly's face darkened. "Don't go looking to take my employment," she said. Grace stared in astonishment. This was the first time she had ever seen Polly look out of sorts.

"I apologize. I wouldn't think of it."

"I'm more than a maid," Polly continued, shoving the seeds in. "I don't do half as many tasks as a lady's maid as I do for Miss Martin and her conservatory."

Grace had seen the state of Thea's shifts far too often to disagree. "Of course." She'd had dreams bigger than service too. Polly's big passionate eyes burned into hers and Grace felt herself unbend. "You know that I used to be a governess. I know what it is to yearn for more."

"It's not the same. A governess is gently bred. You weren't a *servant*," Polly said with a touch of scorn. "Did you think you were the only one in the entire household who wanted more than you had?"

"My path had its difficulties," Grace said, staring at the seeds. Polly didn't know her history. No one did, except for Thea and Lady Harriet.

She shrugged. "Not denying it, I'm sure it was. But you had the means to move on to be a lady's companion. Most don't have that chance. They spend their whole lives dreaming."

Grace was silent.

"We're social climbers, like any debutante wanting to marry up, aren't we? As a governess, you took your meals alone, I bet, but then ate with the family once you were a companion. And now here you are, mistress of the house with your own hand in choosing the menu, let alone your own place opposite of the head of the table."

Grace sucked in a breath. "I've never thought about it in those terms."

"There's nothing wrong in what you've done," Polly said. "It's good honest work."

It had indeed been a climb, though she wanted to tell Polly that she had started from the bottom. But it didn't matter, she realized. What mattered was that she *was* at the top of the household, and that meant she could now help anyone below stairs to get their first step on the rung.

"Tell me, Polly. What is it *you* dream of doing?"

"Of hurrying to get these seeds in the post," she said, a trifle cross.

Chastened, Grace bent herself to the task and decided to accompany Polly on her errand to speak with her more.

"Why do you keep a nominal position as a maid when you really *are* more of an assistant?" Grace asked as they hurried through the streets.

"Miss Martin hasn't asked me to be anything more," Polly said. "And I like bits about being a lady's maid. It's the highest rank in this house below the housekeeper, you know. I would never have had the chance to travel to Scotland if I was an assistant. I would have had to stay here in the conservatory and miss all the fun."

"Some of it was fun," Grace allowed. "But you would do more of what you liked every day if you didn't do any tasks as a maid."

"I care for Miss Martin," she muttered. "I like making do for her, in my way. She took me in when my father wanted nothing more to do with me, you know, and I didn't know where I would end up. She saw me shivering outside the nursery, hawking day-old violets that my father had cast out for not being as fresh as they ought to be, and she took me in. Not many would do such a thing."

Thea was a remarkable soul. It was the sort of thing Grace could imagine her doing, passing a half-starved waif and making a rash decision to hire her.

Then it struck her.

An employment agency. That's what she wanted to do with her time. That was something that would make a difference. For people like her, and Polly, and countless others. People who were qualified but who might not have the chance to gain employment. People who society might think were not quite the thing.

Later that night, when Grace was tucked up beside Thea in bed, she told her about the conversation she had with Polly. "You should talk with her about what she wants. If you make it clear that you value everything she's done, you can offer her a permanent position as your assistant."

Thea blinked. "She never spoke to me about wanting more. But there's much that she can do in the conservatory if she wants a more active role. I would be delighted with her help. I never thought she wanted her position to change. I feel awful that I never noticed." She sighed. "You're right—I need to pay more attention."

"It's never too late. Talk to Polly. She'll appreciate it."

CHAPTER TWENTY-FOUR

Thea stared down at the sprawl of correspondence. She had pushed aside her pots to make room for the letters and invitations that she had received since sending out news of her success with the camellia.

The personal satisfaction was as rewarding as she had expected it to be. Seven and a half years of hoping and experimenting meant that she was thrilled each morning to see new buds on the camellia. Thea had started taking her tea in the conservatory, perched on the padded bench so she might stare at the glorious full flowers in quiet contemplation, reveling in her success.

But the scientific accolades weren't as satisfying. Mainly because they were few and far between, despite the many acknowledgements she received.

The Horticultural Society sent their regrets that they would not consider her for membership, for although her work with the camellia was impressive, she was a woman and therefore not eligible even if she were to garden while standing on her head.

The head gardener at Kew Gardens was interested to hear of her work, but only so that they could offer to purchase the camellia from her. He had written that of course as his gardens were so famous and as they welcomed so many to tour the grounds to marvel at its botanical wonders, it would be a much better use of the plant than remaining in her back garden.

A variety of scientific journals and newspapers replied to her. Some were more gratifying than others. She was invited to share her work in a series of articles in one journal, and another wished to speak with her about her discoveries. A few were condescending, requesting proof that she had indeed grown the shrub from seed to bloom out of doors.

Thea was accustomed to snobbery in the scientific community and had resigned herself to enduring its poor opinion of female scientists. She told herself to embrace whatever interest that *had* been shown, for it was indeed wonderful to share her work with anyone who would like to read about it.

At least it gave Polly more to do in her new official position as Thea's assistant. The essential tasks hadn't changed much for Polly, but now she was helping write out the articles that Thea was planning to submit as a series to the scientific newspaper that she received every week. Grace had been right to suggest that Thea talk to Polly about what she wanted to do in terms of work, learning that Polly liked to help with theory and practical work, instead of correspondence and errands. But then, when was Grace ever wrong? Her insight and her thoughtfulness were wifely benefits beyond measure.

Anthony joined Thea and Grace for a celebratory dinner the week that Thea found out that she had been accepted to do a botanical lecture at the library, but Thea found it difficult to muster the enthusiasm for his congratulations.

"Why are you so dour in the face of such success?" he asked. "I have heard you talk more about that camellia over the years than I have heard men boast about their newborn heirs. This has opened all the doors to you that you wished."

"I am as proud of this plant as if it were my heir," Thea admitted. "But I cannot help but feel a strange sort of disappointment. I thought this would be my opportunity to leave my mark. I didn't want praise so much as I wanted to feel as if I had contributed something. And now that I have…I am left wondering what else is there?"

Anthony poured more wine for her and Grace. "I've told you that you ought to consider other things than botany sometimes," he said. "It's not healthy to be so focused."

She sighed. "I will never give up botany."

"No one is suggesting you give it up. But there is more to life than plants. Perhaps you need to take a little time to think about everything else you want to accomplish."

Grace stared down at her asparagus, and Thea felt a pang. There *was* more to her life than botany, and it was time she started making sure that the people around her understood that she recognized it.

❖

"This is exactly what I used to imagine London to be like if I had the money and time to enjoy it," Grace said to Thea at the eating establishment they frequented on occasion. She took a bite of roast duck and sighed.

Thea wore her hair curled tonight, thick bouncy waves that flattered her face and somehow drew Grace's attention to her lush mouth. Then again, most things about Thea attracted her attention, no matter how much time passed. Grace liked to look at her across the table, in her silk dress that she wore as casually as if it were a work dress, her posture not quite straight from all the hours she spent on her stool bending down to tend to her plants. Thea was beautiful, no matter which milieu she was in.

The past month had been wonderful. Thea had spent less time working in the conservatory, and had been solicitous of her pleasures, conscious of her concerns regarding her loneliness. They had enjoyed Anthony's company at several dinners, and Grace had met some of Thea's other friends at tea. She felt as if they were finally settling into a routine together.

"With winter here, we will of course curtail our activities," Thea said, taking a sip of wine. "There is nothing less pleasant than to tread through London in dreary weather."

"I suppose. But then there are ever so many diversions to look forward to in the spring. The playhouse. Vauxhall." Places she had been as a companion, but not for her own pleasure. There was plenty she hadn't seen or done around London, and it was thrilling that against all odds, now she had the opportunity.

"Yes, perhaps."

Grace put down her fork. "Is there something the matter?"

"Not at all," Thea said, but her eyes were strained. "I am fatigued and looking forward to being home again."

Grace liked being at the eating establishment. They didn't dine out often, and it was a pleasure to while away an evening like this, with crystal chandeliers dangling from the ceilings and velvet seat cushions beneath them, surrounded by the buzz of conversation.

But her enjoyment dimmed. There were times that she felt like she still didn't understand Thea, and this was one of them. She couldn't seem to track the pattern to discover what it was that made her prickle up sometimes.

"An early night would be ideal," Grace said soothingly, though she would have preferred to order a pudding and enjoy the night for longer.

"I dislike when you do that," Thea muttered, scowling at her wineglass.

"When I do what?"

"*Agree* with me."

Grace blinked. "You would prefer I be disagreeable?"

"I meant that you needn't always go along with what I'm saying. We're"—Thea shot a look around them and lowered her voice—"well, you know what we are to one another. When I'm being a boor, you should feel free to kick me under the table and tell me so." She grinned, her ill humors dissipating, and Grace laughed.

Once they were in the privacy of a hackney on the way back to Chelsea, Grace took Thea's hand in her own. "Talk to me," she said. "We don't talk enough."

"We talk every day. We're talking *now*," Thea pointed out.

"I mean about important matters. About our lives. Ourselves."

"We had all the opportunity in the world on the way to Gretna Green and you declined to take advantage of conversation then. But what do you wish to speak of?" Thea's face was in shadows and Grace couldn't tell her mood.

"Do you ever think how extraordinary all of this is?"

"A woman in my bed has been known to happen before, extraordinary as it may seem to others."

"I mean our marriage."

"I take our relationship seriously. You know that."

"I know we committed to staying with each other. But do you truly think of me as a wife?" Thea hadn't said the word at dinner. But then again, it hadn't been the safest place to have spoken openly. Grace wouldn't have braved it either.

"Admittedly, we shall never have the legal trappings. I cannot call you my wife outside of the house, and even within it I must be careful lest the servants overhear. I cannot give you children. We bring each other no dowries." Thea shrugged. "But—you run the household, and I provide the money, which sounds to me much the same as most marriages."

"I wish to do more than household matters. I do not want to be found wanting."

"Oh, I certainly *want* you." Thea slid her gaze down Grace's body.

"You know what I mean! I wish to have a serious conversation." Grace frowned. "When you make jests like that, I sometimes feel like you aren't paying attention to me."

"I am paying inordinate amounts of attention to you. Sexual attention is important to us both."

"Of course it is, but I need more than that."

"You say this, but you are not putting your own efforts forth, Grace."

"What do you mean?"

"We connect under the covers because you are unrestrained there. You communicate better when my mouth is on you than when we are at dinner. You are trying so hard to be a perfect, polite companion, when I would much prefer to hear your real thoughts and feelings."

Grace sucked in a sharp breath. It wasn't entirely unwarranted, which made it sting all the more. "Well, I am trying to communicate with you now. I feel like we are not connecting in the way that I would like us to."

She stiffened. "That's absurd. I have sat down to dinner with you each and every night. I have taken you to Astley's thrice in the past month. We visited the Royal Menagerie. We have walked together and shopped together. What more could you ask for?"

"Those are activities," Grace pointed out. "But here I am in your *life*. Not for sex. Not to ensure that dinner isn't burnt. Not as a partner to do things with, though I appreciate our outings. I want to *connect* with you. I have had relationships before, Thea, and we *talked*. It was what kept us together when we had little else in society's eyes."

Thea shook her head. "You fuss so much all day that it would be a wonder if you ever sat still to find the time to talk! It feels these days as if the furniture exists to shriek your unhappiness at me from a new vantage point each week. The chair in my bedchamber was in front of the window today, Grace. But where will it be tomorrow?"

Grace froze. "*Your* bedchamber? Is it not *ours*?"

"Of course it is. Did I say it was mine? Old habit, I swear."

Was it? Grace was crestfallen.

"Why do you wish to dwell on previous partners, anyway?" Thea asked. "I may have had more lovers in terms of quantity, but I am not harping about yours."

"Because mine were relationships!"

"And more casual liaisons are somehow abhorrent to you?"

"I am the product of such a liaison! I wish it upon no one."

"There can be no such products between us, darling. Are you worried that one woman cannot satisfy me? Trust me in life as you trust me in bed, and I swear to you—I won't disappoint you. Do you trust me, or not?"

"I trust you," Grace said, but it was difficult to choke out the words. "But I wish to be sure that what we have together is enough."

"Or else you will do what—seek an annulment? Upon which grounds? Our beginning was unusual, but I cannot deny that I feel the truth of it in my very bones. There are no grounds of adultery or cruelty. We have consummated the marriage, we have tried to be good to one another. We were meant to cleave together." Her voice was low and raw, her eyes no more than a glitter in the dark of the carriage. "You are my wife, Grace Linfield, and I shall have no other."

"Then why do I feel as if we hardly understand each other sometimes?"

"That must be common in married folks."

"I would never have known how much the camellia meant to you if I hadn't inadvertently interfered with it. Would you have ever mentioned it to me until you saw the first bloom yourself?"

"It isn't always important to talk about the journey of how one gets to success."

"It's important to me. A journey is what brought us together, after all. And it clearly is important to you, because you have been in the doldrums ever since you saw the camellia flower." Grace bit her lip, unsure if she should continue, but then felt a flash of irritation that she had to consider it. If Thea wanted to hear about her feelings, then so be it. "Sometimes I worry that you put so much stock into botany because it became a replacement for everything you ever loved that left you behind. Flowers stay where you plant them, and they thrive because you care for them. But that doesn't mean that success with your plants can replace the pain of losing your family connections. Maybe that's why you haven't been happy." She put a hand on Thea's knee. "You don't like to talk about the things you care about the most."

The hackney pulled up to their townhouse, and Thea rapped on the roof to signal it to stop. Grace stepped outside and was surprised when Thea didn't follow. "I am continuing on to Anthony's," she said, her face impassive as the lamp slashed light across it. "I do not recommend that you wait up for me."

With a clatter, the hackney rolled away, and Grace was left alone.

CHAPTER TWENTY-FIVE

Anthony owned a house in Mayfair where he rubbed shoulders with the fashionable set when he chose to. Thea didn't care what his neighbors might think of her as she alighted from the hackney at quarter past ten at night and strode up to his front door. She knew what she was and what she looked like. They wouldn't like her any better if her velvet was brushed and steamed and her shoes polished up as smooth as glass—they would sneer behind their backs instead of to her face. Her transgressions from her first and only Season would never be forgotten by them.

It didn't matter that one of those transgressions had been with Anthony. They would never treat him with the same abhorrence that they would treat her.

Thea had infinite patience for watching shoots spring out of fresh soil, inch by inch and day by day, but none at all for such snobbery as was found among the ton.

"To what do I owe this pleasure?" Anthony asked as she entered his study.

Anthony was with Michael and Lucius, two dapper gentlemen that he liked to pass the time with while in England, in a loose sort of laissez-faire affaire. None of the men Anthony chose to associate with in private were monogamous.

He and his companions had whiled the evening away together drinking and gaming, a hand of cards still spread on a table and a pair of dice discarded on another, with the remnants of a late supper of bread and cheese and grapes on the sideboard.

"I am in dire need of reasonable conversation and assistance." Thea sighed and sat down on a leather armchair.

"Trouble in paradise?"

"Alas, it seems to be."

Anthony poured her a whiskey.

"What paradise, pray tell, are we speaking of?" Lucius asked, popping a grape into his mouth. He was a heavyset older man with dark eyes and brilliantly white hair, and his cane was propped up beside him. He had been a distinguished captain of the Royal Navy, and Anthony had sailed with him on his ship several times before his retirement.

Thea was not close with either gentleman, though she had known them for years through their relationship with Anthony and had interrupted more than a few evenings such as this in the past. She was too upset to hide the truth from anyone tonight. If she could not trust her own kind, then who could she ever trust?

She gave a brief summary of the events in Gretna Green and afterward, then sipped her whiskey. "Grace is the best person to come into my life. I want nothing more than to make her happy, and yet I can find no respite because I cannot seem to succeed." She glowered into her glass. "I'm not sure that she's happy in London. Or with me. And worst of all, Grace keeps telling me that she wants to *talk*. I cannot imagine her saying anything that won't result in our arrangement coming to an end."

The idea was chilling. She didn't want to talk if that was to be the end result, but why else had Grace brought up marriage tonight when they mentioned it between them so infrequently? Thea had thought they were settling into their life nicely, but Grace must harbor different opinions.

"You're having doubts now, after so many months?" Michael studied her over the rim of his own glass. He was a slim man of fashion, vain about his cravats and his waistcoats and the height of his hair, and was the heir to a shipping fortune which had financed many of Anthony's voyages across the ocean. Thea gathered that he had attended Oxford with Anthony years ago.

"It hasn't been that many months," Thea said.

He shrugged. "More than a fortnight in the arms of one lover feels like forever to me, my dear."

"What if I cannot offer Grace the life that she deserves?" She shook her head. "The fear makes me irritable. I snapped at her tonight.

And look where I am? Instead of curled up in my marital bed, I am back to my old habits, far from home with a glass in my hand." She saluted the gentlemen with it. "It is a wonder how quickly one can feel twenty-one again and just as foolish in the midst of rash decisions."

She had been in a temper when she had decided to go to Anthony's. She should have been more thoughtful. The hurt expression on Grace's face as she stood alone in the street in front of their townhouse haunted her, and she drank deeply once more. Thea would have to make it up to her. Assuming, of course, that Grace hadn't already packed her bags and absconded to safer harbors.

How many times did her impulse need to lead her down the path of regret before she learned her lesson?

"What is it that upset you tonight?"

"At first, I was worried about our finances. Grace doesn't know it, but I can't afford the lifestyle I promised her. Every day I see the crooked stair leading up to our front door but instead of paying for it to be fixed, I whisk Grace away to Astley's to try and make her happy of an evening."

"How do you know that would make her happier than the stair?"

"She has been a governess and a lady's companion for so many years that she has never had the opportunity to pursue pleasure like this. I want to make sure she has everything she ever dreamed of. No one dreams of a fixed stair."

But if anyone did, it would be Grace, with her desire for order. Thea knew it was a problem. She knew she should invest more in the house. But she always told herself that the problems would still be there tomorrow, and why should they not enjoy themselves tonight?

"Is that all you're worried about?"

Thea sighed. "Grace also wanted to talk about her past relationships. What if what we have does not measure up to what she once had with other lovers?" She shook her head. "The very thought terrifies me. I was cold with her when she brought it up. Unforgivably so."

"Your beloved bride is right," Lucius told her. "If you cannot think of these things without fear, then you must talk to each other. It's the only way."

Michael laughed. "I have been married in the molly house twice in the past month alone. Marriage does not mean anything these days."

"Something of a professional bigamist, aren't you?" Anthony smiled. "I think we might have gone through the motions once together, years ago."

"You know how the molly houses are. We enact all manner of ritual together. It's not real marriage." Michael shrugged.

"But mine is," Thea said, with as much dignity as she could muster.

"Come now, no it isn't," he said. "You know better. There *is* no marriage for those such as us. We live outside the law, and always have."

"I stood over the anvil and was handfasted," she snapped. "Grace and I are as married as can be. That is not the point of discussion, gentlemen. I simply don't know if I'm making her *happy*."

For all that she regretted her impulse to come to Anthony's, it felt good to talk. She rationalized having another drink, and then a third, and then decided it wouldn't do at all for her to return to Chelsea in such a state tonight.

"Love and marriage are more than grand gestures over an anvil, darling. There's a day-to-day commitment that goes along with it." Lucius poured another drink. "Or so I've been told. I've never felt inclined to seek a bride, myself."

"But I do rather better with a gesture," Thea protested. "They say everything I want. I gave Grace full control over the household. She may spend as much as she likes, though my purse strings groan in protest. I take her out in the evenings as often as I can, but she doesn't seem to enjoy them as much as I thought she would, given how she spoke of what she wanted of London. How does she not see the affection in how I treat her? Why is she looking for more?"

"Affection?" Anthony raised a brow. "Are you sure you don't mean *love*?"

"Love has no place here, Anthony. We are talking of *marriage*. A pleasant union between two like-minded people with like-minded goals." She took another drink. "I feel in my soul that it is real, but I worry that she does not." But if Grace didn't think they were married, it would rend her heart in two.

Hell and blazes.

Anthony was right. She was in love, wasn't she?

Thea sloshed another finger of whiskey in her glass and tried to drown out the emotion that struggled to well up inside her.

"What is it that you think makes a marriage real?" Michael asked her.

Thea counted the main points on her fingers. "Why, a clergyman must perform the ceremony in one's parish. The banns must be cried for three Sundays, or a license could do in lieu of the banns."

"But you didn't do any of those things."

"No, we eloped in Gretna."

"And what you did in Gretna was perfectly legal and binding according to Scottish law?"

"Well, yes. Except we're women. Grace protested that at the time, and I worry that she still thinks of it as invalid."

He shook his head. "Think of it this way. A century ago, the marriage laws in England were not so different from Scotland today. And what about our grand London tradition of Fleet Marriages? Were they not legal, once upon a time? It was common enough to be wedded by clergy living in parole from debtor's prison, without banns or licence or parish to hinder anyone. My grandparents were thusly married."

"I suppose that is true."

"And what is the only thing that made them illegal?"

Thea felt as if she were being quizzed and didn't like it above half. "The government changed the laws."

He held up a finger. "Exactly. Men in power changed their minds, all because it did not benefit them for people to marry clandestinely, without careful control of inheritance and influence."

"But the law is the law," Thea pointed out. "Regardless of who benefits from it, we all must endure it."

"And yet how can a government determine natural law, such as lust and love? Are those not some of the primary forces behind marriage? Why is it that a man can hang for sodomy in England but not in France? You're a botanist, and therefore a student of natural science. Tell me, does human nature change by border?"

"Of course it doesn't!" Lucius cried, while Thea was still gathering her thoughts. "I have crossed enough borders and enjoyed enough lovers to know."

Michael nodded. "And does a plant follow natural law where it grows, or does it abide by the arbitrary law of government? If plant and animal are governed the same wherever they happen to be, despite our country's borders, then why are some men charged with crimes and others not? Do you not think that the government has some gain when they make such decisions? Why should they be only ones to decide what evolves and what does not?"

Anthony tapped his glass. "And if it is so now, that people such as us have no place within a marriage together, who is to say that it could not be unwritten by a future generation?"

"There is much to think about here," Thea said slowly. "I had not considered such things, but it is encouraging indeed."

"Man can try to govern us, but nature guides us," Michael said. "Nature shows us that our attractions are natural. And if they are natural, then why should they not be held as equal to current society? Why should you not feel as married to Miss Linfield just as well as if she were Mr. Linfield?"

Thea sighed. "I am not sure if Grace feels the same way. It might be better for her if she does not." Her stomach roiled and she worried she would cast up all the whiskey she had imbibed. "Perhaps I should let her think that I do not consider any of this valid. I do not wish for her to be unhappy."

Anthony frowned. "She has an opinion and a choice to make also. It's not only for you to consider. You cannot cut ties with your integrity. No matter what you believe about that moment at the anvil, you cannot deny that you offered this woman your protection and your support. You pledged your life to hers in that moment, and you are bound together by your honor."

Honor. Thea wasn't accustomed to people believing she had much of it.

But maybe she could make it work between them.

She just had to prove to Grace that they were meant to be together.

CHAPTER TWENTY-SIX

Thea evidently had decided to spend the night at Anthony's, for she wasn't there when Grace awoke the next morning. It was either a practical decision, in that it had been too late to safely come home last night, or it was a sign to Grace that Thea was pulling away from the relationship.

Grace scoured the bedchamber for help to understand which way she was meant to interpret things, but all she saw were the cracks in the plaster and the horseshoe above their bed. After their argument last night, it could mean anything. Or nothing.

One thing was certain, however. Thea had been right. Grace had been too hesitant to express herself, and too eager to fit herself into Thea's life as a convenience instead of as an equal. She could also admit that endlessly moving the furniture around hadn't made her feel more settled or secure in the townhouse. There was no perfect arrangement that would ease her worries and help her feel as if she belonged here. That was up to Grace, and to Thea. If she didn't put the work into their relationship, then everything else was a patch of plaster instead of building a whole new structure.

Grace pushed the chair and the rug to move them as best as she could remember from when she had first arrived. Thea had left a shawl draped on the chair, and Grace decided to leave it where it was.

Her heart felt heavy. So much for sharing a life if they could not even share a room without strain, save for their time in bed.

The house felt too quiet without Thea, and yet Grace couldn't bear to wait for her to return. Last night had given her much to think about, and she realized that for all her pushing to talk more with Thea about their lives together, she ought to understand her own thoughts better first.

She wrote a note to Thea to explain where she was, and then left to visit Maeve. She brought her portmanteau with her, the same one that had accompanied her to Gretna Green.

Maeve eyed it with alarm when she set it down in her bedchamber. "I haven't much space if you are planning a lengthy stay," she said.

Grace glanced around the room. It was small, with a narrow bed in a simple wood frame, and walls covered with faded print that peeled at the edge where it met the ceiling. It reminded her of the many places she had stayed with Thea on their journey, but it was missing her joyful presence and sly flirtations. Her heart ached.

"I won't trespass on your hospitality for long," Grace said. "I need a place to gather my thoughts for a day or two."

"And you thought my lodgings an appropriate place to do so? Well, I can't say that I don't welcome it, in truth. The winter in Bath was dreadfully dull. Not a friend to be found, I am sad to admit. Especially not such a friend as I am looking for. Now, let's sit in the parlor with a cup of tea and you can explain."

For all her feelings and thoughts on the matter, it all came tumbling out of Grace's mouth in a matter of minutes.

Maeve tilted her head and looked at her. "This is fascinating. Fancy a liaison to get over her?"

"Maeve!" Grace gasped. "I would never betray Thea in such a manner."

"Good," she said with a little smile. "So you *do* plan to return to her?"

"Of course." She said it without hesitation.

"That is good news indeed, because what you found with Miss Martin is rare and important."

"It is, but I want to be sure that I am contributing equally to the relationship. I think I have relied too much on her in these past few months to set the standard for our marriage based around the life she already has here, instead of establishing a relationship built for the two of us."

"Maybe relying on someone is no bad thing. Especially if that person is your wife."

Grace sighed. "But am I a wife? Sometimes I wonder at it. I felt the bond so strongly when we said the words in Scotland, even though everything was topsy-turvy and no one could have suspected that we would honor our vows. Not even we thought so at first." She looked at her wedding ring. Since the moment it was placed on her finger, she hadn't been able to remove it. It must be a sign. She refused to believe otherwise. "Yet in London, nothing has been smooth at all."

"Your marriage is not a technicality. Yes, it was an accident. A fluke of circumstance. And yet you are as married in your heart as any other couple, because you chose to honor your commitment." Maeve's face was dreamy. "It is the most romantic thing I have ever heard of."

"I worry sometimes that Thea would be happier if we had left those vows behind in Scotland. What if all of this between us has been some impulsive flight of fancy that she now regrets? After all, what matters more—the words we spoke, or our intent to committing to staying together? If it is the words, then we are bound to each other as any other married couple. If it is intent, then there are plenty of legally wedded people who are not nearly as married in their hearts as we are. But I don't wish to stay if it is because she feels obliged." The idea filled her with misery. "You didn't see the look on her face last night," she said, her voice so low that Maeve had to lean forward to hear her.

"Abandoning a wife is a *crime*, Grace."

It was indeed. The newspapers were littered with such calls to find truant husbands. "Neither of us are abandoning the other," she insisted, but a tiny spark of fear remained in her heart. What if Thea did wish to dissolve what they had?

"Then what is that you wish to do right now? To make her jealous? To make her realize your worth? To give you everything your heart desires? Remember, there are no wrong answers here among friends. Whatever you wish to do, I am happy to help."

Grace thought for a moment. "I would rather like to be rebellious."

Maeve set her teacup down. "I am happy to help in any endeavors except for scandal. I do have my own reputation to think of, as well as my mother."

"Nothing too scandalous. A trifle wild, nothing more."

"You are a surprising woman at times," Maeve told her.

She beamed. "I would like to think so."

In the end, they agreed that strolling about London without a maid in tow was the furthest limit that either of them would consider. They sat in a succession of little shops that offered tea or sweets, and then took their time wandering through Bond Street to look at shawls that neither of them could afford. Grace even left her gloves off for a quarter hour longer than she ought to have after they finished tea, and decided that a gentle sort of rebellion was all she had within her.

It felt nice to explore the city with a friend, and to realize that she had been relying too much on Thea for any sort of social activity. It wasn't fair of her to expect Thea to squire her about town all the time, when she had the means to develop her own friendships.

Her own roots.

That was what she had been looking for all along, wasn't it? Though it would always hurt that her natural family would never be part of the new life that she was building.

At the end of the day, after they had dined with Maeve's mother and had brewed another cup of tea, Grace told Maeve about her desires to open an employment agency.

"That sounds like a wonderful idea."

Grace sighed. "I didn't tell Thea about it, which is a terrible hypocrisy, isn't it?"

"Were you still looking for security in case things did not work out between you?" Maeve narrowed her eyes. "Be truthful."

She flushed, miserable at the thought. "Perhaps in part. But I have been afraid to even start thinking on it, because I have no guarantee that I will succeed. That leap of faith is difficult for me. All my life, I have chosen the sure path, my vision clear and my sights set on success. Every step has been so carefully planned."

"And yet somehow, you ended up eloping in Gretna Green with another woman. You can be that person, Grace. Someone who takes leaps, not steps. You need to trust that it will work out," Maeve said.

Trust. Such a simple concept, such a daunting prospect.

But Maeve was right. Maybe she could find it in herself to leap.

And maybe, it would allow her to soar toward things she could never before have dreamed possible.

❖

Thea sat in her conservatory and stared at the camellia through the mullioned window. The bush had bloomed lush and vibrant all winter, with innumerable bright pink and white flowers now studding its branches. She had lain awake for so many nights worrying about the right combination of soil and water and light and shade. She had inspected roots and leaves and stems for infection or rot. She had pruned anything that didn't serve its purpose to nurture and encourage growth.

Now it felt like Grace might be pruning their relationship. She had discarded their marriage as a branch that had failed to grow, and which was now taking unnecessary nutrients from other parts of the plant that would thrive more on their own.

Grace had left, like everyone else in her life.

Now she had nothing except for the plants and flowers that had sustained her during all those other times.

Dusk settled over the garden, and the camellia faded into darkness.

Thea eased herself off the stool, stiff and aching. She hadn't meant to sit in the conservatory for so long, but hours had passed since she had returned home to find Grace's note. It had said that she wouldn't be away for long, but Thea wondered what would happen when she returned. Would she come back to Chelsea to pack up her trunk?

Thea dreaded facing the empty bed. Without Grace, the house was stripped to its essentials. A bed for sleeping. A parlor for sitting. A conservatory for working. She yearned for Grace to fill it again with her presence, to bring life and light and sunshine to the house again. She wanted the conservatory to be used for lovemaking, and the bed a place for discussing their days.

Grace could move every stick of furniture in every single room if it meant that she would come back to her.

Thea discarded her clothes in a pile on the floor and fell into bed, conscious of the empty space beside her. The fear that she wasn't good enough for someone to stay throbbed inside her. Thea tossed the blanket to the floor and grabbed a candle. She must have a bottle of something in the house. Wine. Port. Cooking sherry would do in a pinch.

But a search through the larder revealed nothing but ingredients for lemonade and barley water. And barley water reminded her of their sojourn in Newcastle.

The answer she was looking for wasn't likely to be found in a bottle of brandy anyway.

She curled up in bed again, bringing the blanket to her chin, with nothing but memories and the thorns of her broken heart.

But with the dawn came clarity. In the pale light that streamed through the window, Thea stared up at the horseshoe that Grace had insisted in hauling back from Gretna Green and hanging in their bedchamber. With the iron rusting, it wasn't an attractive piece of décor and Thea had often wished for it to be anywhere else. But it meant a great deal to Grace.

She was determined to make the horseshoe's luck come true for Grace's sake.

Grace had shown her at every turn that she valued her. She listened to her. She encouraged her.

It was even possible that Grace returned the love that she had for her.

But if she wanted Grace to return to her, she owed it to her to be the wife she had claimed to be. She wanted to provide for Grace, but she was going to have to work for it.

And working was one thing she knew she was good at.

After breakfast, she asked Polly to bring Anthony back with her to Chelsea. By the time they returned, she was in the conservatory with a notebook and the contents of her seed library scattered on the table in front of her.

"What's going on?" Anthony asked as he entered the room.

"Please, sit. I need you."

"You're pale. Have you slept at all?"

She dismissed his concern with a wave of her fingers. "I will be fine, but I will need your help to get there. Grace is gone."

"Do we need to find her?" Anthony was on his feet in an instant, worry on his face.

"She left of her own volition, and I know where she is. I want her to come back to me, but I want to prove to her that it's worth it. That *I'm* worth it." Thea took a deep breath and felt more clarity about her situation than she had in years. "I want to sell everything. My seeds. My plants. The orange tree. The wax begonias should fetch a pretty penny, shouldn't they?" She shoved a pot at Anthony so hard that it almost toppled, and he scrambled to grab it before it fell off the table.

"Let's think this through before doing anything impulsive," Anthony said, a thread of worry in his voice. He put a hand on Thea's shoulder and squeezed. "How are you feeling?"

She laughed a little. Through the night, she had wondered if there had been any emotion that she *hadn't* felt. "Thank you for asking. I am perfectly wretched. The tides have risen and I am drowning, out of my depths." She wiped her hands on her skirt and picked up another seed. "But you know me—I don't sulk. I don't dwell. I *act*. Impulse might get me into trouble now and then, but it has also served me well. I know what I am doing, and I am determined to see it through."

"You are a force of nature," Anthony said. "I believe you can do anything you set your mind to."

"Polly, I will need your help to catalogue what I have in the conservatory. Anthony, I need you to tell me who might want some of these other plants, and how much you think they might be valued. I know you sell seeds to other collectors who I might not have been in touch with."

"Are you sure you want to do this?" He looked around the conservatory. "You have spent years building up your collection."

"I want to." She blew out a breath, shaky at the magnitude of the task in front of her. "Frankly, I *need* to. I must admit that although I receive an allowance from my father, it has never been enough. I am to blame for that. I haven't kept with the necessary repairs around the house, and I have spent exorbitant amounts on botany. The conservatory took all the money I had managed to save over the years. I should have kept a closer eye on my finances and sold some of these items a long time ago. But now it's time to move on. These plants brought me comfort in my lowest points, but now they are nothing but a reminder of that time. I need to secure my own future with the only asset I have—botany."

Anthony picked up the quill-bloomed chrysanthemum that she had loaned to Mr. Yates months ago. "There is a good amount of money on this table," he said. "I can make sure you get a fair price from the collectors. I assume Kew Gardens would still be most interested in your camellia."

The camellia.

Her prize. The culmination of almost a decade of dreams.

But she would need to give up the lease on the townhouse if she wanted to provide the life she wanted for Grace. Better to give the camellia away now than to allow it to remain here, to be pulled up and discarded when the next tenants wanted a different color flower in their garden. The camellia, hardy as it was, would survive being uprooted. At least it would be given to a place that understood its value.

The one thing about plants that had always attracted her was the fact that one could always start over and grow something new. New growth might take years, and there was sure to be failure along the way. But sometimes it was important to close the door on the past.

Thea smiled, a frisson of excitement building inside. "Let us begin."

CHAPTER TWENTY-SEVEN

Thea opened the door the next morning to find Grace. Her portmanteau rested at her feet and her reticule was clutched in her hand. Her other hand was raised as if about to knock again.

"Am I welcome?" Grace asked. Her face was pale and pinched.

Grace had come home. That was all Thea needed to know. She was home. She was *here*.

"You never have to ask," Thea said, grasping her hand and pulling her inside. "Wherever I am will always be your home. It should never be in question."

With every fiber of her being, she wanted to prove it to her.

Grace followed her into the sitting room. "I would like that," she said. "But, Thea, I think we need to talk. About everything."

"I agree."

They sat across from one another. Thea stared at Grace's dear face, her sharp nose and long face, and felt the certainty of her love around her like a shawl. *Mine.* She loved this woman. But whether or not Grace would have her was another matter.

There were dark shadows beneath Grace's eyes. Thea yearned to ask her if she, too, had been having trouble sleeping, but stayed quiet. This moment was for Grace. She had returned to Chelsea, but it was for her to say if it would be for good.

Oh, how Thea hoped it was true.

Grace pulled a length of yellow satin ribbon from her reticule and set it on the table. Thea stared. It looked familiar. In fact… "Is that the same one from Gretna Green?"

"I put it in my reticule after the ceremony and have never taken it out again. I couldn't bear to discard it."

Thea glanced down at Grace's hand. Her ring finger was bare, and doubts crowded her heart. She hadn't taken the ring off since it had been put on her in Scotland. Grace fumbled with her reticule and drew out the ring, and Thea was relieved until she put it on the table next to the ribbon.

Was it over, then? She had promised herself to respect Grace's decision to walk away. She wanted to give Grace the opportunity to make her own choices. But emotion washed over like the tides, a swirl of fear and hope and love twisted in an ebb and flow that had her reeling.

"This ring has been glued to my finger since Scotland, but last night it came off when I was applying my face lotion." Grace frowned down at it. "I don't know how it twisted off when it had been stuck fast for months."

"Don't discard what we have shared," Thea said softly, gazing into Grace's eyes. "Please."

Grace picked up the ribbon. "This may be a little bit tricky with one hand." She twisted it around her palm and made a clumsy knot, then picked up Thea's hand and wound the ribbon around her palm and wrist, linking them together. "There we go." She smiled, the first time since she entered the townhouse, and Thea felt like the sun came out from behind the clouds. "Now you cannot run off to the conservatory and bury your problems in the soil."

Thea smiled. "And you cannot jump up to rearrange the furniture instead of telling me what's wrong."

The ring on the table made her nervous, but the ribbon trying them together gave her hope. It reminded her that all married couples had problems that they must work out. The problem had never been that they were two women who were somehow, against all expectation, joined in marriage. The problem was that they were two different women, and they had to learn to fit their lives together.

It was possible. She stared at the ribbon. It *had* to be possible.

"Let us talk," Thea said. "I want to hear everything you have to say."

She wanted to listen to Grace forever.

Grace took a deep breath. "Living with you has been the most amazing experience. But I have been scared. I have lived with the fear that Lady Harriet would ruin the life that I was starting to hold so dear to me. I was so worried that everything would slip away, and I would be left with nothing. I had no way to support myself once Lady Harriet wrote to the employment agencies, and I panicked."

"I wish you had told me how scared you were." Thea's heart panged. "I would have been there for you." Then she bit her lip. It wasn't enough for Grace to tell her. "I wish I had *noticed*. I should have paid more attention to your feelings."

"I kept telling myself that there was nothing you could do."

"Perhaps not. But I would have wanted to share in your feelings and to help you any way I could. Even if that meant sitting next to you and doing nothing."

"But don't you see?" Grace cried. "I haven't done anything grand for you! You have saved me, Thea, time and time again. My sprained ankle. Offering marriage. Even taking me lawn bowling when you realized that I had been left out of such an enjoyment my entire life. No one has ever made me feel so safe. So well taken care of. It is gift above rubies that you have given me, freely and without question."

"I would do it all again."

"You are an amazing woman," Grace said. "And an even more amazing wife." She sighed. "But even though you give and give to me, you do not offer yourself. I must coax any such feelings from you. You shut me out, and I want to be all in."

Thea stared at the ring, the candlelight flickering against the gold and making it gleam. The only way for that ring to go back on Grace's finger was by being honest. Open.

It had never been about the money, or security.

All along, it had been about faith.

"I have been so afraid of you seeing my inner self and finding my roots to be desiccated. Infertile. I didn't want you to run away like I felt like so many people have." The words were hard to say. "You are too important to me."

"I don't want to run away. I needed time to think. And I cannot help but worry—what am I bringing to our marriage? You provide the finances, the house. What am I contributing?"

How could Grace think of their marriage like this? But then Thea remembered the transactional relationship she had with her own parents. How could Grace be expected to think that she wouldn't treat the other relationships in her life the same way?

"Firstly, you are not a boarder. I am not renting you a room in exchange for services. Secondly, you don't have to *do* anything. It's perfectly enough to *be* someone. And the someone that you are is what I need in my life." Thea hesitated, feeling more vulnerable than she had ever been with another person. "You being here is your gift. You *stay*, Grace. You're the only good thing in my life that has stayed. You are the most constant, reliable person I have ever known. It means more to me than I can say."

"Do you trust me?" Grace's large eyes were luminous, and shiny with tears.

"Always. Do you trust me?"

"Yes. I promise. In fact—I love you."

Thea grinned at her. "I love you too."

The words mattered. They slid over her as snug as a blanket. She couldn't remember the last time she had heard them from anyone, but she knew she never wanted to go a day without hearing them again from Grace.

"I worry that I am not good enough for you, though." Thea hated to admit to anything that might dull the shine in Grace's eyes.

To her relief, Grace only shook her head. "You are more than good enough," she said. "You have given me security, when I have had so little of it that I have spent my life living on edges instead of enjoying the center of it. You are so gentle and precise not only with your plants, but with me. You are soft, Thea Martin, for all that you prickle up from time to time." She touched her hand. "We are not made for everyone. But I think maybe we are made for each other."

Thea picked up the ring and slid it on Grace's finger. "I promise to keep you safe," she said. "No matter what. Come, let me show you."

Grace followed Thea into the conservatory and stopped short inside the doorway. "It's all gone," she said, bewildered.

"I sold the seeds and the plants."

"You sold them?"

"I need the money more than I need the plants. We will have to find a smaller townhouse, but the funds I earned will allow us to live in some comfort." She took Grace by the hand. "I wanted to show you that you mean more than anything to me. More than any leaf or flower. You are my priority, and our life together is my focus. Always. I promise you."

"But you can't give up your botany." Grace's eyes were serious. "It's your passion. You have dedicated so much of your life to the pursuit of science. What about your lectures and the articles you planned to write?"

"I can still fulfil my obligations for what I already promised, and nothing prevents me from writing more. I can still grow new things and continue my studies, and I know I would be welcome at the Chelsea Physic Garden if I ever need their space. But when I started to receive offers and opportunities, I wasn't as happy as I had thought I would be. What I like is to grow the plants. I will always study botany in some way, but for now…I feel like opening myself up to new opportunities. The old dreams were wonderful, but there's always the possibility for new dreams to come."

The words felt perfect. They felt like home.

The knock on the front door was thunderous and most unwelcome, as Thea and Grace were curled up in bed. It had been a wonderful few days. They spoke of their hopes for the future, and Grace explained all about her dreams to open an employment agency for second-chance employees like she and Polly had been. Grace's throat was sore from so much talking, but more than talking, she relished all the little ways that they showed their love. Lingering touches in the morning, sweet kisses in the afternoon. She reveled in being closer than ever to Thea.

"They will go away," Thea said, pressing a kiss to Grace's shoulder. "Who on earth could it be?"

"They are likely selling something. Let's pay them no mind."

But by the third round of insistent knocking, Thea groaned and rose from the bed. "I agree with you about giving the servants an extra day off in the week, and I'm glad that we have done so today, but I do wish whoever is at the door would turn around and leave us be without aggravating all of our neighbors."

"We shall see who it is, then we may return to our previous activities." Grace turned her back so that Thea could lace her up.

They went downstairs, and when Thea threw open the door, Grace could barely restrain herself from leaping forward. There was Edie, a snug bundle wrapped in her arms with a tiny pink nose poking out from the blanket, and Mr. Martin stood grinning beside her.

"Good God, Thea, have you no servant in this establishment to see to the door?" Mr. Martin asked, sweeping her into a hug. "We're mighty cold out here and wouldn't mind coming in now. March is no month to keep people waiting."

Thea stepped back. "Of course, come in."

"We are understaffed at the moment," Grace said as they made their way to the parlor, "but we would be happy to make you tea if you would care for refreshments."

"We do not need anything," Edie said. "Oh, Grace, I am so happy to see you again!"

Grace smiled at her. "Words cannot express how happy I am. And who might this young person be?" She touched the baby's flailing hand. Her sweet cousin. Oh, how she longed to say the words.

"This is our son," Mr. Martin said. "Christopher. Thea, you're an aunt!"

Thea shook her head. "But you've only been married…what is it, six or seven months ago?"

Grace winced. She had not told Thea about the letters she had received from Inverley regarding the baby.

Edie lifted her chin. "It was kind of you not to expose our secret," she said to Grace. "But here among family, I am not ashamed."

"What is the meaning of this?" Thea asked, frowning.

"Inverley was not the first place I saw Edie," Mr. Martin said, a little abashed. "We met in London."

"I hope you have not considered me so fast that I would dare to do something so foolhardy as elope with the first gentleman who caught my eye!" Edie laughed, and cuddled Christopher close to her. "I am sorry for the disruption to your family, Miss Martin, but I could not possibly marry your other brother in such circumstances. I had waited the whole summer for Charlie to come home, and we knew we could not explain things to anyone's satisfaction. Scotland was our only chance for happiness."

Thea shook her head. "I never guessed." She touched Christopher's hand. "He has your eyes, Charles."

"He's the best thing that ever happened to me. Well, him and Edie. Couldn't have done it without her."

"Do Mother and Father know?"

"Of course. Couldn't hide it anymore in the last months, could we? We went down to Martin House to introduce the little mite to them before coming to London to show him off to you." Mr. Martin cleared his throat. "They have not been enthusiastic."

"I am surprised you did not write a letter to me with the news. Travel with a child must be difficult."

"We thought it best to come in person," Edie said.

Grace went still on the couch. "Why?"

"You know how Mama is," Edie said. "She was dreadfully unhappy when we returned to Inverley after eloping. She had all of her hopes pinned on James Martin and his inheritance."

"Lady Harriet had some choice words about the matter," Mr. Martin said with feeling. "She wasn't sparing with 'em, either. Made it clear that I'm a ne'er–do–well younger son with not much of anything to offer anyone."

"She does have a good many opinions," Grace said, hands folded in her lap.

"Mama ought not share all the opinions that she has," Edie said. "But somehow she has heard the most *dreadful* rumor about you, Grace. When we visited Charles's family, we were ever so surprised that Mrs. Martin had been entertaining Mama the day before. And all her talk was about you!"

"What did she say?" Thea asked.

Edie turned pink. "Nothing more than vitriol and spite."

Mr. Martin harumphed. "She's been even more unhappy since I told her she had outlasted her welcome at Westhill Grange. She was making Edie miserable, and I couldn't stand to see it any longer. I think that's why she was so put out."

"The visit," Grace reminded her. Had Lady Harriet told Edie everything? How would she feel if Edie knew that they were related? She wanted her to know, but she didn't want Lady Harriet to be the one to tell her.

"She hinted at a *most* untoward relationship between you two. Something far more scandalous than a lady and her companion."

CHAPTER TWENTY-EIGHT

Thea sucked in a breath. She hadn't known what to expect, but it wasn't this. Her parents now knew of her inclinations? They had treated her dismissively enough when they thought her affairs had all been with men. They must have been aghast when they heard the news from Lady Harriet.

"I thought I should warn you right away," Lady Edith said. "Especially on account of all this being my fault."

"It was not all your fault," Charles said. "I daresay I played a larger role in all of this than you did."

Thea stood up. "If you coerced this young lady in *any* way—"

"He didn't!" Lady Edith cried. "He has always been a perfect gentleman. We were a trifle enthusiastic one night in London, and then Mama found out that I had lain with someone and she whisked me away as soon as she could, without knowing who the gentleman in question was. I thought Charles would be in Inverley sooner or later, but he had not realized the implications of our night together, so he did not think he was in any rush."

"Why didn't you come to Inverley sooner?" Grace asked. "Things could have gone very poorly for Edie!" She scowled at Charles.

"I was trying to find a living as a vicar," he said with dignity. "I asked round all my friends, and then all *their* friends, and a handful of their uncles and fathers too. Father always told me to look to the church for my future, and I am ashamed to say that I did not heed him until it was too late and no one would have me. I didn't do well at Cambridge, you know. Bloody good timing that Father gave me Westhill Grange when he did. As soon I heard the news, I knew it meant I could provide for a wife, so I asked Edie to marry me straightaway."

Thea was proud of him. In his way, he had acted as decently as he could have.

"I tried to talk to Mrs. Martin," Edie said, her face miserable. "I told her that Grace was the kindest and most responsible person *ever*, and that I had benefited from her instruction and guidance. But she took that to mean that she had encouraged me toward Charlie in an improper way, and she was even more upset."

Charles cleared his throat. "I understand this is of some delicacy, but, Thea, Father was in a rage. He said he wouldn't continue to support you in such circumstances." He drew a letter from his pocket. "He asked me to give you this."

Hell and blazes. Thea forced herself to stay calm. Her allowance was due next month in April. Although she had sold almost everything in the conservatory, she had counted on the allowance to pay for the bulk of their expenses. Without it, they would be lucky if they could survive a year or two on what she now had in her accounts.

"Thank you for introducing Christopher to us," Grace said. "Where are you staying in London?"

"The Martin family maintains a townhouse in Mayfair," Charles said. "James doesn't know or I'm sure he'd forbid us, but the staff there are kind enough to accommodate us."

"We aren't staying long," Lady Edith said.

"I am sure you will wish to take up residence again in Westhill Grange," Thea said. The thought of it made her want to weep. After all Charles had done, their parents would never think to strip him of the estate. But for one rumor, they had taken everything from her.

"We want to travel," Charles said. "We loved the journey to Gretna Green and are keen to do more. I have friends across England, you know, and I daresay we would be welcome here and there until the little lad is old enough to come with us to Europe."

"I wish you well," Thea said, feeling numb. He had been gifted with a manor house and he wasn't even interested to stay there? The waste of it wrenched her gut.

The silence was deafening once they left.

Grace took a deep breath. "Mrs. Fernsby," she said. "Do you think she has been spying on us the whole time we have been here, feeding information back to Lady Harriet for her to use? I never mentioned it to you, but she knows about our relationship. She hinted at it when I first arrived. I can't imagine how Lady Harriet would ever guess at such a thing otherwise."

"Mrs. Fernsby always had a taste for expensive things. It wouldn't surprise me if she was taking money from Lady Harriet." Thea fell back into her chair. "This is a disaster, Grace."

"What did Mr. Martin mean about your father no longer supporting you?"

Thea sighed. Her last secret. Well, it was no use hiding anything at all anymore. "My parents have provided for me ever since I moved to London. The reason I was summoned to Inverley last summer was for them to tell me that they would revoke my allowance unless I married or returned to live at home. I thought I had found a way around the problem. I wrote to my parents on our way back to London to tell them that you were my companion. I wanted to show them that although I had not married—or at least, not that they would know of—I had indeed settled down. And it worked. Until now."

"Because of me, and the threat of ruination from my aunt." She shook her head. "I never dreamt anyone except our friends would know of such a thing between us, let alone Lady Harriet." She looked stricken. "If this gossip spreads from Inverley to London, how will it affect your relationship with your botanical colleagues?"

"My parents are not likely to tell anyone. But if any of my colleagues discovers any such thing—well, to hell with them. I have my own voice, don't I? If the scientific societies decline to publish my papers, then I can take out adverts in the newspapers to proclaim my findings. If I am never asked to give lectures again, then I can stand on a street corner and cry them out if I have something to say. There is *always* a way," she said fiercely. "What Lady Harriet and my parents want is to deny us a voice. To deny us recognition. If any should cast us out, it doesn't matter, Grace. We will create our own place, if there is none for us to be had. I thought my life was over when my parents denied my return to Inverley when I was young, and I drowned my sorrows in drink and cards and pleasures. But it gave me a chance to discover science, and it was like my life began anew, fresh from the muck of my sorrows."

"It is daunting to think of what might lie ahead."

"It only means that we shall discover something new, together."
Thea took a deep breath. "But first, I think we need to put the past behind
us, once and for all. I think it is past time for us to return to Inverley."

Arabella's seaside cottage was snug, but Arabella and Caroline
welcomed Grace and Thea into their home with as much enthusiasm
and pride as if they were offering accommodations in a grand manor
house. Grace buried her head into the crook of Caroline's neck, the
sound of the ocean pounding in her ears like a heartbeat, soothing and
familiar. The very air felt calmer here, and easier to breathe.

Compared to the journey to Gretna Green, the road to Inverley felt
easy, despite being more than twelve hours in the carriage. Anthony had
leant them his coach again, and Thea, Grace, and Polly made their way
to the south shore of England alone. It felt most daring—but Grace felt
safe by Thea's side.

"It is wonderful to see you again." Caroline hugged Grace tight,
then studied Thea. "You look well, Miss Martin."

Thea rolled her eyes. "Leave off, Caroline. Are we not old enough
acquaintances to dispense with such formality?"

Caroline grinned. "I didn't want to presume, but I am happy to
hear you claim our acquaintanceship."

Thea grimaced. "I apologize for my manners when I was younger.
I was raised to be supercilious. It's a habit I've long since grown out of."

"You are forgiven," Arabella announced, and hugged her. "It has
been a long time since we spoke, and I am delighted that you have
made our Grace so happy."

Thea beamed. "I like to think I have."

"What brings you to Inverley?"

"We have come to face our families," Grace said. "I hear Lady
Harriet is staying in town, and I must have words with her."

"Family?" A puzzled frown spread across Arabella's face. "Lady
Harriet is not family?"

Grace explained her background to Caroline and Arabella.

"Well, this is all most exciting! Inverley hasn't had such a scandal
since—well, since my family inherited and then lost our fortune,"
Caroline said with a wry laugh.

"I have no wish to bring scandal to anyone. But if Lady Harriet wants to blackmail me forever, I may well have no choice." The thought was terrifying. But what more did she have to lose?

"You shan't have to go far to confront her," Caroline said. "She isn't staying at Westhill Grange any longer, though you likely knew that. She is at the Crown Hotel here in town and has not endeared herself to anyone."

Despite the lateness of the hour when they arrived, they went to bed past midnight, exhausted but happy. Letters had all been well and good, but nothing replaced a dear friend's embrace or their voice in her ear.

Their bed was nothing more than a straw pallet on the floor of Arabella's painting room, with a linen sheet and a thin blanket.

"I don't mean to speak ill of your friends, as they are kind to offer us the use of their home, but I must say that these accommodations do leave something to be desired." Thea smiled, and Grace knew she was teasing.

Grace laughed. "It reminds me of the start of our relationship, with all those strange beds along the way to Gretna Green."

Thea gazed down at the pallet. "This is rather less like a bed."

Grace rubbed lavender cream on her face and hands, ran her brush through her hair, and then got under the sheet and curled up next to Thea. "Wherever you are is the place I want to sleep," Grace said, and pillowed her head on Thea's shoulder.

"And yet you have made a ploy already to take all of the blanket." Thea pinched her elbow and then gave it a quick kiss when Grace squeaked in protest. "How are you feeling about tomorrow, darling?"

She thought for a moment. "I don't know," she admitted. "All I know is that you were right to suggest coming to Inverley. There is a certain sense of relief in knowing that tomorrow, I will be able to put Lady Harriet behind me."

CHAPTER TWENTY-NINE

Grace felt a good deal more nervous when she stood outside the Crown Hotel the next afternoon. Her feet didn't seem to wish to move. Her mouth was too dry to speak. All she could do was look up at Thea, who rubbed her hand between her shoulder blades. Thea's touch calmed her.

"You can do this," Thea told her. "If you wish to leave and come back another time, or if you have changed your mind and never want to return here—I will stand by you. But whatever you choose, know that you are capable of facing her. You are her equal, Grace."

With Thea beside her, she felt a surge of confidence that she wasn't convinced would stay for long, so she strode forward and pushed open the door while it still coursed through her.

She spoke to the hotelier and requested to see Lady Harriet if she was in, and she sat in the common room and listened to the seconds tick by on the grandfather clock.

Lady Harriet was an imposing woman. She was tall with raven black hair, her eyes sharp and arresting, her nose in the air and her mouth in a curl that gave her the appearance of someone constantly on the verge of complaining about whoever was not quite in earshot.

"Miss Linfield," she cooed as she sat down across from them, the sneer deepening in an approximation of a smile. "So very charmed to see you again. And who is your friend?"

Grace knew that Lady Harriet knew perfectly well who she was. "This is Miss Martin."

Thea grinned at her. "I am ever so pleased to make your acquaintance."

"I do wonder if we should retire somewhere more private for a tête-à-tête?" She dropped her voice. "You never know who may be eavesdropping in a hotel. The service here is *abysmal*."

Grace would have preferred to stay in public, but the nature of their discussion was delicate enough for her to acquiesce. "I am at your service," she said, regretting the word choice as soon as she said it. It was difficult not to revert into her old habits as an employee.

They removed to a sitting room adjoining Lady Harriet's bedchamber, and Lady Harriet's smile dropped the instant they crossed the threshold.

"Who do you think you are, showing up here?" she snapped. "I suppose this is your base manners showing. Interrupting your betters at their place of residence."

"You trusted my manners enough to chaperone your daughter during the season." Her heart was beating fast, but Grace kept her chin up and her eyes level with Lady Harriet's.

"And look where my misplaced trust got her!" Lady Harriet collapsed onto the sofa and pressed a hand against her forehead.

"Happy, wedded, and with a baby," Thea remarked. "In my opinion, Lady Edith did marvellously well for herself in the end. With my brother, no less."

She slipped her hand between herself and Grace, brushing her fingers against Grace's thigh. It was subtle, but Grace understood it as the comfort that it was meant to be, and she felt some of the tension ease out of her shoulders.

"With your *youngest* brother."

"The younger Mr. Martin may not be the heir, but he is far from destitute," Grace said. "Besides, it was a love match. Edie is happy. Is that not important?"

Lady Harriet scowled. "He is a nobody. The elder Mr. Martin wasn't much of a somebody, but it was a distinguished enough match and came with plenty of money."

"You may tell your friends in Manchester that Edie married into an old branch of an earl's family, however distant the connection and regardless of the fact that her husband is lower in line to inherit than you would prefer." Grace looked at her. "Your vitriol against me is misplaced. Edie has come to no harm."

"But she did not raise to great heights, either. My daughter was fit to wed an earl instead of a mister. If I had hired a different sort of person—a better sort of person—then she would have."

"You blackmailed me into helping you!" Grace exclaimed. "I had no say in the matter. For you to imply that I somehow misled you—"

Thea glowered at her. "Miss Linfield is one of the best people I have ever had the opportunity to meet."

Lady Harriet sniffed. "Of course you would say so. Your parents told me all about you, and your own housekeeper was kind enough to fill in any gaps of my education. How dare you even speak to me?"

"Miss Martin is a perfectly good sort of person," Grace snapped.

Thea smiled. "I am not so good as all that," she said silkily. "You would not wish to cross me, Lady Harriet."

Lady Harriet's eyes were locked on Grace. "If you do not leave Inverley at once, I shall tell the truth about you and your paltry origins."

"Do you want it bandied about that your own sister had an affair with her butler?" Grace asked. "I can hurt you as much as you can hurt me. I have no desire to do so, but if you do not cease your campaign against me, then I shall have no choice."

"Who on earth would listen to a disgraced former companion?" Lady Harriet laughed. "I regret to inform you that you have no such recourse, my dear Miss Linfield. I can ruin you without discrediting my sister. All I need say is that you are of low origins and that you lied your way into working for the best families while hiding your true identity. I can make sure the news travels far enough and ruins you both. It's no more than you deserve, unnatural as you both are."

Grace thought about what Thea had said about creating their own place, if the existing spaces were denied to them. "I would not be so sure about that," she said. "I can speak as much as I want to, to whoever I please. Do you think the gossip rags would not stoop to listen to me? They would sell a great many copies on the back of such a scandal. No one would know the source. You would have no proof that it was me, and no one would discredit the rags even if they make up half of the story to sell more copies. Anyone who has any doubts could check the details with anyone who lived in Manchester who might recall the sudden leave of absence that my mother took in the country the year I was born. Does not the ton have a long memory for such things?"

"You would never slander your own mother. I know your type."
Lady Harriet was pale with rage. "You always thought too highly of
yourself. I know you think yourself too good for such a thing."

"Maybe Miss Linfield would not, but I certainly would," Thea
snapped. "I would also not scruple to embellish the truth. I could ruin
your good name in the space of a week—and I still do have enough
connections of my own in London to ensure that there would be interest
in such a topic of conversation."

"Why does it matter so much to you?" Grace asked. "Why are you
so determined to ruin my life?" She was tense waiting for the answer
to the question that had plagued her for the past year. "I would have
been happy to chaperone Edie for the sake of family alone. Had you
welcomed me with open arms, I would never have thought to turn away
the position. I would have loved and supported you and Edie like the
family that you are to me."

It would always hurt that she had been denied that opportunity.
Her mother and half-sister led a separate life in America, but Lady
Harriet and Edie were right here in arm's reach. Why should she be
denied the opportunity to connect with her cousin?

Lady Harriet shook her head. "You would have been a greater
fool than I thought if you chose to do such a thing for sentiment's sake.
I must say, for all your pretty manners, you do not ape your betters as
successfully as you claim if you think that *sentiment* would ever get
you far in our world."

Was that all it was at the root of it? The fear that help would not be
freely offered if requested? What a sad, sad thing. Grace stared at Lady
Harriet, her fearsome glamor evaporating around her, leaving a tense
and fragile woman incapable of any satisfaction with her lot in life,
always thinking someone was waiting to steal even the barest crumb
from her.

"Your world has every opportunity to be filled with love and joy
and happiness, like mine does," Grace said. "It is a poor life you have
resigned yourself to."

"Feel free to do as you will." Thea said. "I shall do my worst if you
so much as lift a pen to write to your so-called friends about Grace."

"I will be seeing Edie and her child," Grace said fiercely. "No
matter what, I am claiming the relationship to my cousins. I shall not
speak of it in public if she does not wish it, but you will never again

prevent me from seeing my family and telling them what they deserve to know." She lifted her chin. "I do *not* count you among family, Lady Harriet, and I never shall."

Grace felt numb as they left. "I wish to go to the shore," she said, looking up at Thea.

"Then the shore is where we shall go, darling."

They walked for a time, arm in arm, and Grace was relieved when Thea didn't try to speak to her. Her presence, reassuring and steady, was all she needed as she gazed at the swelling sea. Nature was all around them. What care did she have for high society? She had only ever wanted to reach toward that world for security. But now she knew there was nowhere more secure than in Thea's arms.

If only they could stay in Inverley.

She leaned against Thea until their shoulders pressed together and she could speak into her ear, not daring a closer embrace in public view. "You were my rock," she said. "Thank you for coming with me to face her." It meant more to her than she could say. She could never have fathomed daring to confront Lady Harriet, but with Thea by her side, anything felt achievable.

Thea glanced around, then pressed a quick kiss to her temple. "I am here for you. Always." She brightened. "Speaking of rocks, have you ever skipped one before?"

Grace blinked. "I didn't think one could actually do such a thing."

This was what she needed. No more talk of family or of crisis. Thea knew how to distract her and to make her laugh when she needed it most.

Thea entertained her for the next half hour on the sandy shore with the water lapping at the tips of their shoes. She showed her how to choose the flattest rock, demonstrated the flick of the wrist required for the best skip, and showed her time and again that a rock could dance across the waves. It didn't look like it should work—an element of the earth, solid and heavy, didn't seem like it could move across something as changeable as the sea. But maybe such a thing was a sign that opposites were meant to be together. The union of rock and water, material and mercurial. Like herself and Thea.

Grace sighed with happiness as Thea wiggled her bottom against her in a most provocative manner, throwing another rock into the sea.

This was exactly where she was meant to be.

CHAPTER THIRTY

The next day, Thea brought Grace to Martin House.

The walk from Arabella's cottage to the manor house wasn't long, and Thea didn't feel much like talking along the way. She reached out to touch Grace from time to time, grazing her hand against Grace's elbow, or steadying her as they started the gentle climb up the bluffs with a hand to her back. It comforted her to know that Grace was there, as if she were a talisman or a charm.

But of course she wasn't. Grace was so much more than that. She was the sincerest and sweetest person Thea had ever met, and she was lucky each day to have her in her life. The thought of all their future tomorrows together gave Thea the strength to keep walking, even though she dreaded the conversation that awaited her once they arrived.

Would her parents remain calm in their disappointment? Or would Father lose his temper as he had when she was young and did something naughty? A sexual relationship with another woman was by far the most scandalous thing she had ever done. Thea had no real regrets about her parents finding out, for to regret it felt like denying something integral to her being. They already didn't accept her, and this was but one more facet of her life that they did not have to agree on.

To her surprise, the butler told her that her parents were not at home.

Thea blinked. "When shall they return?"

Then she caught a glimpse of Mother at the top of the staircase. Their eyes met for an instant, and then she turned her back and walked away down the hall.

Oh.

Oh.

It was Grace's turn to support her as Thea swayed, her body sagging as if weighed down by every brick that made up Martin House's dour and stodgy facade.

She murmured something to the butler that she wasn't sure was coherent, then she and Grace walked down the steps to the cobblestones. Thea paused at the base of the steps, gazing down the winding path that led back to town. She didn't think she was steady enough to face the walk yet, short as it was. There were plenty of benches in the gardens. Her parents wouldn't begrudge her the use of one to regain her senses.

But if they had refused to see her or to speak to her, then Thea no longer understood what they might think about anything at all. She had assumed that whatever argument was brewing was one they would have in person, instead of being deferred by lies passed through their butler.

Disappointment coursed through her.

"Their reaction has nothing to do with you," Grace said, after they sat down. She took her hand and held tight. "It is born of their own feelings and opinions. But they do not know *you*. They are content to feed their thoughts with rumors, and their memories of long-ago indiscretions. What does that have to do with you now?"

Her eyes, serious and clear, grounded her. Reminded her of what she had now in her life—riches far beyond an allowance or an inheritance. For she had found *love*. "It has nothing to do with me," she repeated, her heart lightening. "You are right. If they are unwilling to even speak with me, then it proves they are not interested in knowing me at all. All they have ever cared about is reputation."

"You are so much more than their opinion."

The day was bright and calm. As it was March, and a cool one at that, the gardens were largely barren. She gazed at the bare sticks and branches and untilled flower beds that spread before them. A swath of bright yellow daffodils was in bloom, their trumpets nodding in the breeze. Overall, the gardens lacked imagination or spirit, having been reproduced according to some other gentleman's vision for his own estate, which her parents must have thought highly of at some point.

Thea didn't recall ever seeing them enjoy the grounds that they had spent so much money maintaining.

Her memories of them were all inside. Nothing challenged them. Nothing interested them beyond the expected.

It was no life for her.

The realization eased something inside her. She had been so upset for so long that her parents had cut off their relationship when she had been eighteen, and deep down, she had always wanted to prove something to them. To earn their love back.

But now she saw that though she had changed, they never would. It was time to let go of the pain and the anger and move forward.

"We ought to do something," Grace said. Her voice was calm, but her eyes were angry.

Thea paused, uncertain. "Do what, exactly?"

"Why—why—let's uproot their gardens!"

"*What?*" It startled a laugh from her.

"Do you think I could rip up that bush?" Grace pointed to a round boxwood shrub, twice her width and half her height.

"Not unless you are hiding a good deal more muscle than I have heretofore seen in our bedchamber."

She bristled. "Then we shall pick their daffodils! Let's take home a bouquet."

Thea doubled over in laughter. "This is the very sweetest form of rebellion I ever saw in my life. I doubt my parents care as much for their garden as I did mine, you know. This won't hurt them. We could take the entire flower bed, and all they would do is hire a gardener to repair any damage."

"I don't care!" Grace cried, rising to her feet. "If your parents want to show that they do not respect you enough to meet with you, then I wish to meet them with the same disrespect, in a language that *you* care about even if they do not."

Grace's eyes snapped fire and her chest heaved, and the sight was so dear to Thea that her heart panged. This woman was ready to ride to war for her, if war could be waged through the gentlewoman's art of horticulture.

Thea raised her hands. "By all means, let us pick a bouquet."

"A big one," Grace insisted, and picked up her skirts to race to the flower patch.

In her verve, she yanked a daffodil from the earth so hard that the bulb came up with it.

"Gently," Thea cautioned. "If you remove the bulb, the plant can't regrow next year."

Grace met her eyes, and pulled another daffodil free, sending soil scattering over their skirts. "I know what I'm doing."

Thea snorted. "Then by all means, pluck away. Far be it from me to deny my wife her pleasures."

"Exactly so," Grace agreed. "Words I intend us to live by."

In the end, they picked an armful each, and staggered home under the weight of them to Arabella's cottage. Thea's sides ached from laughing so much.

"Maybe someday they will wish to talk," Grace said to her later in bed, the thin blanket pulled up to her chin. "There is a lifetime ahead of us, and we can meet it with an open heart."

"You're right," Thea said. "We don't know what lies ahead. The choices they make now might not be the same ones they make next year, or the year after, or the year after that. Nothing is closed off forever."

But there was still family in Inverley that she *did* wish to connect with.

Westhill Grange was some ways distance from Inverley proper, several miles away from Martin House. Thea walked there in the afternoon by herself, the breeze cool on her face. The land around the Grange was uncultivated, but in her mind's eye she could see rows of juniper and spikes of hollyhocks and beds of chrysanthemums, and of course dozens of her beloved camellias.

The house itself was a snug two stories of rough-hewn warm gray stones, with gables that jutted out of the roof and only two chimneys, which made Thea wonder if it was draughty in winter. But draughts or no, it was a charming building on a few acres of prime land, and she must accept that its riches belonged to her brother.

She saw Charles loping around the corner of the house and shouted a greeting to him, which he met with some surprise as she hadn't told him that she was coming to Inverley.

"Thea! I didn't expect you," he said, trotting over to her.

"I thought if I was in town, I ought to pay a call on my brother." She nodded at the house. "It's nicer than I remembered. Congratulations. I suppose it's a lot to handle, is it?"

He frowned. "Why do you say that?"

She shrugged. "Owning a house and land is far different than living in our parents' townhouse in London, is it not? I would reckon it's complicated."

"Too much for a beefwit like myself to understand?" he asked, a tight smile on his face.

Thea realized with a start that he was hurt. She had always thought that their family jests rolled off his back without making much impact on him. "I apologize for calling your intelligence into question. I didn't mean anything by what I said. The property would be a lot for anyone to become accustomed to."

Charles shook his head. "I never liked it when you or James talked about me in that way." His mouth twisted. "I know I'm not the best at books. I never did like learning Greek or Latin, and I don't have a head for sums or figures or dates or what have you from school. But that doesn't mean I'm not smart enough."

"You're right," she said. "Forgive me, I won't engage in such talk in future. Sums and figures and dates are no measure of a man, are they?"

"Edie doesn't think so, either. She likes me just fine. More than fine," he added, his cheeks pinkening. "Never thought such a girl would like me much."

"You are lucky to have each other."

"I am indeed. And to have Christopher as well!" He shook his head. "My life is full of riches these days. I have all that my heart could ever want."

"I am happy for you," Thea said. To her surprise, she meant it. Gone was the pang of jealousy and resentment that she had always felt about her brothers' situation in life. Gone was her jealousy over Westhill Grange. She had found what her heart wanted, too. With Grace by her side, she had plenty of riches of her own. "I want to start again," she said in a rush. "I know we haven't seen much of one another, and I want to change that. I want us to be a part of each other's lives, like family."

"I think it's a dashed shame that we haven't been. Mother was always saying what a disappointment you were. But I've been thinking—what if all that talk is naught but scandalbroth?" His eyes burned into hers. "I know I'm a dashed sight more than what Mother and Father think of me. What if you are too?"

Thea floundered to find words. No one in her family had ever questioned her reputation. But here Charles was, young and enthusiastic and open-hearted.

"I was every bit as scandalous as Mother made me out to be," she said. "I don't want you to think that I have been an angel whilst in London. But that is not the whole of me, Charles. You're right. I am more than what they think."

It was a wonderful thing to say and to share with her brother. She wondered how well she had ever known him. He had been a child when she had left for London as a debutante, and then she had stayed after Father had cast her out of Inverley.

Perhaps they were all more than they appeared. Perhaps she had judged her family too harshly.

"James is still an ass," Charles said cheerfully, "in case you were wondering. But then maybe I'm sore because he gave me a shiner when I came back from Gretna with his intended. I told him flat out though that if he had wanted her, he ought to have put that ring on her finger himself. Can't be my fault that I did it first."

Thea laughed. "I am grateful to start over anew with at least one family member."

He grinned at her. "I'm happy too. And I was wondering if you might be interested in something." He kicked at a stone in the path. "I wouldn't want to take you away from your life in London, so I do hope you will feel free to say no—"

"What is it, Charles?"

"Edie and I want to travel. Going to Gretna Green was the most fun I ever had, and I want to see more of England and Scotland and then to travel across the Channel to France, and Spain." His face was dreamy. "There is nothing like adventure and the great outdoors."

"What is the problem?"

"I don't want to trust Westhill Grange with just anyone. And though I want to be home with Christopher as much as possible to provide him with a stable life until he's old enough to join us on our journeys, I don't want to leave him with just anyone either." He looked nervous. "I was wondering if you would like to maybe stay here?"

"Stay? Here, at Westhill Grange?"

"As much or as little as you like," he said. "Though I would hope it was more often than not. Edie was telling me that Miss Linfield used to be a governess. I wouldn't expect her to do extra work above and beyond what she already does for you as a companion, of course, but it gives me comfort to know that she is good with children."

"I am in dire need of a new living situation, to be truthful. Father did cut me off. I went to Martin House yesterday, and Mother gave me the cut direct from the top of the stairs. I've never seen her look so cold."

"Westhill Grange doesn't have a large income from the rents, but I daresay we could make a living here for the four of us, along with Christopher." He paused. "I would love to have you here, Thea."

"I appreciate the offer. I would like to discuss with Miss Linfield before I accept. She's not exactly my companion."

He shrugged. "Not my business," he said, "but I suspected as much. Doesn't bother me none."

She didn't say anything, but she gave him a quick hard hug.

"By the way, I saw you had a conservatory in your townhouse," Charles said. "We could build one here, you know."

"I would love nothing better." She paused. "No, that's not true. What I dream of, you know, is to have a botanical garden."

"That would be capital!" Charles cried. "But how would you afford it?"

"I have friends who would be willing to send me seeds to start with," she said, already going through her mental catalogue of people she knew who would donate to her. "We could charge visitors to tour the gardens and put the money into the gardens to keep them thriving."

"I think it's jolly," he said. "My only request is one of those hedge mazes. I've always thought them wonderful, you know."

Thea grinned. "I think it's going to be something wonderful indeed. Oh, Charles, thank you!" She hugged him tight.

Something felt different as she walked back to Arabella's cottage. *She* felt different. Whole. Replenished. Mother and Father may never forgive her, but she had started to heal her relationship with Charles. Perhaps it was never too late to discount anyone's feelings from changing.

This was going to be the beginning of a wonderful new life.

Thea couldn't wait to share it with Grace.

They may have been wedded by the most unusual of circumstances, but loving her accidental bride gave her life greater purpose than if any of it had been planned.

EPILOGUE

Ten years later

The botanical gardens at Westhill Grange were young when compared to many of the great gardens of England, but Grace liked to tell anyone who would listen that their quality was unparalleled. The grounds were lush and boisterous, with a mix of flowers, shrubs, and trees, and an area for herbs and medicinal plants that had been gifted to Thea courtesy of the Chelsea Physic Garden.

Grace loved to wander through the expansive gardens, for at any given time, Thea had some project that she was cultivating or experiment that she was growing. It was fascinating to see the changes that each turn of the season wrought, and the further changes that evolved in the garden year after year.

The gardens were somehow both peaceful and exciting, and it warmed Grace's heart to hear the appreciation of the crowds that thronged the gardens in the summer, and to read the accolades in the scientific papers that Thea showed her when they visited Inverley's lending library each month.

She could not be prouder of her wife for all of her accomplishments. Her *wife*.

Grace twisted the ring on her finger as she watched Thea prodding at the soil near the magnificent line of camellias that bordered the garden. The hair that was forever escaping Thea's chignon had strands of grey in it that sparkled in the sunlight now. Grace thought she was more beautiful than ever, though Thea grumbled about the fine lines that had emerged near her eyes and had taken to using Grace's lavender cream at nights in efforts to smooth them.

"Are you going to watch all morning, or are you going to help?" Thea called out to her.

Grace lifted the bag of compost, redolent with orange peel from the batch of marmalade that the cook had made this week from their orange trees, and walked to where Thea stood.

"Can you remember when we started, and all that was here was a straggly patch of chrysanthemums?" Thea wiped the sweat from her brow as she gazed across the lawns.

"And the old bowling green." Grace bumped her hip against Thea's as she set the compost bag down. She started to trowel the mulch from the bag to the soil, careful to spread a thin layer. "The new one that you insisted on is much straighter."

"You're being humble, darling. You only say that because you've started to win all the lawn games at Christmas. Admit it, you've developed skills over the years."

"Those days are long gone now. Look at how much work you have done through the years."

"With your help," Thea said. "And with the help of all the gardeners you have hired for me. They have been indispensable."

Grace's employment agency had grown into a well-established business, providing opportunities to as many people as Grace could find who needed a second chance in their life. Inverley swelled in size every summer to accommodate the visitors who came to the seashore, and Grace was always busy placing people in new opportunities in the hotels and businesses that catered to people on holiday.

"Why are you thinking of the old days?" Grace asked after she had finished with the last camellia.

"I like to remember when we first moved here, and everything was fresh and new. It felt like everything had changed."

"Everything did change."

"Somehow, it still feels new, no matter how long we have been at Westhill Grange. I used to think Inverley was stagnant, but I think it was just that I was unwilling to change."

"That very first summer in Inverley will always be special to me," Grace said softly. "The summer that we met."

"And to think that but for the want of a pin, we may never have fallen in love."

Grace was grateful for the twist of fate that had brought her to Thea, and which had brought her the gift of family. Edie had not only welcomed her with open arms when she learned that Grace was her cousin, but she had made her the godmother of her next two children.

"I always worried that those thirteen pins would be unlucky, but instead they gave me the greatest fortune I could ever imagine."

Thea kissed her. Grace closed her eyes and felt the warmth of the summer sun seep into her skin, and the warmth of Thea's love seep into her heart.

"We make our own luck, darling. We always have."

Grace leaned her head against Thea's shoulder. "And we always will."

About the Author

Jane Walsh is a queer historical romance novelist who loves everything Regency. She is delighted to have the opportunity to put her studies in history and costume design to good use by writing love stories. She owes a great debt of gratitude to the local coffee shop for fueling her novel writing endeavors. Jane's happily ever after is centered on her wife and their cat and their cozy home together in Canada.

Books Available from Bold Strokes Books

Broken Fences by Jo Hemmingwood. Former army sergeant Seneca Twist has difficulty adjusting to civilian life until she meets psychologist Robyn Mason and has a place to call home. (978-1-63679-414-3)

Never Kiss a Cowgirl by Ali Vali. Asher Evans dreams of winning the National Finals Rodeo in Vegas, and Reagan Wilson wants no part of something that brings back the memory of what killed her father. (978-1-63679-106-7)

Pantheon Girls by Jean Copeland. Cassie Burke never anticipated the detour life was about to take when a meeting with a prospective client reunites her with a past love and reignites the star-crossed passion they shared twenty years earlier. (978-1-63679-337-5)

Roux for Two by Aurora Rey. For TV chef Chelsea Boudreaux and hometown boy Bryce Cormier, love proves as tricky as making a good pot of gumbo. (978-1-63679-376-4)

Starting Over by Nance Sparks. Jennifer has no idea if she can mend Sam's broken soul after the sudden loss of her wife, but it's never too late for starting over. (978-1-63679-409-9)

The Accidental Bride by Jane Walsh. Spinsters Miss Grace Linfield and Miss Thea Martin travel to Gretna Green to prevent a wedding, only to discover a scandalous passion—for each other. (978-1-63679-345-0)

Three Wishes by Anne Shade. A magic lamp, a beautiful Jinni, and a cursed princess make for one unbelievable story. (978-1-63679-349-8)

Undiscovered Treasures by MJ Williamz. For Cyl and her friends Luna and Martinique, life's best treasures often appear when you're not looking. (978-1-63679-449-5)

Curse of the Gorgon by Tanai Walker. Cass will do anything to ensure Elle's safety, but is she willing to embrace the curse of the Gorgon? (978-1-63679-395-5)

Dance with Me by Georgia Beers. Scottie Templeton mixes it up on and off the dance floor with sexy salsa instructor Marisa Reyes. But can Scottie get past Marisa's connection to her ex? (978-1-63679-359-7)

Gin and Bear It by Joy Argento. Opposites really can attract, and as Kelly and Logan work together to create a loving home for rescue cat Bear, they just might find one for themselves as well. (978-1-63679-351-1)

Harvest Dreams by Jacqueline Fein-Zachary. Planting the vineyard of their dreams, Kate Bauer and Sydney Barrett must resist their attraction while battling nature and their families, who oppose both the venture and their relationship. (978-1-63679-380-1)

The No Kiss Contract by Nan Campbell. Workaholic Davy believes she can get the top spot at her firm if the senior partners think she's settling down and about to start a family, but she needs the delightful yet dubious Anna to help by pretending to be her fiancée. (978-1-63679-372-6)

Outside the Lines by Melissa Sky. If you had the chance to live forever, would you take it? Amara Rodriguez did, and it sets her on a journey to find her missing mother and unravel the mystery of her own heart. (978-1-63679-403-7)

The Value of Sylver and Gold by Michelle Larkin. When word gets out that former Boston homicide detective Reid Sylver can talk to the dead, the FBI solicits her help on a serial murder case, prompting Reid to assemble forces once again with Detective London Gold. (978-1-63679-093-0)

When It Feels Right by Tagan Shepard. Freshly out of the closet Marlene hasn't been lucky in love, but when it comes to her quirky new roommate Abby, everything just feels right. (978-1-63679-367-2)

Lucky in Lace by Melissa Brayden. Straitlaced stationery store owner Juliette Jennings's predictable life unravels when a sexy lingerie shop and its alluring owner move in next door. (978-1-63679-434-1)

Made for Her by Carsen Taite. Neal Walsh is a newly made member of the Mancuso crime family, but will her undeniable attraction to Anastasia Petrov, the wife of her boss's sworn enemy, be the ultimate test of her loyalty? (978-1-63679-265-1)

Off the Menu by Alaina Erdell. Reality TV sensation Restaurant Redo and its gorgeous host Erin Rasmussen will arrive to film in chef Taylor Mobley's kitchen. As the cameras roll, will they make the jump from enemies to lovers? (978-1-63679-295-8)

Pack of Her Own by Elena Abbott. When things heat up in a small town, steamy secrets are revealed between Alpha werewolf Wren Carne and her human mate, Natalie Donovan. (978-1-63679-370-2)

Return to McCall by Patricia Evans. Lily isn't looking for romance—not until she meets Alex, the gorgeous Cuban dance instructor at La Haven, a newly opened lesbian retreat. (978-1-63679-386-3)

So It Went Like This by C. Spencer. A candid and deeply personal exploration of fate, chosen family, and the vulnerability intrinsic in life's uncertainties. (978-1-63555-971-2)

Stolen Kiss by Spencer Greene. Anna and Louise share a stolen kiss, only to discover that Louise is dating Anna's brother. Surely, one kiss can't change everything…Can it? (978-1-63679-364-1)

The Fall Line by Kelly Wacker. When Jordan Burroughs arrives in the Deep South to paint a local endangered aquatic flower, she doesn't expect to become friends with a mischievous gin-drinking ghost who complicates her budding romance and leads her to an awful discovery and danger. (978-1-63679-205-7)

To Meet Again by Kadyan. When the stark reality of WW II separates cabaret singer Evelyn and Australian doctor Joan in Singapore, they must overcome all odds to find one another again. (978-1-63679-398-6)

Before She Was Mine by Emma L McGeown. When Dani and Lucy are thrust together to sort out their children's playground squabble, sparks fly leaving both of them willing to risk it all for each other. (978-1-63679-315-3)

Chasing Cypress by Ana Hartnett Reichardt. Maggie Hyde wants to find a partner to settle down with and help her run the family farm, but instead she ends up chasing Cypress. Olivia Cypress. (978-1-63679-323-8)

Dark Truths by Sandra Barret. When Jade's ex-girlfriend and vampire maker barges back into her life, can Jade satisfy her ex's demands, keep Beth safe, and keep everyone's secrets…secret? (978-1-63679-369-6)

Desires Unleashed by Renee Roman. Kell Murphy and Taylor Simpson didn't go looking for love, but as they explore their desires unleashed, their hearts lead them on an unexpected journey. (978-1-63679-327-6)

Maybe, Probably by Amanda Radley. Set against the backdrop of a viral pandemic, Gina and Eleanor are about to discover that loving another person is complicated when you're desperately searching for yourself. (978-1-63679-284-2)

The One by C.A. Popovich. Jody Acosta doesn't know what makes her more furious, that the wealthy Bergeron family refuses to be held accountable for her father's wrongful death, or that she can't ignore her knee-weakening attraction to Nicole Bergeron. (978-1-63679-318-4)

The Speed of Slow Changes by Sander Santiago. As Al and Lucas navigate the ups and downs of their polyamorous relationship, only one thing is certain: romance has never been so crowded. (978-1-63679-329-0)

Tides of Love by Kimberly Cooper Griffin. Falling in love is the last thing on either of their minds, but when Mikayla and Gem meet, sparks of possibility begin to shine, revealing a future neither expected. (978-1-63679-319-1)